she deserved his protection, his care, all the comfort he could give her. *Ask me,* he willed. *Care, comfort, the strength in my body—they're yours for the asking.*

But that was not what she asked. Raina lifted her chin, her eyes pleading with Gideon to use his power on her behalf, whatever power he had to steer the course of events.

Her silent, desperate plea clawed at his heart. The power she wanted didn't extend to her. He was the chairman of the Pine Lake Band of *Chippewa.* Yet there was no promise he could make—*honestly*—to allay a white woman's fear. And there was precious little he could give her in exchange for her tears.

SUPER ROMANCE

Dear Reader,

Once again, we're proud to bring you a lineup of irresistible books, something we seem to specialize in here at Intimate Moments. Start off your month with award-winning author Kathleen Eagle's newest American Hero title, *Defender*. In Gideon Defender you'll find a hero you'll never forget. This is one of those books that is bound to end up on "keeper" shelves all across the country.

Linda Turner completes her miniseries "The Wild West" with sister Kat's story, a sensuous treat for readers everywhere. Award-winner Dee Holmes once again demonstrates her skill at weaving together suspense and romance in *Watched,* while Amanda Stevens puts a clever twist on the ever-popular amnesia plotline in *Fade to Black.* We have another Spellbound title for you this month, a time-travel romance from Merline Lovelace called *Somewhere in Time.* Finally, welcome new writer Lydia Burke, who debuts with *The Devil and Jessie Webster.*

Coming soon—more great reading from some of the best authors in the business, including Linda Howard, whose long-awaited *Loving Evangeline* will be coming your way in December.

As always—enjoy!

Leslie J. Wainger
Senior Editor and Editorial Coordinator

Please address questions and book requests to:
Silhouette Reader Service
U.S.: 3010 Walden Ave., P.O. Box 1325, Buffalo, NY 14269
Canadian: P.O. Box 609, Fort Erie, Ont. L2A 5X3

AMERICAN HERO

Kathleen Eagle

DEFENDER

Silhouette®
INTIMATE™ MOMENTS®
Published by Silhouette Books
America's Publisher of Contemporary Romance

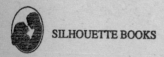 SILHOUETTE BOOKS

ISBN 0-373-07589-8

DEFENDER

Copyright © 1994 by Kathleen Eagle

This edition published by arrangement with Harlequin Enterprises B. V.

® and TM are trademarks of Harlequin Enterprises B. V., used under license. Trademarks indicated with ® are registered in the United States Patent and Trademark Office, the Canadian Trade Marks Office and in other countries.

Printed in U.S.A.

Books by Kathleen Eagle

Silhouette Intimate Moments

For Old Times' Sake #148
More Than a Miracle #242
But That Was Yesterday #257
Paintbox Morning #284
Bad Moon Rising #412
To Each His Own #428
Black Tree Moon #451
Diamond Willow #480
Defender #589

Silhouette Special Edition

Someday Soon #204
A Class Act #274
Georgia Nights #304
Something Worth Keeping #359
Carved in Stone #396
Candles in the Night #437
'Til There Was You #576
Broomstick Cowboy #848

Silhouette Books

Silhouette Christmas Stories 1988
"The Twelfth Moon"

Silhouette Summer Sizzlers 1991
"Sentimental Journey"

KATHLEEN EAGLE

is a transplant from New England to Minnesota, where she and her husband, Clyde, make their home with two of their three children. She's considered writing to be her "best talent" since she was about nine years old, and English and history were her "best subjects." After fourteen years of teaching high school students about writing, she saw her own first novel in print in 1984. Since then, she's published many more novels with Silhouette Books and Harlequin Historicals that have become favorites for readers worldwide. She also writes mainstream novels and has received awards from Romance Writers of America, *Romantic Times* and *Affaire de Coeur*.

For Charlie Murphy,
who served the Standing Rock Sioux Tribe
as Chairman,
And in memory of his wife, Kay,
fellow sojourner to the Dakotas way back when;
fellow teacher, working mother, old friend.
Who knows where the time goes....

Prologue

Gideon Defender instinctively hit the deck at the sound of gunfire. The first person he'd learned to defend was himself, and this wasn't the first time he'd had to eat a little dirt in the process.

"Damn." Tribal game warden Carl Earlie dropped to his knees at Gideon's side. "Don't see nothin', but my ears are ringing pretty good. How close would you say that came?"

"Too close for comfort." Another bullet zinged over Gideon's head, scattering chunks of oak bark as it ricocheted off the trees. He grabbed the back of Carl's belt and jerked him down. "Eeeez, that forty-acre forehead of yours makes a nice, shiny target."

Carl's eyes widened. "You think they're shootin' at *us?*"

"You know anything else that's in season this time of year besides Indians?"

Carl thought about it, then turned down the corners of his mouth and shook his head. "Naw, you're gettin' paranoid,

Chief. Nobody's out to shoot us." Flashing a quick grin, he stuck his head way up on his scrawny neck, looking around like some big-eyed ring-necked duck. "You know what I think is—" Another shot rang out, and the duck became a turtle. "I think I got a job to do. Somebody's poachin'."

"Just stay down, Carl." Gideon spared him a warning glance. "And don't call me 'Chief'."

"Sorry. If they heard that, I guess you'd be the one they'd aim for, huh?"

"Not if they're poachers. Poachers'd go after you first, mistaking you for a moose."

"Get outta here, Ch—"

Gideon touched his fingers to his lips and cocked one ear toward the sound of footsteps. Glimpsing the sprinting shooter, they exchanged nods, scrambled to their feet and followed. To anyone who didn't know him, it would have been surprising that a man of Carl's considerable girth was able to move nearly as quickly and almost as quietly as Gideon did, but they shared the heritage of native woodsmen.

"Taking a little venison, Marvin?" Gideon asked as they approached the man.

Marvin Strikes Many stepped between his challengers and his kill as he tucked the butt of his rifle into his armpit and carefully pointed the barrel at the ground. "My kids are hungry."

"It's fishing season," Carl said. "And you're a damn good fisherman."

"I saw this buck, and I happened to have my rifle along, so I took a shot." Marvin threw his shoulders back and wedged his thumb between his overlapping belly and the waistband of his jeans, assuming a cocksure, hip-shot stance. There was something about the combination of skinny legs and droopy gut that ruined the effect, but Marvin seemed oblivious to that fact. "You call yourselves Chippewa, but you talk about licenses and seasons, just like the whites. I have a right to take this meat home to my family."

Gideon eyed the deer carcass. He almost wished he could let the man take the meat and go his way. A few years ago, that was exactly what he would have done. But these days he couldn't pick and choose on a whim. The tribal chairman's hat was a tight fit for a man who was used to taking some pretty broad liberties. He'd spent most of his life doing things his own way and telling anyone who didn't like it to go to hell. Nowadays he had to choose his words more carefully, even though he couched them in the same tone he'd always used when he was challenged. What was once considered offensive was now authoritative.

"You have to go by the rules, Marvin. The Pine Lake Band has rules."

"And the state has rules," Marvin recited. "And the feds have rules." He shifted his weight from one foot to the other. "You gonna slap me with a fine, Carl?"

"Got to, Marvin, you know that."

"The Strikes Many family has its own rules. The Pine Lake Band doesn't speak for us." Marvin jabbed his forefinger in Gideon's direction. "You might be chairman of the Pine Lake Band, but you've got no say over the Strikes Many clan, Defender. We're White River, and we didn't ask to be put in with you guys."

"*We* didn't invite *you*, either," Carl said.

"All right, all right." Gideon didn't like being pointed at, especially by a man toting a hunting rifle. Times like this he wanted to throw the damn chairman's hat back into the ring, land one punch and walk away.

But he took a deep breath and calmly made his case. "The fact is, the feds included your clan in the Pine Lake Band,

Marvin. That all happened way before my time, so I had nothing to do with it. You wanna complain to somebody about your tribal affiliation, complain to the Bureau of Indian Affairs. Let me know if you get anywhere with them. Meanwhile, I'm tribal chairman, and I've got some say over you."

"You didn't get *my* vote." Marvin gave a smug nod, convinced he'd just delivered a crushing blow. "Nobody did. Election Day, I said the hell with you guys, and I just stayed home."

"Well, we sure missed you, Marvin. Tell you what—next time around, why don't you run against me?"

"Run for chairman of Pine Lake?" He gave a mirthless hoot. "Might as well run for chairman of the Pine Ridge Sioux."

"C'mon, Marvin, we're related closer than *that*. We're all Chippewa, right?" Silently cursing himself for sounding exactly like a politician, Gideon indicated the deer with a quick chinjerk. "Let's dress this guy out. We'll give the meat to some of the elders."

"I gotta take your rifle, Marvin." Carl held out his hand. Reluctantly, Marvin surrendered his weapon. "Could be worse. I could impound your pickup."

"One game warden's just as bad as another, doesn't matter whether he works for the tribe or the state." Marvin unsheathed his hunting knife and wagged it at Gideon. "You think you're gonna make this deal with the state, selling our treaty rights down the river, you can think again."

"Point that thing somewhere else, Marvin, or I'll break it in half. Now, you know that all we're trying to do is work a compromise. We're not selling anything. But either way, you've got to get it through your head that you can't do this." He nodded toward the carcass. "We've always had some kind of rules for the hunt. *Always*."

Carl laid a conciliatory hand on Marvin's shoulder. "Hell, man, we thought somebody was shootin' at *us*."

"I didn't know you were within range."

"Thank God for small favors," Gideon muttered. He unsnapped the knife sheath that was fastened to his own belt. "Give me a hand here, Carl."

"We'll take care of this," Carl said, offering an insider's smile. "You've got business to tend to over at the lodge, right? You don't wanna keep the pretty lady waitin' too long."

"She's my *sister-in-law*, Carl."

"I know that, but your brother's dead. Been dead awhile now. And the way I remember it, you saw her first."

"If anybody ever wants to write my life story, I'll tell 'em to give you a call. You remember more than I do." He had to walk away from that infuriating grin. Carl had known him too damn long. "And that chapter would only run about a page and a half."

"Yeah, right." Carl's gesture invited Marvin to start the gutting process. "You've been stallin' around long enough, Chief. Go tend to your business now."

"Quit calling me—" Gideon turned and cocked a finger in Carl's direction, but he couldn't quite keep a straight face in the presence of that cock-eyed grin "—*Chief!*"

Chapter 1

Her name was Raina, but perched on a ladder-back oak chair in the rustic lobby of Pine Lake Lodge, she was all sunshine. She could easily have been the solitary woman in one of those stippled paintings, the kind that seemed to equate fair women, white dresses and blue water with pure serenity. The lodge's big front window framed her quite nicely, with the lake in the background. Streaming through the glass, the afternoon sunlight embroidered her dark blond hair with threads of gold. She wore a flowered sundress and a straw hat with a big sunflower tacked to the band. Beneath the droopy yellow brim, all Gideon could see of her face was pink nose, pink lips and small white chin.

Standing in the dark shadows of the lounge, he tuned out the jangle of the slot machines at his back as he watched her flip through the magazine that lay open on her lap. Her lips moved slightly as some noteworthy bit of information caught her eye. Despite the passage of more time than Gideon had the heart to mark, the sweetly familiar habit hinted of the same old Raina. Soft and yielding, those lips had given him much pleasure the few times he'd been permitted to taste them. But in recent years she had pressed them only against his cheek and only briefly, then smiled and made some polite remark about being glad to see him.

Only snatches of her first words ever registered with him. She had a way of bombarding his senses, and it usually took him a moment to get his mental bearings. But this time he'd gotten the drop on her. This time, much like a time long past, he'd been the one to see her first....

She looked like a fish out of water—a goldfish that had somehow escaped the confines of a giant crystal brandy snifter and fallen into a shot glass. Seated on a stool in the company of two women who were polishing the bar with all four elbows, the lady with the big blue eyes seemed a mite uncomfortable. Gideon knew the other two—Kristy Reese and Charlotte Croix—both seasoned teachers, both single and neither a stranger to the Duck's Tail Tavern. But the young blonde was new to the north woods, and Gideon was an expert guide. He knew all about taking fish out of the water, and he hated watching them struggle.

He felt especially charitable tonight. After he loaded up the jukebox with quarters, he was going to take this one off the hook.

"How's the three-R's business lookin' this fall, ladies?" With a subtle nod he suggested to Charlotte that she move over one stool. "Have you filled up all those little desks yet?"

"Gideon." Charlotte smiled, gave a quick, knowing glance at Gideon's chosen target, then obligingly vacated the stool to give him a clear shot. "It's been a while since we've seen you around here. Did you venture out of the woods just to check up on us?"

"If this is still the same Duck's Tail, I'm not out of the woods yet." He claimed his seat, acknowledging Charlotte's collaboration with another nod, this one more deliberate, more courteous. "Came in to see if we pulled in any new faces this year. Not that it isn't a pleasure to see the old faces, too. Well, not *old* faces," he amended with a deferential smile. "Returning faces. Friendly faces of old acquaintances who shouldn't be forgot."

"Nor offended when they can introduce you to a pretty new face," Kristy said. "Raina McKenny, meet Gideon Defender. If you ever get the urge for a real wilderness experience, Gideon's your man."

Charlotte's chortle nearly caused her to choke on her drink. She recovered with a rejoinder that got a giggle out of Kristy. "He has an excellent reputation for satisfying all kinds of wild urges."

Charlotte was trying hard to sound like the voice of experience, which gave Gideon his chance for a good laugh. With a mischievous sparkle in his eyes, he nodded in her direction. "This one's hoping I might take a run at hers someday."

The remark drew an indignant scowl, but his order for another round made the proper amends.

"Care to dance, Raina?"

"Well, I . . ."

Gideon waited while she exchanged meaningful glances with her companions. It wasn't like she was asking permission—after all, this was what they'd come for, right? To meet guys. It was more like, *Any last words of warning, girls? Any particular aberrations I should be apprised of before I take the plunge?*

When neither of them came up with anything, she slid off the stool and looked up at him, like a small female Daniel offering to go quietly.

Gideon cupped his hand under her elbow. "Nothing wild, I promise. I just stuck about five bucks in the jukebox. I picked all slow tunes."

Her tentative smile seemed real enough. "Is that supposed to be reassuring?"

"It's supposed to be romantic. I've been in the woods a long time, and I've had nothing but all-male fishing parties all summer." Locking her gaze with his, he took her hands and slid them over his shoulders, as though he were putting on a necklace. "I was about ready to put on an apron and dance with one of them, like they used to do in the old days at the trappers' rendezvous."

"You enjoy dancing that much?" He'd put both his arms around her. She promptly withdrew his left one and made him do the tea-spout pose with her. "I was taught this way."

"Really? How about this?" He made a silly face and started them rocking side to side.

"Are you serious?"

"Hell, no. Just trying to make you smile." And this time her smile came easily. "There. That took some of the tension out of your shoulders. I could feel it." He spread his hand over the middle of her back, pulling her closer. "Damn, guess I shouldn't have mentioned it. You stiffened up again."

Casting him an apologetic glance, she made a deliberate attempt to relax. "I don't know anyone here very well yet. I'm really not very... good at this sort of thing."

"Not much of a barfly?" She shook her pretty head, and he chuckled. "Not much nightlife in a small town. You from the Twin Cities?"

"Yes."

"Teacher, right?" She gave a tight nod. "First year?" Another nod. He pulled in the teapot spout and held her hand against his shoulder. This time she didn't object. He figured he'd hit on a compromise.

"What made you decide to start your career at Pine Lake Indian Reservation, of all places?"

"They offered me a job."

"Not your first choice, huh?"

"I wanted to start out in a small school, and I've always loved the northern part of the state." She glanced up at him, still unsure, but clearly, as far as he was concerned, attracted. "And I wanted to come to a reservation."

"Really." He slid his hand down her spine and let it rest at the small of her back. He led with his hips. She wanted to follow merely with her feet, but he was having none of that, and he could feel it the minute her hips stopped resisting the rhythm. He smiled and settled in. She was going to give him a run for his money, but he would reach the payoff window eventually. "Well, here you are. How do you like our music?"

"It's—" she drew a shallow breath and gave a soft sigh "—familiar."

"You've heard this one somewhere before?" She nodded. "How about our dancing?" She looked up. He indicated the two of them with a suggestive chinjerk. "*Our* dancing."

"I like it," she confessed. Unwilling to lose the ground he'd gained, he drew her only a fraction of an inch closer. She acknowledged his restraint with a smile. "I like it very much."

He had held her close on the dance floor, touched his cheek to hers, and later that night he had tasted her lips. And in the months that followed he'd found himself, much to his surprise, going for broke. Not only had he tried to make it with her, he'd also tried to make her love him. Unfortunately, he'd made a few mistakes. Maybe more than a few—he'd been good at that then. But he'd made up for it by introducing her to the Defender who could do no wrong—his brother, Jared.

When she finally looked up, she peered straight at him and smiled, as though she'd known he was there all along. His boot heels sounded an unhurried rhythm across the hardwood floor of the lobby. She closed the magazine, set it aside and slowly rose from the chair. He would greet her in the customary fashion, he thought. He would simply, properly shake her hand.

But her way was to greet him with a sisterly embrace and a peck on the cheek, and he gave in to it without objection. Her smile was easily mirrored, her greeting easy to echo, but her withdrawal came too quickly. His response lagged by a heartbeat. His hands lingered on her back just a little too long, and she beat him to the punch at stepping away.

"I wasn't sure you'd gotten my message," she said as she adjusted her hat. "It's not so easy to reach you."

"Easier than it used to be. I have an office indoors these days."

She nodded, and it bothered him that she seemed to smile only on cue, her eyes devoid of anything but the recognition of the rudiments of an acquaintanceship, an acknowledgment of the fact that they had seen each other only occasionally over the years.

With a shrug he told himself to shift into the same gear. "But things have been pretty hectic lately, and I'm in and out. Actually, I got two messages this morning—one that you were coming, the other that you were here. I couldn't tell how old that first one was."

"It was kind of a spur-of-the-moment decision. I wanted to get away, but at first Peter didn't want to go on vacation at all. He didn't want to leave his friends.'' She sighed as she turned from him, snatching off the hat as though it had suddenly become troublesome. "You know how kids are at twelve, nearly thirteen. Suddenly their friends become their whole reason for living."

"Is he twelve already?" He didn't know why the number should hit him so hard. It was just a number. With a casual click of his tongue he tried to shoo the whole thing into an insulated mental box. "Almost a teenager. My God, that's really hard to believe."

"I know. I don't know where the time went. All of a sudden he's a young man, and I... Sometimes I just want my little boy back." She brushed her hair from her temple in a nervous gesture, then summoned a bright smile. "Anyway, we hit on this idea, that we would just come up here for a week or so and explore the woods. Try boating on a little bigger lake than we're used to and maybe do some fishing or something."

"Not your first choice, huh?" The echo of his old challenge made him chuckle. It made her blush, which at last added some real color to her smile and told him that she remembered, too. He laid his hand on her shoulder and offered a sympathetic squeeze, then a teasing jiggle. "Come on, Raina, when were you ever interested in fishing?"

"I've always enjoyed the water. And the woods," she averred amiably.

But his hand lingered on her shoulder and drew her in closer, not so much physically as intellectually. It seemed as though she sensed his willingness to be her ally. "Truthfully," she began quietly, "Peter doesn't really know any other Indian kids. We live in the suburbs, you know, and he's definitely in the minority. He's beginning to have mixed feelings about his heritage—doesn't seem to know whether to take a serious interest or to pretend to be—" her eyes shifted from his face to the front desk and back again, and she shrugged, unwilling to name an alternative "—something else, I guess. I don't know how to, um... Well, he's at that difficult age. With Jared gone..."

She spoke her husband's name so softly that Gideon could barely hear it. With Jared gone, what? he wondered. With Jared gone, Peter was probably the only Indian left in the upscale suburb he'd lived in all his life. With Jared gone, Peter was surrounded by people who didn't look much like him, including his mother. So with Jared gone, just who was going to tell Peter to stay away from mirrors and he'd be fine? Jared, for all his smarts and all his talents, had been the Chippewa who was not a Chippewa. That was his chosen alternative. If he'd lived a little longer, Jared would have helped his son learn the ins and outs of avoiding mirrors. And, Gideon had to admit, nobody did it better. It had once been one of the many accomplishments Gideon had envied his brother.

Gideon shoved his hands into his back pockets and banished all negative thinking about his brother with a quick shake of his head. A dead brother could do no wrong. Respect was due his memory. Respect and then some.

"So where's Peter now? You brought him with you, didn't you?"

"He's up in the room, playing video games." She glanced at the wide staircase with its dark, rustic banister. "He insisted on bringing them along."

"He doesn't want to rough it too hard?"

She shook her head and gave him an indulgent, just-between-adults look.

He let it pass. The boy could have his video games and his hiking in the woods both, no problem. He could have a little taste of life on the rez, maybe use it in a school essay in the fall, and tell his friends all about how his uncle, the chairman of the Pine Lake Band of Chippewa, had taken him fishing. The boy was welcome to take all that back with him. And then some.

Respect, *and then some.*

No, Gideon didn't really give a damn about the boy bringing his video games. But he did give a damn about being ignored.

"It's been over two years, Raina. I haven't seen either of you since the funeral."

"You know where we live," she said breezily.

Too breezily. His flat stare was intended to remind her that he'd never been there. He was never invited.

He wasn't sure she got the point.

"You do get down to the Cities once in a while, don't you?" she asked. "I saw you on TV recently. You were in St. Paul, I believe."

"Meeting with some people from the Department of Natural Resources about this treaty issue."

Okay, maybe he was being a little stubborn. Going back to the Cities was never easy. The best way to avoid old haunts was to stick to a business agenda. He never looked anybody up. Never tried any of the restaurants people suggested, never even stayed overnight unless he had to. But when he did, there were times when... "I thought about calling you."

"I've thought about that, too. About coming back, about establishing some sort of ties." Too quickly, she added, "For Peter's sake."

"Of course. For Peter's sake." Too quickly, he smiled and gave an open-handed gesture. "So, for Pete's sake, here you are. And you look great, as always."

"You do, too. Your job seems to agree with you, Gideon."

"It agreed with me better when I was a hunting and fishing guide, working for a good outfitter. Back when I first met you, I think that might have been the best job I'll ever have." With a look, he told her that he didn't expect anyone else to be impressed.

"Now, here I am, bucking tradition. Too young to be a tribal leader. But they voted me in, so what the hell." He caught himself patting his breast pocket for the cigarettes he'd all but given up, and he nodded toward the restaurant. "Let's go get some coffee."

She tipped her head in assent, and he gestured for her to lead the way.

"Rumor has it that you're a refreshing change," she said as the hostess seated them near a sunny window. "Quite progressive, in fact." She declined the proffered menu. "Just coffee for me, please."

"Yeah, well..." He spared the waitress a two-finger sign and a nod. He was suddenly more interested in telling Raina what he was about these days, since she'd brought it up. If she hadn't been impressed back then, maybe she would be now.

Not that it mattered anymore. But just for the hell of it...

"The longer I hold this job, the more respect I gain for traditional thinking. The only problem is, the rest of the world doesn't get it." He braced his forearm on the edge of the table and leaned closer. "They're into money power. They don't understand traditional values. They don't have any respect for spiritual power."

Raina nodded, her eyes alight with interest. "That's why we're here. Peter needs to know more about what it means to be Chippewa. Without Jared, I—" Her voice dropped into that confessional tone again. "I'm kind of at a loss, because, you know, *I'm* not ..."

He watched her align her flatware with the edge of the table, and he wondered which part of what she'd just said embarrassed her. He didn't think it was the Chippewa part—at least, he'd never gotten that impression from her before. Maybe it was her being at a loss for the insight she was seeking on Peter's behalf. Or maybe just being at a loss for her husband.

He eyed the cigarette machine like a coyote sizing up a rabbit hutch. Then he shook his head and sighed. "For somebody who always had a knack for doing the right thing at the right time, my brother sure picked a bad time to check out."

"It wasn't his idea to have a heart attack." She raised her eyes to his and smiled softly. "I know you miss him as much as we do, Gideon."

He nodded once, almost imperceptibly. "So you're looking for Uncle Gideon to do a little straight-talking, man-to-man?" Less than comfortable with the assignment, he arched an eyebrow as he snatched a toothpick from the holder on the table, peeled off the cellophane and stuck the poor substitute for what he really wanted into the corner of his mouth. "Do you have any idea what I was like when I was twelve-goin'-on-twenty?"

"Hell on wheels would be my guess."

"And you'd be right on." His smile faded. "Peter knows he's adopted, right?"

"He's thrown that up to me once or twice lately. 'You're not my *real* mom.'" She leaned back as the coffee was served. "I try not to show it, but that one really hurts."

"I don't know much about kids, Raina. If I heard him say something like that, I'd probably...." Probably what? He'd hardly known his own father, so he was short on memorable examples. "Well, I'd probably say the wrong thing."

"I probably already have." She added cream to her coffee and stirred until the mixture was well past blended. "Listen, I know you're busy. I don't expect you to entertain us. I thought if Peter could meet some people, maybe some kids his age, and participate in some of the—"

"It might be a little risky." Avoiding her eyes, he sipped his coffee.

"Why?"

"Because he might run into—" He was tempted to say *more complications than culture,* but that would sound like a defeatist attitude. "Some problems, maybe. You never know. A lot of people are up in arms over this treaty issue. We don't have much land left, but we've got a treaty that says we've got major hunting and fishing rights, and we're suing the state over it. So the non-Indian landowners and the resorts and the sportsmen's groups, they're making all kinds of threats. The tourist trade is down this summer because of all the controversy." He wrapped both hands around the mug of coffee, took a deep breath and admitted with a sigh, "It's not a good time to learn about being an Indian."

"What *would* be a good time? When there is no controversy?"

He chuckled. "Good point. We'd need a time machine to take us back a few hundred years, wouldn't we? But I don't know about—" *Right here, right now.* What he should have told her was that he didn't have the time. That would settle it, at least for the time being.

But he had a strange feeling that the die had been cast and that there was no point in trying to change the numbers that had come up. They would just come back. Sooner or later, the same combination would turn up again. Raina, Peter and Gideon. Along with maybe a ghost or two.

Gideon glanced at the door, as though he were expecting someone to come through it and rescue him. Jared, maybe.

The brother who did everything by the book. *Read it to me, brother. Where do I go from here?*

"It might be a better idea if we got together someplace else. Neutral territory."

"Neutral? I don't understand, Gideon. Am I unwelcome here? This was my husband's home."

He gestured with an exception-taking forefinger. "It was a place your husband put behind him, with very little time spent looking back."

"Not on my account. I never really understood why he stayed away. Believe me, I never asked him to. In fact, if he'd wanted to, I would have—"

"It doesn't matter anymore. We made our choices, the three of us, and it worked out the way it worked out." He leaned back in the booth, taking a moment to study her, to wonder what she would have done if he himself had asked her. Since he'd denied himself the chance, he didn't want to know the answer, but there had been many a time when he'd taken an awful kind of pleasure in torturing himself with that question, and others.

But those were the days when he'd taken his pleasure where he could get it. No more.

"So you're back again. Full circle, Raina." And she would find that things had changed some. Gideon had changed. He tipped the coffee mug, studied the contents as though he were reading tea leaves, then nodded. "You need a fishing guide, I guess I'm your man."

"I'm not asking you to just drop everything on such short notice. I mean, I know you're much too..."

"Too what?"

"Too busy now. I'm sure."

"You're not sure." He shook his head slowly, half smiling, taking a new and perverse pleasure in protracting her discomfort. "Not about me, Raina. You never were."

* * *

He tried to dismiss the uncomfortable sense of foreboding that plagued him as he followed her up the stairs. If he could handle himself around lawyers and politicians, he could surely deal with a twelve-year-old kid without getting warm in the face and sweaty in the palms. 'Course, maybe that was just a reaction to following Raina up the stairs. He had to remind himself that she wasn't taking him to her bedroom, the way he used to dream she would back when he was a man of large cravings and little character. She was asking him to do her a service, not to service her, and, damn his own hide, it was the least he could do.

But seeing the boy for the first time in over two years, actually seeing the boy with the controls of a child's game in his hands and what had to be man-size tennis shoes on his feet, was a real gut-twister. Before the boy even opened his mouth, he reminded Gideon of Jared. Spitting image, just in the way he moved his hands and the way he spared only a glance for the two people who had entered his domain when he was clearly occupied with important business. Like father, like son, Gideon told himself ironically. He found himself digging deep for an easy, breezy smile as he offered the boy a handshake.

"How's it going, Peter? You remember me?"

"Sure." One last jiggle on the game control elicited an artificial explosion from the TV. Peter gave a victorious nod, switched the machine off and accepted Gideon's greeting. "You're Uncle Gideon. You took my dad and me fishing once."

"Seems like a long time ago, doesn't it?"

"It was. I was just a little kid. I remember, though." Peter stepped back as he measured a foot and a half of space between his hands. "I caught a fish that was like *this long.*"

"Close." Gideon shoved his hands in his pockets as he looked the boy over. Damn, he'd gotten tall. "The three of us had fun that time, didn't we?"

"Yeah, I guess it was pretty good."

"Wanna try it again?" With a gesture, Gideon invited Raina to join in the reunion. "Take your mom along this time?"

"I guess that's what we're here for." Peter shot his mother a sullen look. "It was this or else get dragged to someplace like Disney World."

"Peter actually chose Pine Lake over Disney World," Raina confirmed.

"Well, that doesn't surprise me. Lots of people choose Pine Lake over Disney World." Gideon clapped a hand on Peter's bony shoulder. "A born fisherman just naturally knows where to come for the best walleye fishing in the country."

"But we realize you have tribal business to attend to, Gideon, and Peter and I don't want to get in the way of your—"

"You won't be in my way." Gideon slid his hand away from the boy's shoulder, disappointed that his friendly gesture hadn't changed the guarded look in Peter's eyes. He turned to Raina. "But we've had a little trouble lately, just so you know. A couple of incidents down at the public boat landings made the local news."

"I haven't heard about any real violence," Raina said.

"No violence so far. Just some verbal confrontations between some of the so-called sportsmen's groups and some of our people." He shrugged. "Rednecks versus Indians. Same old story. A lot of name-calling. Some threats tossed back and forth. The kind of stuff you don't want your kids to hear." *Anybody's* kids, he thought, recalling the vulgar words thrown around like hot potatoes in a game no kid needed to be taught to play. "Adults setting the kind of example you wish kids didn't have to see."

"Kids know how to form their own opinions," Peter claimed.

"Anybody ever ask you for yours?" Gideon asked. He was inclined to try laying a friendly hand on Peter's shoulder again, but the look in the boy's eyes warned him not to push. "I mean, like your friends or your teachers at school? They know you're Chippewa, right?"

"They know I'm an Indian."

A distant look came into the boy's eyes. Gideon knew exactly what it meant, and he knew why Raina glanced away. She knew, too, but not from experience. And that was what troubled her most.

"Do they have a problem with that?" Gideon asked gently.

"No way, not my friends," Peter declared defensively. Then, with a shrug, he qualified his claim. "One guy asked me why Indians think they should have special fishing privileges, like higher limits and using spears and some kind of nets."

"Gill nets," Gideon supplied. "So what did you tell him?"

Peter shrugged again. "I told him I didn't know anything about any special privileges. I've only been fishing about three times in my entire life, and I used a pole." He looked to Gideon for confirmation. "I did, didn't I? I don't remember any weird kind of nets or anything."

"You used a rod and reel, and I had you casting pretty good for such a little guy."

"I can't exactly see me throwing a spear into the water like some kind of wild man."

Gideon laughed, even though, deep down, he hurt for the boy's choice of words. "You're not much of a wild man, huh?"

"Maybe with a joystick, but not a spear. Besides, from what I hear, if Indians get to use spears and nets, pretty soon there won't be any walleye left in the lakes."

"Really?" Peter's assumptions echoed the accusations being bandied back and forth in the media and the halls of the Minnesota legislature lately. It chilled him to realize that it wasn't just the so-called sportsmen he had to worry about. It was the kids Peter's age who had no reason to question what they were hearing. The books from which they learned their history told a distorted story. Popular culture had turned his people into stereotypes and foolish-looking mascots. The critics were legion, and there were so few Indian voices left to be heard.

And for Peter, who was growing up surrounded by caricatures and critics, it must have been scary to hear all this stuff about Indians, then look in the mirror and see himself, living and breathing inside real Chippewa skin. It had to make him wonder, *What the hell is this all about?*

And Jared had neglected to leave the answer book behind.

Which left Gideon.

He gestured instructively. "Spearfishing is a sport that non-Indians indulge in during the winter, so they've made sure it's legal then. But spearfishing for our people is a food-gathering skill. We have traditionally practiced it in the spring for hundreds of years. And there are still plenty of walleye."

"Yeah, but they say there won't be if you guys get your way." Hearing himself, Peter instinctively looked to his mother for help, then shook his head, as though coming to his senses. "I mean, if the Indians get this treaty settlement thing."

"Who says that?" Gideon asked.

Peter shrugged. "I don't know. Some of the guys whose families have lake cabins and stuff."

"What *they* say and what's true are often two different things. Our people have never endangered the fish, and we don't ever intend to."

Now it was time, welcome or not, for Gideon to lay that friendly hand on Peter's shoulder again. The boy did, indeed, need him.

"I think your mother's right. It's time you did a little fishing with your uncle Gideon."

Chapter 2

Gideon had taken her fishing only once before. They'd had a good time together—the *best* of times. And the worst, as well. As she pulled on a comfortable pair of khaki slacks, Raina remembered how the day had begun all those years ago with an admonishment from her roommate, Paula, to "dress warm."

She had bundled up in her down-filled jacket and her insulated boots. The snow pants she'd borrowed were so thickly padded that she could barely bend her knees as she climbed into Gideon's battered green pickup. Lifting her onto the blanket-covered seat was like tossing an armload of satin pillows onto an army cot, he'd teased.

Oh, she remembered that deep, rich chuckle close to her ear. She couldn't have worn enough layers to protect her from the quick shiver that exciting sound had sent shimmying from the side of her neck to the tips of her toes. Gideon had always had a way with shivers, a way that continually challenged her to anticipate his next move. It had been a talent too titillating, too unpredictable.

It had scared her silly.

And silly was the way she remembered behaving when she'd ventured reluctantly onto the frozen lake. The glare from the distant winter sun had nearly snow-blinded her. Despite Gideon's assurances that the ice was well over a foot thick, she hadn't been able to forget that it wasn't all ice. That there was still water down there somewhere. Deep, cold, breath-stealing water that would swallow her up if her foot found a patch of thin ice....

"It could happen," Raina insisted. She tested her footing and found that, sure enough, ice was ice, and it was slippery. "I've read about shifting currents, treacherous weak spots."

"I've got a treacherous weak spot, darlin'." He was unloading fishing gear from his pickup, but he managed to shift the tackle box and cooler to one arm so he could steady her with the other. "Deep down in my heart, and I think it's got your name on it."

"What a line." She laughed as she slipped her arm around his waist. "So corny it's actually sweet," she quipped, playfully bumping hips with him as they slip-slid toward the little fishing shack he'd said belonged to a friend of his.

"Mmm. Sweet corn makes a good side dish, don't you think?"

"What's the main dish?"

"You are."

She looked up, feigning surprise.

He dropped a quick kiss on her pouty mouth. "Come on, now, you should've seen that one coming."

"I did. I decided to accommodate you, since you're the host."

"Guide," he corrected. "The man who's gonna show you the way, sweetheart."

"The way to...?"

"Heaven." He gave a sly wink as he shoved a key into the padlock on the door. "Or supper. Take your pick."

She was tempted to tell him that she really wanted heaven. Might as well admit it right off the bat. Everything about him said sexy. The way he walked, the way he laughed, the way he wore his jeans, everything. The trouble was, Raina was wary of heights. She believed in working her way up, testing all the footholds along the way. Meanwhile, she wanted a third choice. She liked the word *maybe*. Maybe later, in a few weeks or months, after they'd shared lots of suppers and made commitments, maybe *then*.... Heaven sounded awfully good to her.

With Gideon, nothing came easily, not even a simple supper. He did make ice fishing look simple, even with a spear, which required a larger hole than the icehouse would allow. So he dazzled her with his skill several yards away from the house, and then they took his catch inside. She was surprised to find that the little house actually had chairs and a card table inside. There was a small heater, and Gideon had brought a camp stove for cooking. Once he'd gotten the appliances going, he squatted next to a hole that had been drilled in the middle of the floor and began chipping away at the ice that had formed since the last time the icehouse had been used.

"What's that for?" Raina asked. "Don't we have enough?"

"No appreciation for the sport," he complained to the hole in the ice. "This is our excuse for being out here. Otherwise we look pretty stupid, sitting out here in the middle of a frozen lake." He grinned up at her, his hands braced on his knees as he prepared to stand. "Officially, it's your line that's going down here. I'm giving you the chance to catch the big one, darlin', so you can brag to your friends."

"A hook at the end of a line is my best chance," she agreed. "Obviously I'll never have your talent for spearing."

"It takes practice. Either that or you have to be born to it." He stood, ducking to avoid bumping his head on the low roof. His baiting smile loomed over her. "As you've probably heard, some of us just naturally come complete with the necessary equipment."

"You might find this hard to believe," she said, returning a coy smile, "but some of *us* are perfectly content to let you carry that particular burden around with you constantly."

He chuckled appreciatively as he rummaged through his tackle box, and she figured she was racking up points for her side. He handed her several pieces of tackle.

"Ah, yes." She looked them over, ostensibly weighing them in her hands. "The hook, line and sinker are so much less cumbersome."

"Maybe." Going about the business of setting a line, he sank into an ice-fisherman's crouch. "But I'll bet you're gonna ask me to bait yours for you."

She returned the bits of tackle he'd given her, with a prim "If you insist." She didn't know what to do with the stuff, anyway. She unzipped her jacket.

"Here, I'll trade you."

It surprised her when he produced a pint of whiskey from his box of supplies, sampled it, then extended it her way. "Help yourself. Warm yourself up inside."

"I'm fine, thanks." She wasn't sure what bothered her about it. Maybe it was just the idea of nipping from a bottle, or the fact that she'd felt as though she were on a roll with her clever repartee and suddenly he'd suggested a different kind of fun. The kind that made her nervous. "A little too warm, in fact."

"Nice and cozy, isn't it?"

He didn't seem to notice the change in her tone. Which was fine. She didn't want him to. She wasn't a kid anymore, and he surely wasn't. In fact, she found it hard to imagine that he ever had been.

He took another drink, then pointed with the bottle toward the hole. "Your job is to watch that line. I'll fry up the first course while you catch the second." Again he offered the whiskey. "Maybe *you* haven't heard, but this is part of the fun of ice fishing."

"I don't know how you can drink it straight like that," she said, shaking the bottle off with a grimace.

"Your trusty guide will show you how." He took a longer sip this time. "Easy as sin, once you get past the initial burn."

"With sin, the burn comes later, doesn't it?"

"When I find out, I'll give you a holler." His naughty grin was enticing. "All it takes is one belt to chase the chill."

"I'm not cold." In answer to that grin of his, her indulgent smile probably looked prudish. "Neither are you."

"No, but I'm sinful." And it didn't bother him one bit. Neither did her prudishness. He favored her with another of his charming winks. "And you're not quite sure whether it turns you on or scares the hell out of you."

Rather than admit to both, she stood silent, and he went about his cooking. She was more interested in watching Gideon than watching the fishing line. His broad shoulders seemed to fill one whole side of the ice shack. His size dwarfed the little camp stove over which he happily busied himself cooking their meal. The truth was that every move he made turned her on, even the occasional nip he took from the bottle. He probably didn't realize that in high school she'd had a reputation for being somewhat aloof. She glanced at the hole in the ice and smiled to herself. The term "cold fish" had been bandied about, actually. Not that it mattered, since she'd dated only boys she could count on to be, well, almost as scrupulous in their behavior as she was.

All right, the truth was that the boys with the *un*scrupulous reputations never asked her out. Not that they hadn't flirted with her once in a while, and not that she hadn't occasionally flirted back. But going out with her would have been a waste of a precious Friday night with the family car.

Apparently her reputation hadn't preceded her when she'd come to Pine Lake. The thought almost made her laugh out loud, and the joke was on her, for imagining a locker-room network that extended this far. It was time to grow up, she told herself. Time to stop playing games. Time to try a different kind of...

"You've got a bite there, daydreamer."

"What?"

Arms folded over his chest, Gideon stood there grinning down at her. "If you weren't afraid to touch the thing, you'd have felt it."

"What thing?"

"The *long* thing—" the look in his eyes grew deliciously devilish "—that I dropped in the hole for you, sweetheart." He chuckled. "Your hook, line and sinker."

"Oh." She reached for the line. "What should I do? Pull on it?"

"Too late now. You lost him. You scared him away with that word *pull*." He sucked air through his teeth, as if the word pained him. "Use a light touch, honey. Jigging works better." He turned back to his cooking, clucking his tongue in mock disgust. "Remember that when he gives you another chance."

In the end they had to make do with his catch, which made the freshest-tasting fish dinner Raina had ever eaten. She took off her snow pants and used them for a chair cushion, and she and Gideon played cards and listened to country music on the radio. Gideon got a little tight and played the ham, crooning along with every tune while he slapped his cards on the folding table with a flourish and beat her three hands of whist out of five.

Then he pulled her onto his lap and started in with some playful kissing. Together they quickly heated up the ice-house. Before she knew what was happening she was straddling him, and he was holding her hips steady while he rocked himself in her cradle, pushed her jacket aside, opened her shirt and suckled her breast until she moaned with exquisite pleasure.

"Pretty as an angel," he muttered, then nuzzled her hair aside from her ear and whispered, "but are you willing to give the devil his due?"

"What devil?"

"You're sittin' on his lap, honey."

"I doubt that." She combed his long, thick hair back from his temples with her fingers. His hair was as black and as beautiful as a raven's wing. "I'll buy 'sinner,' but not 'devil.'"

"Sold," he said softly as he unsnapped her jeans. "To the lady with the shiny halo."

"No, I'm not...no." Her zipper was halfway down before she stayed his hand with hers. But he turned her hand and pressed it against his own zipper and let her feel the hard bulge straining beneath it.

"You wanna pull on something, pull on my belt buckle, okay?" He slipped his hand inside her jeans, and the zipper gave the rest of the way. He tucked his thumb over the elastic at her waist. "Do this to me," he entreated, his breath warm against her neck.

"Gideon, we can't. Not now." She tipped her head back and gulped cool air. The plywood ceiling seemed so close. "Not...here."

"Not here and now?" His hand stirred at her waist. His low voice sounded somehow menacing. "Or not you and me?"

She slid her hand away from his lap and put her arms over his shoulders. Her pulse was racing so wildly, she wasn't sure she could achieve her indulgent, goddess-of-good-sense smile, but she gave it a shot.

"Have you drunk enough to make you forget that the floor is made of ice here?"

"No." The heated look he gave her was far from contrite. "I'm not drunk."

"I didn't say you were." She wanted him to kiss her. Just kiss her, and maybe... "Gideon, don't look at me like that. It scares me."

"I want to make love to you." He tightened his hand at her waist, and the heat in his eyes made her mouth go dry. "Why would that scare you?"

"If you could see the look in your eyes..."

"I'm hungry for you, Raina."

"It's more than that."

There was a predatory gleam in his eyes, and she suspected the whiskey was responsible for that. She liked having control, and this man threatened to take that from her. He made her scare herself. He made her want to let go, just for a moment. And something told her that a moment would be all it would take. He belonged to the wilderness and the wildlife. And Raina's world was much too tame for him.

"I could make it much more." He nuzzled the promise into the valley between her breasts and made her catch her breath. "I could make you hungry for me."

He already had, but she wouldn't indulge herself. Not with icy water lapping at a hole in a floor of ice in a rickety shack in the middle of a frozen lake in the middle of absolutely nowhere. Lord!

Her hands trembled as she pushed against him. "Please don't do this, Gideon."

She slid off his lap awkwardly. His hand shot out, but only to keep her from stumbling into the hole in the ice. "Watch your step, little girl."

"I'm not a little girl."

"My mistake," he muttered, eyeing the breasts that were only partially curtained by her open shirt.

"But I'm certainly not..." Not what? She felt foolish. He was fully dressed. She was the one totally disheveled, panting, on the verge of screaming and moaning at the same time.

"Check your other line, honey." He nodded toward the hole in the ice. "The name of the game is catch and release."

"I'm not playing a game," she said.

"Neither am I."

That was all it took with Gideon Defender. "Please don't." The words seemed to drive him back into the woods.

They had run into each other at a party a few weeks later, and he had introduced her to his brother. Then he'd stepped aside and quietly watched, as though he were testing for her reaction. It was a move she'd resented, and she'd told him so, the same night she'd told him that Jared had asked her out and she'd accepted. He'd expressed no surprise, offered no objections, mentioned no regrets. Not that it would have mattered, since she'd made up her mind. But it had hurt. Just a little.

Jared had never asked her how she'd felt about his brother. Other than a certain physical resemblance, the two brothers had little in common. Jared had a different brand of charm. More practiced, perhaps. More polished. He had gone to the University of Minnesota in Minneapolis, while Gideon had, for the most part, preferred to stay in the north country among the people he'd grown up with, in touch with the life he knew. In the end, Jared had chosen Raina's world. And Raina had chosen Jared.

They'd both wanted children, and when a pregnancy hadn't occurred soon enough to suit Jared, they had adopted Peter. Raina hadn't questioned the decision when Jared announced that the opportunity for a baby had unexpectedly presented itself. His low sperm count was an issue he neither wanted to discuss nor fret about. He'd had some childhood health problems that he didn't care to discuss, either. They had been blessed with a perfectly beautiful son, and all was well.

For a time after that they had been a fairly typical suburban family. Raina had quit her job to stay home with Peter until he started school, and then she'd only worked outside their home part-time, while Jared had worked too hard. He'd found less and less time to be at home as his time, unbeknownst to him, slipped away quickly. Eventually there had been no chance for visits to Pine Lake, and then suddenly, irrevocably, the time was gone.

At least, *his* time was gone. At first Raina had had to remind herself that hers was not. But not lately. Ever since adolescence had overtaken her son and transformed him like some kind of fairy-tale curse, she had no trouble remembering that she had miles to go and challenges to meet.

Like another fishing trip with Gideon.

"Are you ready, Peter?" He'd been in the bathroom forever. A year ago, sixty seconds in the shower and he was out. "You know, your hair doesn't have to be perfect. We're going out *fishing*. Uncle Gideon said he'd pick us up at the dock in—"

The door finally opened, and her son deigned to emerge. His beautiful black hair was still wet, so she assumed that the new pimple on his chin was the reason for the stormy look in his eyes. He was hoping for *hair* on his chin, he'd informed her a few weeks ago when she'd tried to tell him that the occasional pimple was not the end of the world. A man's beard, he'd said. Not a wimpy zit.

Raina was not ready for either development. Not quite yet.

"Why don't you just call him Gideon?" Peter's scowl was ominous. "He's not your uncle."

"He's *your* uncle. He's your father's brother."

"Yeah, well…where did you hide the damn hair dryer?"

"Peter, please don't talk like that." She handed him the blow-dryer, and he mumbled his thanks. "You told me that this was where you wanted to come. We're here. The next step is to venture beyond this room."

"It's been a long time since I've been up this way." Barefoot and so far dressed only in his favorite ripped-knee jeans, he plopped on the rumpled bed he'd claimed as his, then fell back as though he'd just run a marathon. "I mean, I was just a kid. I don't know *him*. I don't know anybody here, and I feel like I'm supposed to. It's weird."

"I know." She sat down beside him and patted one knobby knee. "You miss your dad."

"You always wanna blame everything on that." He pushed up on his elbows and looked her in the eye. "It's *not* that."

"Tell me what's wrong, then."

"Nothing's wrong. Why does something always have to be wrong? I just—" Dramatically he flopped back down again. "It isn't like what I thought it was gonna be."

"You haven't been out of the room yet." She knew it was no use to ask what he was looking for. He didn't know. "Let's go see what it's going to be like. Give it a chance. If it's no good, we'll go home."

He sat up. "Is there a damn plug around here?"

There went her chance to use the bathroom. "Try—"

"Following the lamp cord, I know." He dived for the head of the bed and tossed pillows over his shoulder like an overgrown pup burying a bone.

She laughed and shook her head when he announced, "Pay dirt." Then he flopped on his belly and hung his head over the side of the bed, brushing his hair forward. "You know what, though?" He tucked his chin and turned to look at her upside down. "He seems pretty cool."

"Who?"

She held out her hand for the dryer, making an offer she hoped would hurry things along. It was the kind of thing he might have asked her to do for him a year or so ago. Now he might be offended. Then again, he might take her up on it. She never knew which way he was going to jump next.

"Uncle Gideon." He plunked the dryer in her hand. "*Gideon.* You know what Dad told me once? That his brother got all the looks, and he got the brains."

"Your father said that?" She turned the machine on low and directed it at his nape, gently finger-combing his hair and feeling favored by his willingness to confide a remembrance, and to still let her coddle him once in a while.

So Gideon had all the looks, huh? He was the younger of the two, but physically, Gideon was the big brother. He'd certainly never shared Jared's taste for expensive clothes, and she remembered Jared teasing Gideon about his need for a barber once. His hair wasn't as long as it used to be, but it was still shoulder-length, still an attractive expression of his own personality. But nothing, surely, that Jared would covet in any way.

"That was a strange thing for him to say. Your dad was very handsome, and Gideon is . . ." She shrugged. "Gideon is Gideon."

Peter peeked up at her. "What's that supposed to mean?"

"It means it's been a long time since I've been up this way, too." She smiled and turned the dryer on full blast.

Gideon was waiting, as promised. He was sitting at the end of one of the lodge's boat docks, basking in the sun and chatting with a boy about Peter's age. Below their dangling tennis shoes was a fishing boat with cushioned chairs and two outboard motors—one for trolling.

Gideon turned when he heard footfalls treading the planks. They were late, and Raina half expected him to check his watch and ask where they'd been. But he smiled as he hopped to his feet and tapped the boy on the shoulder, coaxing him to follow suit. Raina liked the way the spokes at the corners of his eyes made his smile seem even brighter, and the easy way he handled himself put everyone else at ease, too. From the look of him, it appeared that the years had been kinder to Gideon than they had been to his brother. But then, maybe it was true, Raina thought. Maybe Gideon had all the looks.

"This is Oscar Thompson. He's been camped out in my office ever since I told him I was thinking about going fishing pretty soon." The two boys shook hands. "That was last May, wasn't it, Oscar?"

Oscar shrugged. "Before school was out."

"See there? And here we're going fishing already. Fishing lesson number one—" Gideon squinted into the sun and brandished a finger "—patience. Everyone wants to go fishing with me, because everyone knows..."

"He's got a good boat," Oscar put in.

"...that ol' Gideon knows exactly where to go lookin' for Mr. Walleye. Plus, I've got some extra tackle."

He took a pair of aviator-style sunglasses from his pocket, put them on as though he were preparing to read a sign and made a production of surveying Raina from head to toe. "So, I see Mom's wearing the proper fishing attire, all nicely coordinated. Matching shoes and hat."

Raina compared his cutoffs and T-shirt with her neatly pressed yellow blouse and khaki slacks. "Heck, I'm casual," she said. "Don't you like my fishing hat?"

"It's very... yellow. But I think we can fix that in a real hurry. Right, boys?"

The round of male chuckles would have bothered her if it hadn't been exactly what she'd come looking for. For Peter's sake, of course.

"What about a license?" Gideon asked.

"License?"

"Fishing license. See, the three of us are okay because we have tribal ID." He arched an eyebrow in Peter's direction. "You brought yours along, I hope?"

Peter cast an accusatory glance at the person he considered responsible for the boring technical details of his adolescent life—his mother—as he reported, "I didn't know I had one."

"You do," she said. "I brought it."

"You've got yourself a good secretary there, kid. If you're smart, you'll pay her well." He turned to Raina. "But no fishing license, huh?"

She shook her head.

He shook his, too. "And you look just all heartbroken about it. We can get you one over at the tackle shop."

"I'll just go along for the ride this time."

"Good woman." Gideon clapped a hand on each boy's shoulder. "Then we're set."

Raina let the *good woman* comment go unchallenged. She didn't want to question anything, justify anything or fish for anything. Just going along for the ride was exactly what the doctor had ordered. It was early evening, the best time of a summer's day. The sun's slanted rays became bright flashes in the water. When the boat was moving, she could close her eyes and catch the wind in her face while her hand trailed in the cool wake. When they anchored in the shallows, she could simply enjoy her son's growing excitement for the relaxing sport as Gideon patiently tutored his casting arm.

"Good catch." Gideon gave Peter a shoulder slap of approval. "Now take him off the hook and throw him back."

Peter looked up in near horror. "Throw him *back?*"

"We're fishing for supper for the four of us." Gideon appraised the small wriggling crappie that Peter had just pulled proudly from the water. "That's guy's not worth bothering with. We want nice, pan-sized—"

"Gideon, I think that's a wonderful fish!" Raina sharpened her bright tone with a defensive edge. "A beautiful fish. I think we should have it stuffed and mounted."

"This isn't like bronzing his baby shoes, Raina. We're looking for food." He nodded toward the cooler containing the fish Oscar had already caught. "Right, Pete?"

"I guess so." Peter looked at his catch again. "He's too small, huh?"

Those motherly instincts would not rest. A quick justification tingled on the tip of Raina's tongue.

But Gideon headed her off with a warning glance. "Put him down in the water and see if he's gonna make it. We don't return dead fish to the lake."

Peter complied, his face brightening when, revived by the water, the little fish flipped its tail and swam away. "There, see?" Gideon watched the boy's first catch in six years head out to the middle of the lake. He promised himself it wouldn't be the last one for this season. Not by a long shot. "He's a survivor, like us. If we catch you next year, brother fish, you'll make a fine meal."

They dropped their lines again. Once Peter had caught a pan-worthy fish, Gideon put in at the public boat landing, where he would take his boat out of the water. There was no one else waiting to use the boat ramp, and his pickup and trailer were parked in the public parking lot. Soon he would be cooking up a meal for Raina and the boys. Soon he would be able to show her that he had a little place of his own now. He'd been looking forward to this day for a long time.

Gideon cut the motor, while Oscar took up his assigned post in the bow and prepared to catch a mooring. As the boat drifted toward the dock, Gideon smelled trouble. The odor came from the four young men who were hanging out right where Gideon planned to step ashore. The signs were all there—the four accusatory stares, the folded arms, the set of the jaws. The gist of the quick comments passed among them was easily interpreted visually—Gideon didn't need to hear those words. He had heard it all before.

"I'll tie her up, Oscar," Gideon said quietly.

But it was too late to switch places. "I've got it," Oscar muttered, reaching for a piling as the boat drifted in to the dock.

They could have been ordinary boaters or fishermen—and most days they probably were. They sure didn't look like anybody's idea of a gang, but the tough-kid posturing was there—the insolence, the confidence in bully power.

The first man to speak wore a Redskins T-shirt. "You got any illegal nets in there, chief?"

"Do you know who you're talking to?" Oscar looked up, scowling as he slipped the nylon rope around the post. "He *is* the chief."

"I don't give a damn if he's Tonto himself," the man said as he adjusted the bill of his Twins cap. "You guys out spearing fish today?"

"Nobody's spearing any fish." Gideon grabbed the piling, planted one foot on the dock and rose to tower over the gang's spokesman.

"Oh, yeah? So you claim." The man stepped back, his friends covering his flanks as he jabbed a finger at Gideon. "You guys better drop this little plan to get special privileges for yourselves. There's no way you're gonna start netting and spearing in these waters. The sports fishermen in this state won't stand for it."

"You're in my way," Gideon said calmly.

"No, you're in my way." The man settled one hand on his hip, but on the other hand, that finger was still jabbing. "You're trying real hard to get in *my* way."

Gideon returned a level stare. "This gesture shows me that you have no manners. Touch me with it, and you will have no finger."

The man sniggered, then checked to make sure he wasn't alone and sniggered again. But the finger came down.

This was a public landing. Gideon had half a notion to punch this blockhead's lights out. He could take him easy, and the three jerks backing him to boot. A few years back there would have been no question. Just impulse. But now, besides the fact that he had a woman and two kids with him, he had to remember who he was and what he stood for.

Damn. Standing for more than just Gideon Defender could be a royal pain sometimes. He couldn't walk away and

leave Raina and the boys with the boat as long as these guys
were standing there. He was going to have to back down and
take the boat back to the lodge rather than load it up here
and take his guests up the road to his cabin. He didn't have
his own dock. Couldn't afford it. This was prime tourist
territory. Thanks to all the damn treaties, the Pine Lake
Band was land poor. Three thousand meager acres and some
hunting and fishing rights were all they could call their own.
The only dock space they actually owned was at the lodge.

Public landing? Hell.

"You need any help getting your boat out of the water,
Gideon?"

No one had noticed the timely appearance of Bill Lucas,
a conservation officer with the Minnesota Department of
Natural Resources. The gang of four didn't seem too pleased
when they turned to find him walking up behind them.

But Gideon was glad to hear his old friend's voice. "Not
if these boys would just step aside so I can go get my
pickup."

Bill's uniform probably had something to do with the way
the small crowd parted for him. "You boys have a problem
with that?"

"No problem at all," the Redskins fan said, "unless
they're taking more than their rightful limit."

"How does that concern you? I don't see a badge on any
of you."

"I own a cabin on this lake." The claim was made by one
of the three backups. "Along with my dad, that is. That's
how it concerns me. All this talk of the state cuttin' some
kinda deal with the Indians, I was just tellin' this one here,
we're not gonna stand for any gill nets, and none of their
spearfishing, either."

"You talk to your legislator about it. You call the attorney general's office," Bill suggested. "You don't bother

these people. This is a public landing. We don't want any—"

The Twins cap got another adjustment as its wearer did some more posturing. "We just want to let 'em know what's comin' down the pike if they don't drop this thing. You know what happened in Wisconsin."

"We're trying to avoid the kind of trouble they had over treaty rights in Wisconsin. Same treaty we're dealing with here. In the end the court sided with the Indians, and the state lost big." Bill glanced his friend's way. "Gideon here's Chippewa. He can go over to Wisconsin and do all the spearfishing and gill netting the tribal code allows."

"Yeah, well, go on over to Wisconsin, then, 'cause you ain't gettin' anywhere with that here." The four started edging away as the summer cabin owner made his final point, driving his finger toward the dock like a nail. "We won't stand for it here."

His buddy added his concurrence—a quick glare and another adjustment of the baseball cap—and the four sauntered down the dock toward a club cab four-wheel drive pickup that was parked at the end.

"His family's probably been coming up to their summer cabin on the lake for what—two, three generations?" Gideon's gesture was one of empty-handed frustration. "You know how long *my* family's lived on this lake year-round? You know how many generations, Bill?"

"No, do you?" Bill raised his palms and chuckled as he shook his head. "No, don't answer that. You'll be reciting the whole history for me again."

"For you guys it's history, for us it's tradition."

"Either way, anybody can see you've got a good case." Bill shrugged. "Anybody with an open mind, that is. Seems like the more we talk this compromise up, the more guys like that dig in their heels. Never gonna change his mind."

"Then we'll end up in court."

Bill nodded. The department recognized that possibility. And dreaded the likely outcome.

Gideon turned his attention to the boat and the three people who were waiting for him. He leaned down to offer Raina a hand.

"Catch anything?" Bill asked Oscar, who was still in charge of mooring the boat.

Oscar smiled. "Supper."

And that had always been just what fishing meant to Gideon's people. Supper.

Chapter 3

Supper was a joint project. Gideon had done some shopping with the intention of pleasing his guests at any cost. Raina was amused by the choice of skim milk or whole, butter or margarine, white potatoes or red. "Or rice. If anyone hates potatoes, I've got rice." He offered every salad leaf imaginable, dark bread or light bread, three flavors of ice cream, for which he was sorry he didn't have any marshmallow cream.

"Marshmallow cream?" Peter pretended instant nausea.

"Hey, that stuff's good, man," Oscar said.

"Are you starting a restaurant?" Raina wondered with an appreciative smile.

Gideon shrugged. "I know kids have sensitive taste buds."

"I'll eat anything," Oscar promised. And he did. He ate *everything*.

"Me too." But Peter asked for *his* fish—the one he'd caught himself—red potatoes and blue cheese on his salad.

The blue cheese was one request Gideon hadn't anticipated. "Next time," he promised.

Raina liked his house, and she made a point of telling him so. It had no feminine touches and didn't need any. Made of logs and furnished with a functional combination of old chairs and new stereo equipment, it was comfortable. And it was Gideon.

After supper he and Raina sat on the little screened porch at the back of the house, enjoying the chorus of crickets, listening to the water lapping at the shoreline, sharing coffee. He had a view of the lake, which glistened with the pink and purple shades of twilight, but he possessed no pricey piece of lakeshore. He didn't have much of a yard, but he was within shouting distance of the end of the neighbor's dock, where the boys sat, dangling their feet in the water like Tom Sawyer and Huck Finn.

"When you guys get tired of donating blood, there's a can of powwow cologne up here," he called out. Through the dusky shadows, he smiled at Raina. "Specially formulated to ward off the Minnesota state bird."

"Mosquito repellent?"

"Want some? I think there's a hole in the screen somewhere." She shook her head. "Not your scent, huh? Yours is more flowery." He leaned across the arms of the wicker chairs they occupied, the arm of his touching the arm of hers, and drew a deep breath. Another mistake, he thought, as his blood rushed to harden his sex. That scent was all it took. "The same one you always wore."

"One bottle lasts me a long time," she said, as though it might possibly be a relic from years past. "Actually, I haven't worn it in a while. I haven't been dressing up much, or..." It sounded like an apology. "Perfume is one of the frivolities I'd all but given up lately."

"Nice touch for a fishing expedition." He wanted to keep his thoughts to himself, so he teased, "Classy bait."

"It wasn't—"

"Intentional, I know." It was working its magic on him, anyway. "I don't know what to make of this visit, Raina. After all this time, you suddenly show up with—"

"Peter. I came for Peter's sake." By way of apology, she touched his arm. "That's becoming a familiar refrain for me, isn't it? And it's not the whole truth." Her sigh seemed distant in the near darkness. "I never intended to stay away. I enjoyed teaching here. We had friends here, and Jared's family, of course. I suggested to him once that we leave the rat race and come back here. I thought maybe he'd like to offer the Pine Lake Band his legal services, and I could go back to teaching." She sighed and shook her head, remembering her husband's answer. "'You can't go home again,' he'd say. And that always bothered me."

"Why?"

"Because I was afraid it was because of me that he stayed away. Because of me that he was so—" she waved her hand, the gesture evaporating into the shadows "—driven to succeed. And that's what killed him. That's what—"

"Are you looking for credit or blame?" His tone sounded sharper than he'd intended. He tempered it. "Either way, you're way off base. Jared was always ambitious. I'm surprised he came back here when he did, even for a short time." He remembered Jared's explanation. The high school history teacher had quit in the middle of the school year, and Jared needed to earn some money so he could continue with law school. "But if he hadn't, he wouldn't have met you."

"If you hadn't introduced us . . ."

"It might have prolonged the agony for, what, another week?" He'd told himself they would have met, anyway, even though she was an elementary schoolteacher. For some reason, Gideon had wanted it to be *his* idea when she met his brother.

"What agony?"

"You and me." He chuckled, remembering. "Fire and ice."

"You were the one who had a thing for ice."

"You bet I did."

"And a thing for fire*water*."

"That, too," he admitted quietly. "Which wasn't your style. And neither was I."

"Nor I yours. So you introduced me to your brother."

After several moments of seemingly respectful silence, he asked, "Do you miss him, Raina?"

She turned, ready to challenge his insolence, but the words dissolved on the tip of her tongue when she saw the distant look in his eyes. And the sadness.

"Do you ever think you hear his voice and go looking out the window, just for a second actually expecting him to be there?"

"Your voice sounds exactly like his on the phone." She remembered his call early one morning. No hello, no name, just a voice, a continuation of a dream. He'd said he was sending her some old yearbooks. She'd struggled to find more than a two-word answer. "A bit unsettling in kind of a bittersweet way," she told him now in the hope that, if he remembered, he would forgive her reticence after the fact.

But he had other recollections to share.

"We were close when we were kids, up until he went away to boarding school. They wanted me to go, too, but..." He shook his head, the way he had back then. "No way. I'd heard all about how strict those nuns were. Make you study so hard you get cross-eyed. When Jared had to get glasses, I got to say 'I told you so.' I don't know why, but he really liked that. Studied so hard he had to have glasses."

Gideon slid down and rested his head against the back of the chair. "He was there for three or four years before they sent him home. They found out he had a heart murmur, and I guess he'd been sick with pneumonia, and they were scared something might happen to him. He looked okay to me. All I know is, it nearly killed him right then, 'cause he was making straight *A*'s. He said the school here was too easy for him." Gideon shook his head slowly, rolling it back and forth against the chair. "Damn show-off. Too *easy* for him. I was lucky to graduate."

"He said you hated school."

"He was right. Damn desks were too small."

"He thought he'd outgrown his heart problem," she recalled. "At least, that was what he told me."

"He knew it all, my brother. Knew all there was to know about everything. Damn walking encyclopedia." He turned his head her way. "I used to think he could probably walk on water and recite the Bible backwards if he wanted to. And it was the kind of thing he just might do if somebody challenged him to." His smile was a bright spot in the dark. "Me, I couldn't see taking up a challenge unless there was some fun in it."

"We saw so little of you after we were married, Gideon." She looked him in the eye, challenging him for the truth. "Why was that?"

"You were busy, and I was...you know, knockin' around." He turned his attention to the ceiling. "You think you've got all the time in the world, you know? You tell yourself, maybe next summer, maybe Christmas. Last time I talked to him, I called to tell him I was running for chairman. I thought, if I got elected, we'd kinda be—" with a wave of a hand, he minimized the notion "—on equal footing in a way."

"In what way?"

"I don't know. Importance, I guess. Here we're like an apple and an orange, but I'm thinkin'—" He cut off the comparison so abruptly, she thought he'd bitten his tongue. "Forget I said apple. I didn't mean apple. I'd give anything just to have one day back—one *hour*."

"What's wrong with 'apple'?"

"You know, red on the outside, white on the inside. Some of the more traditional Indians get disgusted when—" He gave a quick shrug. "I remember calling him that a time or two, along with a few other things. I had no right to judge my brother. Right now, today, I'd like to hear some of his answers. But damn him, he took them all with him."

"Tribal law wasn't his field," Raina said quietly.

"Doesn't matter. He'd have the answers. He always did. *Good* answers, not just bull—"

"I miss him, too, Gideon." There, she thought. She'd finally answered his original question. She'd made him work for it, too. It was the biggest chunk of himself he'd ever shared with her. He'd earned some trust. "So does Peter. Peter has so many questions about so many things. Things I only know about secondhand."

"Because you're a woman?"

"And because I'm not Chippewa." She sighed. "And also, I guess, because I know very little about his background. Jared was able to make all the arrangements through the tribal court, even though he was born in a Minneapolis hospital. That's where we got him. He was so little, so..." Her wistful smile faded. "Anyway, I know he needs...someone like you." She shook her head. "No—*you*. He needs you, Gideon. You're his uncle. You *are* Chippewa, and you're—"

"Hell, lately some people have called *me* 'apple.' Taste of my old insult, comin' back at me." He chuckled humorlessly. "Anyway, I can't replace—"

"We're not looking for a replacement," she assured him. "Or answers, really. Peter needs to learn how to find his own answers."

"What does he want to know? Who his parents are?" He peered at her, his eyes burning with the question. Abruptly he turned away. "The answer to that is you and Jared."

"He knows he's adopted."

"He knows you raised him. That makes you his mother."

"He needs to learn more about his Native heritage, Gideon. And with Jared gone..."

"Jared didn't know his heritage from—" Jared had answers, but not *those* answers, damn it. Those were the answers Gideon had. At least, he had *some*. A few. "Look, Raina, the problem is that this whole treaty rights issue is pretty dicey right now, and people are circling their wagons up here." He chuckled. "Some analogy, huh?"

"It's an interesting choice of words."

"These are interesting times. It can be tricky just figuring out who your friends are. Tell you what—we'll take in the powwow tomorrow, give Peter a taste of smoked fish and frybread. How's that?"

"Will you take us canoeing before we go?"

"I could," he supposed. "With a canoe you can avoid the boat landings. One of these days I'm liable to blow my cool and bash somebody's face in. Then I'd sure as hell make the front page of every newspaper in the state. And not the way I'd want to."

She touched the back of his hand with her cool fingertips. "After what I saw today, I don't know how you've resisted this long."

"No choice." Her soft touch had the same effect on him as her scent had. Old reflex, he told himself. The evening shadows covered for him nicely. "Anything I do reflects on the people. Gotta mind my manners." He smiled playfully. "Mostly."

"I won't ask what 'mostly' means."

It meant that as long as he was playing the gentleman escort, he would behave himself and dress the part. Gideon's idea of dressing up coincided in some ways with Raina's. He broke out a bottle of men's cologne that reminded him of the north woods on a chilly spring evening. He thought he could detect a hint of spruce, a touch of balsam and a splash of fresh water from a swift, icy current. And he wore his dress shoes—moccasins with floral beadwork—and his hairpipe choker with the abalone shell tickling his Adam's apple. The small leather bag he wore tucked inside his shirt was generally not for show, but the beaded belt was.

Damn, he felt good-looking.

It was too hot for the sport jacket he usually wore for official occasions. And the jeans, well . . . short or long, jeans were always Gideon.

The powwow was held in a traditional circular bowery. The focus was music and dancing, and the costumes splashed color in every corner of the fairgrounds. The prizes for the dance contests drew dancers from out of state, and even though styles had blended in recent years, Gideon was able to point out the differences between the American Chippewa and the Canadian Cree moccasins, both with floral beadwork. He noted the Ojibwa influence on the local Dakota designs, as opposed to those of their Western Lakota cousins. There were even visitors from the Southwest, and Raina was impressed with Gideon's knowledge of Zuni, Hopi and Navaho silver work, which was available for sale at some of the stands.

Peter was interested in everything that was going on around him—the costumes, the dance steps, the people, the food—but Raina could tell he was feeling a little awkward. He was like a saddle horse's colt catching a glimpse of a herd of mustangs. Was this really who he was? If he left his mother's side, would those strangers let him run with them, or would they kick up their heels in his face and leave him standing there looking stupid?

"What do you like to eat, Peter?" Gideon asked as they approached the chow wagon. "Corn dogs or Indian tacos?"

Peter checked the list of choices on the sign next to the sliding window. "What's frybread?"

Gideon's glance told Raina that she'd neglected her son's culinary education.

"I don't know how to make it," she explained.

"You take a bunch of bread dough, smash it down, cut a piece off—" his quick hands made air frybread as he explained "—make a slit, drop it in hot lard...." He peered through the window. "You got any fresh frybread in there, Ron? I mean *fresh.*" Shoving his hand into his pocket for money, Gideon turned to relay the cook's nod to the outside world. Then, in competition with the fan inside, he shouted into the window again. "We've got a guy out here who's never had frybread."

A round, sweaty, bespectacled face appeared in the window, followed by a paper plate with the sought-after sample. Ron adjusted his glasses and gave Peter the once-over. "*This* guy's never had *frybread?*"

"Boarding-school kid," Gideon said as he pushed some bills across counter. With a conspiratorial wink, he handed Peter the plate. "Spends all his summers at Disney World."

"Geez, poor little guy. What did he cut his teeth on?"

"Mouse tail."

Peter nearly choked on his first mouthful of frybread. Gideon laughed and slapped him on the back. "If you like this part, we'll have the works. Indian tacos. How about it?" Peter nodded, and Gideon ordered three.

"Two for me," said a voice at Gideon's back.

"Marvin, hey." Gideon wasn't sure Marvin Strikes Many would accept his handshake. But it was powwow time, time to socialize, so Marvin relented.

Gideon breathed a sigh of relief. He wanted everything to go smoothly today. No politics, no taking any stands. He shoved his hands in his back pockets and grinned. "Is your oldest boy around? I've got someone I want him to meet. My brother Jared's boy, Peter."

Peter was a little slow on the uptake with the older man's proffered handshake, but he had a mouthful of frybread to contend with.

"And this is Raina, Peter's mother."

Marvin nodded, then gave the universal Indian lip gesture toward the bowery, where the afternoon elimination rounds were taking place in the dance contests. "Tom's over dancing right now. Competing in men's traditional. It's his first year in twelve-to-eighteen."

"Is that Arlen Skinner judging?" Gideon frowned slightly, craning his neck to get a look past the lineup of younger boys dressed in colorful double bustles, waiting outside the circle for their turn to dance. "Haven't seen him around in a while."

"Some of us parents got together and asked him to come out and judge the dance contests," Marvin reported with a clear sense of satisfaction. "Arlen's one of the real traditionals. He knows how it's supposed to be done."

Gideon watched the old man take one of the boys aside and demonstrate a dance step, shuffling his moccasins in the grass.

"He sure does. It's good when the old ones do the teaching." He glanced Peter's way and gave an instructional nod. "It's good when the young ones pay attention to them."

"Arlen can still bring a buck down with an arrow."

"He uses a compound bow," Gideon pointed out as he indicated, again with a nod, that Marvin should help himself to the first two plates of Indian tacos Ron had served up.

"Nothing wrong with taking advantage of an improvement." Marvin handed his money through the window and claimed the plates. "But Arlen still knows his culture. Knows his rights, too." Hands full, he nodded his goodbyes and headed for the bowery.

"Good seeing you, Marvin," Gideon said to the man's heels. "Glad you've got no hard feelings over that deer."

Marvin plunked his plates on a bleacher seat, turned and watched the threesome wander from the chow wagon to the pop stand before he took exception to Gideon's assumption under his breath.

"What're you mutterin' about, nephew? Complainin' about the judging?" Arlen Skinner gave a dry laugh as he hiked his arthritic bones up to the plank seating and pulled a cigarette from his shirt pocket. "Your boy did real good."

"We've been working on his costume. Can you use some chow?"

The old man shook his head. "Could use a match, *nini-ninqwanis.*"

Marvin fished in his jeans pocket for a match for the man who called him his nephew. With his free hand he waved his son down. "Got something over here for you to eat."

He offered Arlen a light, but his attention strayed back to the motley trio at the pop stand. Motley from his perspective, anyway. "What do you think about the way Defender's trying to trade off our treaty rights?"

"I don't pay much attention to politics." Arlen blew a stream of smoke and turned a cursory glance toward the man who held Marvin's interest. He registered his reaction with a grunt. "Looks like he's got himself a pretty white girlfriend."

"That's his brother's wife," Marvin informed him. "His brother Jared. The one that moved to the city and died of a heart attack."

"You mean the lawyer? That's his wife?" Arlen pulled the cigarette from his mouth and took another look. "She don't look Indian."

"Nope." Marvin wagged his head. "The boy sure takes after his dad."

"His dad?" Arlen squinted, staring harder now in a manner that would have been rude, had it not been necessary. "You're talking about the lawyer? The lawyer was that boy's dad?"

"Hardly looks like a half-breed."

"If that's Jared Defender's boy, and if that's his only son, then he's no half-breed. He's my grandson." Arlen took another drag on his cigarette, squinting through the smoke for a last look before he finally turned away, muttering, "The one my daughter gave away."

Chapter 4

Gideon had promised to bring his canoe over to the lodge the following morning, and they planned to launch their outing from there. Raina had popped down to the little grocery store early and put together a picnic lunch, but she was beginning to think she would have to make a second trip if Gideon didn't show up soon. Peter had already eaten half the fruit she'd bought. He was working on a banana when Gideon called to say he would be a few minutes late. What he'd planned as a quick stop at his office was turning into a little more than that, he explained. Raina graciously refrained from mentioning that he'd long since passed a few minutes. Instead, she told him not to worry about it.

"He says he really wants to go, and we'll be doing him a favor if we hang in and wait," Raina reported as she hung up the phone.

"Jeez, Mom, he's like the president of the tribe. He's probably got a lot of stuff going on all the time." Peter dropped the banana peel into the wastebasket, propped his feet up on the chair opposite the one he occupied and checked the grocery bag for another selection. "I wonder what Mark and Eric would say if I told them my uncle was a tribal chief."

"I'm surprised you haven't told them," she said absently as she turned for a backward inspection of her outfit in the mirror. She wasn't sure she liked the way the blue looked tucked into the white. "Can you see my shirt through these shorts?"

"Kinda." Peter was more interested in slurping every drop of juice dripping from the plum he'd just bitten into. "It came up in a class once." His mouth was still half-full, so the words sounded juicy. "Social studies." He swallowed and licked his lips. "We were talking about current events. One of the other guys heard the name Defender on the news and asked if I was related. I said I didn't know."

"Why did you say that?"

"'Cause I don't." He shrugged and popped the rest of the plum into his mouth. After he spat the pit into the wastebasket, he allowed, "Not by blood, anyway. Figured I can say I'm related, or I can say I'm not. Depends on how you look at it and who's askin'."

"What would you say now?" she wondered, the shorts forgotten.

He had to think about that one. "I guess I *feel* like he's my uncle."

"Good." She tried to ruffle his hair, but he leaned away. "Did you enjoy the powwow?" she asked.

"Sure, it was okay." He reached for the TV schedule that was lying on the table next to the grocery bag. "I think I'd like to try spearfishing."

"It's legal during the ice-fishing season," Raina recalled. "Maybe this winter we can come back and ask your uncle Gideon to—"

"Oscar says the best time for spearing is in the spring." After a quick scrutiny, he tossed the schedule aside and snatched up another banana. "He says there's supposed to be a big celebration, traditional ceremonies, stuff like that. And there will be, once all this argument about who's got the say over how Indians do their fishing is settled. Oscar says it's a treaty right, and it's got nothing to do with state laws."

"They're working on some sort of compromise so that the Chippewa can resume the practice peacefully, without—"

The knock at the door prompted another mirror check, which confirmed Peter's assessment. The blue *did* show through the white shorts. "Too late now," Raina muttered on her way to the door.

But the man on the other side was not the one she was expecting. This one was wearing a uniform, a sidearm and a badge.

"Mrs. Defender?"

"I'm Raina Defender, yes."

"Cletus Sam. I'm a tribal police officer." He nodded politely, then glanced over her head, into the room. "I'm looking for Peter Defender. I'm carrying a court order for his—"

Court order? Raina folded her arms, squared her shoulders and took a wide stance in the doorway. "Peter hasn't done anything. He's been with me ever since we got here."

The officer produced a piece of paper with an official letterhead. "The judge issued an order for him to be taken into the custody of—"

"Custody?" Raina stepped back into the room, instinctively falling back to protect her child as she examined the document with Peter's name on it, signed by Judge Gerald Half. The names registered clearly enough, although the judge's was not familiar to her, but the rest made no sense.

She scanned the document again, but her eyes were working faster than her brain. "What does this mean—'the terms of the Indian Child Welfare Act,' and this part about biological family members?"

"May I come in, ma'am?"

Raina gave a tentative nod. "I don't have the papers with me, but I assure you that I can prove that I am legally Peter's mother."

"All I know is the boy is an enrolled member of the Pine Lake Band of Chippewa."

"Yes, he is. So was my husband. We adopted Peter when he was a baby, and it was all perfectly leg—"

"Are you Peter?"

The policeman turned to the table, where the boy sat with the first bite of his second banana still in his mouth, looking from one adult to the other in total confusion. He nodded hesitantly.

"You wanna come with me?" Officer Sam asked, as gently as he might have petitioned a much younger child. "We're just goin' over to see Judge Half, over to the court."

"I didn't do anything," the boy said quietly.

"Nobody says you did, Peter. The judge will explain." Officer Sam nodded to Raina and spoke just as quietly. "You can sure come, too, ma'am."

But Raina's voice was on the rise. "Gideon Defender is Peter's uncle. He'll straighten this whole thing out as soon as he hears—"

"Maybe he will, Mrs. Defender. But the court is separate from the chairman, so I've got to do like the judge told me." He gestured toward the paper, which was still in Raina's hand. "Gideon's office is right across the street, though, so you can go right on over there and see what he has to say. I mean, it's not like anybody wants to do any—"

"I'm interested in hearing what this *judge* has to say." She perused the document again, but the words wouldn't stay in focus, and the paper seemed to burn her fingers. "This is ridiculous. Peter has nothing to do with welfare, or whatever that act is supposed to mean."

She stared at the man, hoping to convince him, searching for the magic words that would make such perfect sense that he would take his paper and go back where he'd come from. "I'm the one who's raised him. I'm his *mother.*"

"Yes, ma'am." The officer turned to Peter again. "Nobody is going to hurt you, son. You're not in any trouble. The judge just wants to see you in his office. He'll explain everything."

She was doing all right until the judge asked her to wait outside his office while he talked with Peter. "I have no jurisdiction over you," the portly man with bulldog jowls explained. "Only the boy."

Over her objections, Cletus Sam directed her to a chair, but it was on the other side of the door to the room she ought to be in. The room where Peter was. This was not defensible. She definitely had parental rights. *Legal* rights.

Gideon's blue pickup was parked across the street. Right across the street! Surely he could see what was going on here. Why wasn't he doing something about this? Raina fumed to herself. Getting herself in a huff expanded her confidence as she marched past the receptionist and through the door labeled Chairman's Office.

Taken off guard, the receptionist was a little late in sliding her chair back from her desk. "You can't walk in without—"

Standing next to his desk with a handful of papers, Gideon turned in surprise. Dressed in a Timberwolves T-shirt and cutoffs, he clearly hadn't planned to spend the morning on official business. He looked poised, in fact, to set the rest aside.

"Gideon, thank God," she breathed.

He smiled sheepishly as he selected one paper and put the rest in a desk tray. "I'm sorry to keep you waiting, Raina. I think that phone has eyes. I ought to know better than to—"

"Gideon, what in heaven's name is going on?" She closed the door and approached him tentatively. "Did you know that your judge sent a policeman over to the lodge to arrest Peter this morning?"

Gideon's eyes widened incredulously. "*Arrest* . . . Peter?"

"Yes." She nodded once, then shook her head in confusion. "Well, take him into custody because of some child welfare law that says he can just take *my* son into *his* custody. I don't understand how—"

"Where is he now? Where is Peter?"

She gestured with an unsteady hand. "Right across the street." In two strides he was at her side, turning her toward the door while she was still sputtering, "You have to *do* something, Gideon."

On his way past the receptionist's desk he tossed a letter under her nose. "You know what to do with this, Rosie?"

"Sure. Slam-dunk it into file thirteen."

"No, you send out the standard reply. The Pine Lake Band has no intention of depleting the lake of all the fish, which were here before the Chippewa, who were here long before the North Woods Anglers Club started its annual fishing derby, *which* we wouldn't dream of interfering with, et cetera, et cetera." Half of him was guiding Raina toward the outside door, the other half reaching back, still pointing to the letter. "Those guys spend a lot of money at the casino."

"They say they're going to *boycott* the casino," Rosie pointed out. "Maybe you ought to call this guy, or else maybe—"

"Tell them we hope they'll reconsider. Just say—"

"Excuse me, Gideon." Raina tugged on his arm. "Peter doesn't understand what's going on any more than I do, and he's probably scared."

"Thanks, Rosie. Gotta see what the hell's goin' on across the way here."

Gideon opened the front door and ushered Raina into the late morning sunlight. "The Indian Child Welfare Act," he explained as they walked. "That's the law they're probably talking about. It's a federal law, and in Minnesota there's also a state law. The idea is to keep the children from being taken away from the tribe."

"What are you talking about, Gideon? We adopted Peter when he was a baby. Jared and I—"

"He's Chippewa. Somebody must have taken a notion to file a complaint of some kind."

"A *complaint?*"

They waited at the curb, both of them watching a car cruise by. The driver gave a nod, and Gideon returned the greeting. Then he turned to Raina. "I'm not sure why anyone would in this case, but you might need an attorney. We'll have to—"

"There's nothing to complain about. That judge has no right to take my son. Gideon, did you say something, or did someone approach you about—"

He shook his head. "I didn't know anything about this. As long as Jared was alive, there was no problem. Now, maybe there could be." He sighed as he stepped off the curb, thoughtfully eyeing the sign across the street that said LAW AND ORDER: Pine Lake Band of Chippewa. "Let's go see what kind of a problem. And how big."

They found Peter and Arlen Skinner occupying two chairs in the judge's chambers, exchanging sidelong glances as though neither was quite sure what to make of the other. Raina didn't know what to make of any of it, but she was relieved to find that Peter hardly looked scared, although he did still look confused. At Gideon's request, the judge admitted her into the office. He introduced the old man, Arlen Skinner, as Peter's grandfather.

"Grandfather?" Raina echoed softly, trying the word out on her own tongue. She knew she was supposed to approach an elder with a respectful handshake, but her feet wouldn't move. She knew she wasn't supposed to stare, but she couldn't help it.

Peter's biological grandfather?

"Here's the paperwork on this so far." The judge handed Gideon a file folder.

"Why didn't you talk to me about this before you served any papers, Judge?" Gideon looked the documents over, but he had a good idea what they would say. "This was some pretty fast work."

"Since the boy was in the neighborhood, seemed like the sensible thing to do was serve the papers first, ask questions later." The judge exchanged nods of previously determined agreement with the old man sitting quietly in the corner chair. "Peter here is a member of the Pine Lake Chippewa. He was enrolled by Tomasina Skinner, his birth mother. She didn't name his father. She's got him down as half Chippewa, so apparently his father wasn't a member of the band."

"Is she..." Raina glanced from the judge's face to Gideon's and back again. "Is she trying to take him back now?"

"My daughter was killed in a car wreck," Arlen said evenly. "Eight, nine years ago now."

"Judge, my husband and I adopted Peter when he was a baby. Jared actually made the initial arrangements, but I understand that Peter's mother—" The words, coming from her own mouth, stunned her. *She* was Peter's mother.

She turned slowly, like a player just enlisted for blindman's buff. A rising mire of uncertainty threatened to engulf her as she thrust her pleading gesture first in the judge's direction, then briefly toward the old man. But finally, as though she were awakening, recovering a full awareness of herself, she drew her hand back to her own chest.

"I..." She injected her voice with what starch she could muster and explained softly, "*I* was told that Tomasina, whom we never actually met, was allowed to choose the...to *choose* adoptive parents for Peter, and she chose us. We were looking for a child to adopt, and because Jared was Chippewa, we were...we were..."

She hated her senseless emotionalism when what she needed was coolness and poise. She cleared her throat and forbade her voice to crack.

"We were even... We gave him his name and everything."

She didn't have to do this, she told herself. There was no need to plead her case to these people, especially since the look in Arlen's eyes was decidedly unmoved. *Don't even try,* she wanted to say, but she was afraid.

"It was all perfectly legal," she insisted quietly instead. She turned to Gideon, whose familiar face did not threaten her composure. "After all, Jared was an attorney, wasn't he, Gideon? So it *all* has to be in order, because Jared never left any loose ends."

She took the slight bob of Gideon's chin as an endorsement. She turned to the judge, and calmly she concluded, "I know I'm a single parent now, but Peter is legally my own son."

Judge Half was unruffled. "The boy's also Arlen's grandson."

Son and grandson were not the same, Raina told herself, which enabled her to recover her manners and offer the old man a belated handshake. Arlen Skinner briefly permitted the courtesy, then withdrew his hand.

"Forgive me. I'm happy to meet you, Mr. Skinner. And I'm more than willing to..." She smiled at her son and fell back on her mother's prerogative to speak for him. "I know Peter's very glad to meet his grandfather, too. He never knew Jared's father, and mine is..."

Peter lowered his eyes and restlessly braced his hands on his knees.

Gideon was watching Peter.

Judge Half was surveying the order he had issued.

"All right, what's really going on here?" Raina demanded quietly. "Why did you send a policeman after my son?"

"Arlen asked the court to claim custody of his grandson on his behalf." The judge's dark eyes conceded nothing, deeply impregnated as they were with the power of Solomon. "Peter is Chippewa."

"So was my husband. Gideon's brother." She spun around, seeking his help. "Gideon?"

But he appeared to be studying the blank side of the document the judge held in his hand. "I'm guessing the tribal court is exercising its right to claim custody of a Pine Lake Chippewa child living in a non-Indian home." He looked up. "Right, Judge?"

"That's right." Judge Half extended his beefy hand toward Raina. "I understand how you feel—"

"Gideon, whose side are you on? Peter is your..." Her hands curled into fists as she remembered Peter's claim. He could be related or not related—whichever he chose. Maybe Gideon saw it the same way.

But she did not. She was Peter's mother. Period.

"We'll call our attorney and get this whole thing straightened out today, Peter. I'm not going to let them do this."

"I guess the question of whose side you're on—" Judge Half glanced sidelong at Gideon "—might be on a lot of people's minds, Mr. Chairman."

Gideon sighed. "The boy lost his—" He swallowed hard and cast a quick look ceilingward. "He lost his father just two years ago." He drilled Judge Half with a challenging stare. "We'd be hard-pressed to take him away from the only living parent he's ever known, wouldn't we, Judge? Hell, he's twelve years old. This is no time to be meddling in his—" Abruptly he turned his attention across the room. "You ready to raise another teenager, Arlen?"

"Marvin Strikes Many pointed him out to me at the celebration." The old man shifted in his chair, spreading his hands wide. "I didn't interfere with my daughter's decision to give her baby up for adoption, even though I didn't think it was right. She said the baby would go to a good Indian home. Jared Defender, she said, so I thought, okay. A good Indian home. I was sorry when I heard he'd passed away. I wasn't doin' too good myself then, so I didn't get to his funeral or nothin'. I never knew he was married to a white woman. Never thought to ask." He spared Raina a quick glance, then spoke to the judge. "I keep to myself, mostly. Never pay much attention to other people's business unless it crosses over into mine somehow."

Judge Half folded his arms over his chest. "Did Tomasina tell you much about the boy's real father?"

Arlen shook his head. "She wouldn't say who it was. All she ever said was, 'This is what he wants, too. Give the kid half a chance,' she said. I thought maybe she got some money out of it or something, because she always wanted to move to the big city, and that's what she up and did." He grunted with disgust and shook his head again. "But now, I don't think it's right, my grandson being raised by a white woman."

"What's wrong with a *white* woman?" Raina demanded, the trepidation gone from her voice. "I'm a good mother, and Peter is my son. You can't take my *son*. I don't care what this crazy law—"

"Raina." Gideon touched her arm. "Believe me, the judge has the authority to take this matter—"

She shook him off. "I *won't* give up my son!"

"I know." His hand dropped to his side. "Under the circumstances, I'm sure some kind of compromise—"

"Compromise!" Raina clipped, as sharply indignant as any mother cat surrounded by males threatening to devour her young.

"Sounds a lot like the word *settlement*," Arlen muttered. "Which is a word some of us are getting pretty tired of hearing."

"Let's not confuse *that* issue with this one," Gideon said. He rested one hand low on his hip and nodded toward the court order still held menacingly in the judge's hand. "What are we lookin' at here, Judge? Temporary custody while the lawyers cinch up their briefs, right? I'm the boy's uncle, and I'm also a resident of Pine Lake and an enrolled member of the band. I'd say I'm a good prospect, wouldn't you?"

"You want me to appoint you his guardian?"

Raina stepped forward. "Peter doesn't need—"

As a subtle warning, Gideon laid his hand on Raina's shoulder. "Temporarily."

"Hey, I gotta get back to school by September eighth," Peter put in. It was his first real comment, and it surprised

Raina that getting back to school was his first concern. But she was relieved to hear him speak up so sensibly for going home.

"We'll have time to get in some fishing, maybe a little camping before school starts," Gideon said. He slid Raina a glance that said *trust me,* while he turned his negotiations from the judge to Peter, skillfully including Arlen in the verbal circle he was drawing. "Your grandfather can teach you to dance Indian. That's what you came up here for, right? To learn about your culture?"

All the while he kept his hand on Raina's shoulder.

She'd never known Gideon to be such a smooth talker. For the first time she could see a commonality between brothers. She noted that Arlen hadn't refused the suggestion yet.

Gideon sidled quickly over to Peter, tapped him on the arm with the back of his hand and inveigled some more. "So here you've got yourself a grandfather into the bargain. Pretty cool, huh?"

"Pretty damn confusing," Peter grumbled as he stood slowly. He looked up at Gideon, implicitly accepting him as an ally. "Can these guys really...uh...take me away from Mom?"

Raina closed her eyes briefly, clamping down on the terrible burning in her throat. She would not lose it now. *She would not.*

"Judge Half is a fair man, Peter. He's got to sort though all the claims and the circumstances." He laid his hand on the boy's shoulder. "You're right, it's confusing, but we'll get it straightened out. It'll just take a little time." Gideon turned to the man who had the final say. "What about it, Judge?"

"You're her brother-in-law," Arlen injected. "I don't know if that's such a good idea."

"I'm the tribal chairman, Arlen. It's not like I'm gonna skip town."

Arlen looked at Raina, then turned to the judge. "Maybe she might try to take off with him or something."

"Take off!" Raina ignored the look of warning in Gideon's eyes. "If we leave, we won't be *taking off*. We have every right to leave here whenever—"

"Nobody's gonna take off," Gideon, the self-appointed voice of reason, insisted. "You don't mind staying with me for a while, do you, Peter? Your mom will be staying at the lodge."

Peter looked at each face in the room, one at a time. Finally he shrugged, then gave his head a quick shake. Unsure, uncomfortable, even a little unsteady, he was willing to defer to the man with the plan. At least Uncle Gideon— *Uncle* sounded better all the time—was not a stranger.

Gideon kept a judicious distance from Raina, but his eyes sought hers, and he offered quiet reassurance. "It'll work out."

She glared at him.

He glanced away. "You got something you want me to sign, Judge?"

The judge produced another document, which he filled out and finally slid across the desk for Gideon's signature.

"I wish my dad was here," Peter said as he assumed a detached stance from which to observe the proceedings. "He knew everything there was to know about the law. You'd hand him a court order, he'd hand you an injunction—" he snapped his fingers "—like that."

Gideon looked up, a trace of regret in his eyes, and he smiled. "Guess you'll have to settle for me. I'm no lawyer, but I know a little bit about a lot of things." He nodded toward Arlen, who hadn't moved from his chair. "Kinda like your grandfather."

"I know it's not right for her to take him away," Arlen said stubbornly. He folded his arms and shifted in his chair. The look in his eyes said this was only round one. "You'll need your Indian ways," he told Peter. "You'll be a man soon."

"But I don't know if I want to *live* up here. Summer might be okay, but—" Peter looked at the judge. "Don't I have something to say about all this?"

"Sure you do." Judge Half slipped the paper with Gideon's signature on it into his file. "Everybody gets a say in my court." He nodded in Arlen's direction. "I want you to spend some time with your grandfather, too, now that you two have finally met. You'll see to that, Gideon? And meanwhile, I've got to study up on your background a little bit. I'm just a judge. I'm not a lawyer, either. Like the chairman, I don't know everything there is to know about anything." He brandished the file. "Got some studyin' up to do."

Raina's brain was as wobbly as the hindquarters of a rhino shot with a tranquilizer gun. She hadn't seen the blow coming, and she was still reeling from it. Gideon kept telling her to stay cool, but his voice seemed distant. Peter had little to say, except that he didn't mind riding in Gideon's pickup "to keep up appearances," while his mother followed them back to the lodge in her car.

There they set about packing up Peter's clothes.

"You got an extra TV that I can hook this up to?" Peter showed Gideon the controls to his video game.

Gideon shoved his hands into his pockets as he scanned the cords and buttons on the control box. "I only have one TV. Does it have to be some special kind?"

"I have a converter." Peter glanced at Raina.

Without even seeing it, she could feel that visual check-in from child to mother, that Don't-I-Mom? look. Sitting on the bed, carefully folding each shirt, she looked up. There was an unspoken concern in her son's eyes, as though he were seeing her differently as he prepared to take his first significant leave of her, and it scared her.

But he smiled at her as he reported, "At home I have my own TV."

"I don't watch TV much," Gideon said. "It's yours for the duration."

"Yeah." Peter reached behind the TV and unplugged his equipment. "Whatever that means."

"It means until this custody thing gets straightened out," Gideon said. "It gets complicated, doesn't it, being an Indian?"

"Hey, I'm just minding my own business, eatin' a banana, and in comes this cop." Twirling the converter cord like a lasso, Peter nodded toward the door. "Pretty soon I've got a grandfather named Arlen Skinner, who tells me his daughter was my mother, and her name was Tomasina, and she's dead, and then my uncle gets to be my guardian, just *temporarily....*" He turned to Raina, giving her a puzzled look. "And I'm wondering, how come I never knew any of this stuff?"

"I didn't know about your grandfather," Raina said. She laid her hand atop the pile of folded shirts, splaying her fingers over the soft cotton. "The adoption—your adoption—was a private arrangement, which is perfectly legal in this state. Your dad handled the technical end of it, and when the time came, we both went to the hospital to get you." A warm surge of nostalgia flooded her as she recalled cradling her baby in her arms for the first time. So much beautiful black hair, she'd said. Such tiny, delicate fingernails.

"I remember the caseworker's name was Susan something, but I was never told your birth mother's name. I've often thought about her and wondered—" She shook the speculations away. She now knew the answer to the final question. *Wondered what ever happened to her.*

"We were given some medical information, but that's about all. I was just so glad to..." Raina looked at her son and smiled. "I was just so glad you were ours, Peter. Maybe I was afraid to rock the boat, I don't know. But I've never deliberately kept anything from you. I've answered all your questions as best I could."

She picked up the shirts and rose from the bed. Gideon and Peter both watched her every move, as though they were suddenly fascinated by her ability to pack a bag. As though they'd forgotten that mothers did such things. "That's why we came, remember?" she continued. "To answer some of your questions. If I'd known about your grandfather, I would have told you. And I have no idea whether your dad knew about him." With a glance she invited Gideon to answer for his brother.

But he skirted the invitation with a shrug. "Arlen's never been what you'd call a sociable fellow."

"Is he as mean as he looks?" Peter wondered.

"He just looks *old*," Gideon said. "And he *is* old." That was about all he could say for sure about the man, besides the fact that he was a "traditional," and he was reclusive, even among his own people. What little contact he'd ever had with Arlen Skinner had been accidental and had always made Gideon feel a bit uneasy.

"No, I don't think he's mean." Even now he had to make a concerted effort to shake off the uneasy feeling. He'd long since learned to arrest such feelings by distancing himself from personal ties. He could put Arlen into perspective by thinking of him as one of the elders. One whose realities dwelled, for the most part, in the past. One who remained behind as a reminder. One who deserved respect.

"Arlen's lost a lot over the years," Gideon said. "The older people remember how the land was appropriated by waves of newcomers. Around here, it wasn't so much the land but the timber they wanted first. Villages were a nuisance to the loggers, and logging drove the game away, anyway, so some of the bands agreed to move farther north. Our little band resisted.

"This is prime real estate." Gideon glanced out the window at the lakeshore below. "But we didn't know anything about real estate. We just knew we belonged here. We couldn't keep the miners out next, or the farmers, but in those days the United States didn't care that much about the hunting and fishing, so they said, 'We'll pay you for the land, but you can keep on hunting and gathering on it.'" He shook his head and chuckled at the irony of it all. "None of our people ever saw much of the money. Coincidentally, the Chippewa owed the white traders almost exactly the amount the government was paying for the land. So why not cut the red tape and send the money directly to the creditors? Makes sense." His full mouth turned down at the corners, and he nodded in a parody of understanding. "Eliminated a whole step. Went down in history as an early attempt to make government carry out its duties efficiently. But the Chippewa didn't much care for the way it worked out, so we've seen more than our share of red tape ever since.

"Anyway, with all the logging and the farming, the game kinda disappeared, so the Chippewa had some pretty hungry times. Most of the bands were relocated, but some families hung tough here by the lake. Guys like Arlen remember real well that after the loggers and the traders and the farmers, along came the weekend sportsmen, then the lake cabins. We didn't have much land left by then, but we still had our hunting and fishing rights. People like Arlen, the older ones, they just kept to themselves and watched over what was left.''

As Gideon watched now. Long, silent moments passed as he watched a fishing boat head out from the lodge. In the Land of 10,000 Lakes, evidently Pine Lake had become everybody's current ideal recreation spot.

''What do you think he wants, Gideon?''

''Arlen?'' Gideon turned from the window to find both Raina and Peter looking to him anxiously for the answer. He felt a little foolish. Maybe they didn't see any connection between his story and Arlen's demands. Maybe for them there wasn't any. ''Guess he wants a grandson. *His* grandson.''

''Which means—'' Raina gestured, hopeful of something simple and straightforward ''—visits, right? He wants to be able to see Peter periodically, the way... the way grandparents do. The way they *should*. I have no problem with that, and I'm sure Peter—''

''I'd like to get to know him,'' Peter chimed in. ''As long as he's not as mean as he looks. Heck, I guess that's how I'm gonna look when I get to be old, you know? I'm gonna look a lot like him. I'm *related* to him by blood.'' A first for Peter, that much clearly impressed him. ''Maybe he could come and watch some of my swim meets this year. Some of the guys' grandparents come all the time.''

''You're a swimmer?'' Gideon smiled. It was the phrase *related to him by blood* that got to him. And pride, and a strong sense of the circle. Maybe his sad historical tale had played a part in prompting this show of optimism.

''Yeah. Swimming and soccer.'' Peter turned to his mother. ''I gotta be back by the time soccer practice starts. You remember the date?''

"I have it written on the calendar." She shot Gideon a look that pleaded for reassurance. *He'll be back in time, won't he? Tell him he will, and tell me this will all be settled and we'll be on our way home soon.*

Home, Gideon reflected. His idea of home was a far cry from Raina's. Not better. Not worse. Just *different,* and the difference would take some serious getting used to for Peter, if it came to that.

"How about taking Oscar out in my canoe?" Gideon suggested. "He's been bugging me again this morning."

"All four of us?"

"Four would be crowded," Gideon acknowledged as he crossed the room to lay claim to the large duffel bag Raina was zipping shut. "You're a swimmer. Oscar's a paddler. Between the two of you, the important bases are covered."

Raina glanced up. "You've got something else to do?"

"Some calls to make."

"Yes," she said, as if she'd just remembered. "I guess I do, too."

"Hey, you're comin' over to my place with us. I'm responsible for him for—" Gideon shrugged apologetically "—probably for just a few days. Nobody said you can't be with us while I have, uh . . ."

"Custody of my son," she said bluntly.

"I'm his uncle," he reminded her, feeling the pressure of stretching his light tone beyond anything he felt. "Could be worse."

"You're also the tribal chairman. You ought to have some . . ."

"Pull?" The notion made him chuckle. "Tell you what, we're gonna take Peter's stuff over to my place and pick Oscar up on the way." He laid his hand on Peter's shoulder, carefully, as though he were testing the boy's forbearance. Peter lifted his eyes to meet Gideon's, offering

tentative trust. The big hand tightened in a gesture of reassurance. "Then we'll see how much pull this guy can manage on a canoe paddle. What's your event?"

"Event?"

"Isn't that what you call it in swimming?"

"Butterfly and breaststroke."

"Hey, I'll bet you can paddle that thing all the way to
Canada."

They had shared Raina's picnic lunch on Gideon's porch.
Afterward, the boys had gone out in the canoe, and the
phone calls to the attorneys had been made. Independ-
ently, the counsel for the Pine Lake Band and Raina's
lawyer came up with similar pronouncements. It sounded
like a "sticky" situation.

"*Sticky* just means they're gonna charge more." Gideon
opened the refrigerator door and gestured for Raina to stash
the remaining lunch meat inside.

"Easy for you to say. Yours is on retainer." She offered
him the last of the plums. When he shook his head, she
tucked the fruit into the crisper. "Did he sound as confi-
dent as mine sounded doubtful?"

"Our attorney has dealt with the issue before. Yours
probably hasn't."

"I've heard about it, of course, but I'm not sure I understand...*completely*." She closed the refrigerator door,
leaned back against it and stared him down across the narrow width of his kitchen. "You explain it, Gideon. Just
what is it we're dealing with?"

He braced the heels of his hands on the edge of the sink
behind him and took a deep breath, as though he'd been
backed into a corner and now had to make an official statement. "The Indian Child Welfare Act was passed in 1978,
and basically what it says is that the tribal court has the right

to—" he lifted one shoulder, as though the right were self-evident "—become involved the way it just has. Used to be that Indian kids were being siphoned away from their people, first into boarding schools, then non-Indian foster homes and adoptions.

"Finally, the people said, 'no more.'" He tilted his head slightly, his eyes looking for the kind of understanding that ordinarily would have come naturally to her. Quietly, he told her, "They said, 'You take our kids away, we've got nothing left.' So recently they got this law passed to protect Indian families and to preserve the integrity of Indian nations."

"This all sounds very—" she sighed, gesturing impatiently "—philosophical and political and . . . and it sounds like an interesting topic for discussion, but this is *my child* we're talking about."

"I know." He laid his hand on her shoulder in a gesture that was pure brotherly love. "I can't see the judge taking him out of a good home after almost thirteen years."

"He could do that?"

"I don't know." Technically, the answer was yes, but the judge's *will* to do it was another question, and of that possibility, Gideon could honestly say, "I don't know."

"What do you mean, you don't know? You're a tribal leader now, for God's sake. If you don't know, who *does?* If you can't do anything about this, who—"

"Raina." Gently he squeezed her shoulder, then let his hand fall to his side. "This is a complicated issue. We're going to take it one step at a time, and—for Peter's sake—you're going to stay calm."

But he took half a step back, because her defensive stare accused him of taking something from her. "I think the judge is going to want Peter to have a chance to get to know his grandfather, but I don't think he'll decide to turn the boy's whole world upside down, take him out of school, take him away from—'' he glanced at the top of the refrigerator and the cabinet above it, searching the high places in his kitchen for some assurance to offer ''—his mother. I just can't see him doing that now.''

''Excuse me, but I'd like to hear something a little more decisive, a little more positive, than what sounds like a cloudy forecast from your crystal ball.''

Stung by her sarcasm, he shrugged. ''Call your lawyer back, then.''

''I didn't like . . . what I heard in his voice. . . .'' Tears welled in her eyes, and her voice came dangerously near cracking. Her lips trembled as she drew a deep breath, searching for something that would steady her. ''. . . any better.''

What he saw in her eyes embarrassed him, and he glanced away. It wasn't easy for her to admit to a fear that might bleed her of her strength. He was afraid to touch her. He was afraid that if she fell apart and the pieces of her scattered across the floor, he wouldn't be able to put them together. He wanted to fix things for her, but he didn't know how. Arlen Skinner saw her as an outsider, and she sure as hell looked like one.

But this was Raina—Peter's mother, Jared's widow and Gideon's . . .

Gideon's *what?*

Sister-in-law. That was enough. She was family. The Indian way, he needed no more explanation, no other excuse. It didn't matter who he was or what office he held, she was family, just like Peter, and she deserved his protection, his care, all the comfort he could give her. He took both her shoulders in his hands, effectively pinning her to the refrigerator. *Ask me,* he willed. *Care, comfort, the strength in my body—they're yours for the asking.*

But that was not what she asked. She lifted her chin, her eyes pleading with him to use his power on her behalf, whatever power he had to steer the course of events.

Her silent, desperate plea clawed at his heart. The power she wanted didn't extend to her. It was for Peter and Oscar, even Arlen. But it was not for Raina. He was the chairman of the Pine Lake Band of *Chippewa*. And there was nothing he could honestly say to allay a white woman's fear. There was no promise he could make—honestly—and there was precious little he could give her in exchange for her tears.

He pulled her away from the refrigerator, drew her close until her shirtfront touched his, until he could feel the small, delicate impressions of her breasts through the layers of cloth. He slid his hands over her shoulders slowly, maintaining the lock his eyes had on hers, giving her fair notice, ample warning. Her eyes slid closed, and a tear escaped. One sparkling tear slipped down her cheek. He caught it on his tongue, tasted its wonderful saltiness, murmured something about her liking this better, this would be better, this would be...

A kiss. That was all. There was power in it for him, but little promise for her. Maybe she knew that. Maybe she didn't. When he felt her arms encircle him, he didn't care either way. All he wanted was the taste of her sweet mouth deep inside his, the feel of her tongue against his, and the dampness—the dampness of tears and kisses and opportunities long ago denied him. But the need for more than that swelled low in him, slow in him, gathering strength from the response her lips made, moving with his. His soft, involuntary groan expressed the depth of his need. He held her tight and pressed himself against her, letting her feel what he had to give. This and more, his hungry mouth promised. Don't be afraid. Don't...

Raina tore her mouth away on a desperate gasp. "Oh, no, not this." Her quick, frantic breaths fluttered against the base of his throat. She clung to him even as she denied him. "Gideon, we can't let this happen."

He drew back slowly, thinking—hoping—he hadn't heard her right. They'd put their arms around each other and shared a kiss, for God's sake. It tasted good. It felt good. It was what they both needed. What could be wrong with something that felt this right?

"Peter," she began as she sidled away, still gripping him at the waist for support. "Peter might..."

A thousand retorts raced through his mind, but he allowed none to pass his tongue. He couldn't afford to. The state his head was in right now, he couldn't be sure which one would cut itself loose first. Something about her or himself or the two of them together. Or something about Peter. Or Jared. God help them all, he thought as he finally stepped back. With everything that had happened already, this was a tangled mess.

But the kiss was right. That was all he knew. No matter what the source of confusion in her eyes, no matter how much fear and hurt glittered in them like glass splinters, there was a glimmer of something within her tears that told him the kiss was right.

We can't let this happen?

Didn't she realize it was more than fifteen years too late for that?

Chapter 5

Raina returned to Pine Lake after spending two days tying up loose ends at home. Her neighbor couldn't be expected to take care of the place indefinitely, which was exactly the kind of time frame Raina was looking at now. *Indian time.* It was the leisurely pace Jared had been determined to put behind him when he'd left the reservation. He'd often complained that the stereotypes hounded him—the notion that Indians never got anything done on time. That if they showed up at all they were always late. Good workers once they got started, but undependable. Unpredictable. Inconsistent.

She'd heard all the modifiers and qualifiers, too, and she'd watched her husband try to ignore them whenever speaking up might cause a rift with someone with whom he did business. She'd watched him try to change minds that didn't want to be changed, to try—without offending anybody—to kick holes in cherished images and long-held assumptions. All he'd gotten in return for his efforts, besides a lot of stress, was the occasional, presumably complimentary observation, that he certainly had come a long way from those roots of his.

Roots like *Indian time*. There had been many times when she'd wished Jared could slow down and smell the roses, maybe rediscover the meaning of Indian time. But he'd set his course for changing times, and he'd followed it religiously to the end.

He'd left her with more house than she and Peter could manage easily. She'd been inclined to sell it, but friends had advised her not to make any major changes immediately after her husband's death. Now she hired a lawn-care service and a home-security agency to tend it while she was gone. She couldn't say how long it would be. All she knew was that she had to stay close to her son. She had to accede to someone else's terms, to someone else's schedule—or lack of one. All things in good time. In Indian country, good time meant Indian time. And the reality was that, no matter what her husband had endeavored to be, her son was physically, legally, undeniably, Chippewa.

But he was also a twelve-year-old boy, and he was hell-bent on acting like one. When Raina returned to Pine Lake, she learned that Peter was "on restriction" for the weekend.

And, for the first time in over two years, she hadn't been the one to make the decree.

"Whose restriction?" she demanded. "The court's?"

"Mine," Gideon said simply as he passed Peter the potatoes he'd helped prepare for supper. "Since my experience with kids is pretty limited, I'm not used to sleeping with one eye open." He arched an eyebrow over that one eye, and Peter quickly lowered his. "But I'm learning fast."

Raina sighed. She'd thought her son had learned his lesson the last time he'd tried using the basement window instead of the door for an exit. "Did you sneak out again, Peter?"

"Me and Oscar did." He served himself a generous helping of potatoes. "We went to check out the casino, but they carded us, so we just hung out. This place is really quiet at three in the morning."

She gave Gideon a look of apology. "I forgot to warn you that Peter is a night owl."

"I've been known to do some hootin' with the owls myself." Gideon sawed on his well-done beef with a table knife. "I know all the haunts around here and probably a few tricks you haven't thought of yet, Peter. So I'm way ahead of you."

"Did you get grounded, too?" Peter asked.

"Didn't get caught too often." Gideon glanced at Raina. "Didn't have anyone out looking for me. My dad wasn't around, and my mom wasn't up to it." He turned a hard look Peter's way, tapping a forefinger on the table to make what he hoped would be a memorable point. "So when I *did* get caught, I got searched, handcuffed and hauled off to jail."

"For what?"

"Petty stuff. Kid mischief." He nodded confidently. "Mistakes you're too smart to make, Peter. Myself, I was a slow learner."

"Seems like you turned out okay."

Gideon leaned back in his chair and put his hand to his mouth. His eyes shifted from Peter's face to Raina's and back again as he wiggled his front tooth until it came loose with a click. He withdrew it and showed them the empty space.

Raina's eyes widened. Peter laughed, as thoroughly delighted as he had been when he was six years old and Gideon had magically produced a quarter from his ear.

"My goodness, Gideon, I'd never have known," Raina marveled.

"You would have if you'd seen me about ten years back, when I couldn't afford a false one." He popped the tooth back in place and smiled, as splendidly as ever. "Indian Health doesn't cover the cosmetic stuff."

"How'd it happen?" Peter wanted to know.

"Lost it in a fight. It could have been worse. It could have been an ear or an eye." Gideon pointed the blunt-tipped knife Peter's way in passing, then set it back to work on his meat. "There's a lot of bad stuff going on after dark. A lot of ways to get hurt."

"Around here?" the twelve-year-old voice of experience scoffed. "This place is like the outback at night. You oughta try the Cities."

"I have." Gideon noticed the question in Raina's eyes. He shrugged. "If a guy's looking for trouble, he'll find it wherever he goes," he said before he took a bite of meat. But the question hung in the air until he dismissed it without looking up from his plate. "I lived in St. Paul for a while. Didn't like it much."

"We didn't know you were living so close by."

An old wound melted away when he looked into Raina's eyes and saw honest bewilderment. He smiled wistfully. The *we* part wasn't exactly true, but it was good to know that she didn't realize that. And that *she* hadn't known.

He'd said he didn't want her to know, but he'd often wondered whether Jared had mentioned it to her after all. Gideon had needed his brother then, but he'd never been able to say it in so many words. He'd also thought a lot about his brother's wife. He'd thought about the baby they'd adopted, the home they'd made for themselves, the family he wanted to be part of in some small way. Staying away had never been harder than it was then.

She read it in his eyes—at least, some of it. "Jared didn't tell me. Were you there for...?"

"I was only there for a short time. It didn't work out." Nothing had been working for him then. With an abrupt gesture he dismissed the recollection and turned to Peter. "So you see, big city or backwoods, you're probably not gonna come up with too many tricks I haven't tried. You might as well save yourself the trouble."

"Like you're just about to tell me you wish you had," Peter supposed, challenging Gideon to a stare-down. "You did your own growing up, and you did it your way. Why don't you leave me alone and let me do mine?"

"Why don't I?" Out of a hundred reasons, he was supposed to pick the best one right there on the spot. "Because your dad was my brother, and your mom..." He'd taken the first easy choice, then skidded when he hit the hard part.

With a wave of his fork he backpedaled, settling on what was indisputable, figuring he was entitled to all the prerogatives of the man in charge. "Because I signed some papers saying I wouldn't. At least, not for the time being."

"Yeah, well, I don't see why they let you just—" Peter slid his mother a help-me-out-here glance "—take over on me all of a sudden."

"I should've seen this coming, I guess." Gideon pushed peas and carrots across his plate with an ineffectual fork. "This legal hassle. I should have realized that, with Jared gone, something like this might come up."

"Yeah, well..." With perceptiveness honed by years of parent-handling, Peter recognized Gideon's self-doubt as the chink in the fortress. "This is supposed to be temporary, and you act like you think you can be my dad. Like you can just tell me what to do." Seizing the moment, he fired his zinger. "But you can't. My dad *would've seen* this coming, and he wouldn't be letting any of it happen."

Gideon took the blow with a level stare. "What would he have done if he'd caught you sneaking out at night? Anything different from what I'm doing?"

"That's not exactly the point."

"It *is* exactly the point." It really wasn't, but Gideon decided to make it the point by virtue of the authority Judge Half had unwittingly vested in him. "I'll stand in for him the best I can as long as . . ."

Raina and Peter were both staring at him now, wondering if he knew something they didn't. *As long as* what?

He went for the open-ended option, hoping it covered the bases innocuously. "As long as need be."

Now drop it, he warned Peter with a paternal look that seemed to come naturally, without a lick of practice.

"We talked about paying your grandfather a visit," Gideon said, easing smoothly into a different subject. No less sticky, just different. "You still wanna do that, Peter?"

"I guess so."

Gideon turned the offer over to Raina. "We were just waiting for you to get back so you could go along if you'd like to."

The suggestion clearly surprised her. "Do you think I'd be welcome?"

"I think we need to try to get along." Gideon spared Peter a patently inclusive glance. "With each other and with the old man. I'm betting that a genuine, friendly overture will earn you some points with the judge."

"Earn *me* some points?" Raina's look challenged him, and her follow-up smacked him hard. "You're maneuvering on my behalf, Gideon? When I'm not even part of your constituency?"

Surprised less by the remark itself than by the way it stung, he sighed. "Just trying to pour a little oil on the water, that's all."

* * *

Arlen Skinner lived in a three-room house tucked deep in the woods at the end of a gravel road that turned into a dirt track about three-quarters of a mile before it became part of his side yard. Visitors couldn't call ahead, since Arlen had no phone, but Gideon assured Peter that his grandfather was usually home. And that there were people checking on him regularly.

One of the programs Gideon had started since he'd taken office involved adding a home-visiting assignment, not only to the duties of the tribal health workers, but also for the tribal employees whose jobs had them traveling the reservation byways. People like game warden Carl Earlie paid routine visits to the tribal elders.

At a time when increasing numbers of the younger generation of Chippewa were looking for off-reservation opportunities, elders like Arlen Skinner were not to be ignored by Gideon's administration. Even though profits from the casino had made it possible to provide housing for many of the elderly within the small town of Pine Lake itself, Arlen preferred to stay in his own house, isolated as it was. Gideon was a strong advocate for respecting the elders' reluctance to change the way they'd always lived. He paid as many personal calls as he could, mostly for his own benefit, he was quick to say, for there was much to be learned.

But he had always seen that Arlen was on someone else's route rather than his own.

The old man was sitting on his porch, his chair tipped back against the weathered siding on the front of the house. He was surrounded by wood shavings, plastic pails and bundles of willow and birch, and he was working with strips of birch bark. He looked up as the three expectant visitors approached. Lowering the front legs of his folding chair to

the plank porch, he nodded a solemn acknowledgment of
their presence.

Clearly neither side knew what to expect of this meeting.

Gideon reached past the steps and wordlessly offered a
handshake. Raina knew well enough to follow suit, but Peter, suddenly reluctant to take center stage, hung back.

"Shake hands with your grandfather, Peter," Gideon in-
structed.

Peter promptly complied, stubbing the rubber toe of his
high-top tennis shoe on his way up the wooden steps.

"Do you speak Ojibwa?"

"No—" Awkwardly stuck for a way to address this new-
found relative, Peter tried, "Sir."

"Call me *nimishoomis*," the old man said, then trans-
lated, "'Grandfather.' I'm not a 'sir.'"

"*Nimishoomis*," Peter repeated carefully.

"Can you make coffee, *ninaoshishan?*"

Peter didn't need a translation. He knew that he was being addressed grandfather to grandson. "You mean like in
a coffeemaker?"

"I mean like on a stove. Show him," the old man ordered Gideon. "You won't have any trouble finding the
kitchen. Everything you need is there. When you come out,
bring yourselves some chairs." He waved a strip of bark toward a folded chair leaning against the house and offered
Raina an invitation by way of a nod. "I have one here for
Mrs. Defender."

She opened the paint-splattered chair and set it next to the
small, green Formica-topped kitchen table that was spread
with Arlen's work-in-progress. Gideon ushered Peter into
the house. The door closed softly behind them as Raina
took her seat across from their host.

"Raina," she said quietly, perching like a shy forest
creature on the edge of the folding chair.

Arlen spared her a questioning look.

"My name..." She cleared her throat nervously as she folded her hands in her lap, feeling a bit like the girl with the impeccable school record who'd been called to the principal's office. She took a deep breath and offered a tentative smile. There was no call, she told herself, to feel nervous. "Please call me Raina."

"Raina," Arlen said, testing the name out much the way Peter had done with the Ojibwa word he'd been given.

"Rain, with an *a* on the end."

"That could almost be an Indian name." It might have been a compliment, but there was no smile on his slash of a mouth. Only a hint of one, maybe, in the dark depths of his eyes. "Rain, with an *a* on the end," he echoed. "I know some people by the name of *Reyna,* but they're not 'rain with an *a* on the end.' They're Indian, though. Part Indian, anyway."

He eyed her curiously.

She fidgeted, the backs of her thighs sticking uncomfortably to the metal chair. She smacked her knee, flattening a mosquito, and regretted her choice of madras plaid walking shorts for this outing.

"Do you have a great-great-grandmother way back who was part Indian or something? Maybe your grandmother named you after her." One corner of his mouth turned up just slightly. "Raina."

"None that I know of," she said airily, offering him her own smile and hoping to set an example. "I used to teach at the Pine Lake School, though. Back when I first met my husband. Does that...help?"

He slid a strip of bark between his fingers, considered her face and finally nodded once.

"Jared," she supplied obligingly. "My husband. Did you know him?"

"Not really. I knew his dad, long time ago. I used to stay with my wife's people." He tipped his chin in a vaguely westerly direction, pursing his lips as though his idle hands were too busy to make the gesture. "Over by where they got that new school now. She was from the Strikes Many clan. After she died, I came back here. But I lost track of those Defender kids. This one moved to the Cities. That one got to be chairman somehow." He shrugged. "I lost track."

"Do you have other children besides—" unsure of the reference, she gentled her voice to the point of near downiness "—besides Tomasina?"

"Two sons," he reported. "Both went away, looking for jobs. One other daughter, married one of them Oglalas, moved to South Dakota. Peter's mother was the youngest." She could tell he was testing her. When she didn't take exception to his choice of the word *mother*, he confided, "The wildest, looks like."

"Do you have other grandchildren?"

"Five. Don't see any of them that much." He couldn't quite hide the fact that he felt slighted. He shifted in his chair. "So you used to be a schoolteacher. And your husband was a big-shot lawyer?"

"I wouldn't say he was a big shot. He worked very hard." Gently, as was her way, she added, "And he died very young."

"A lot of Indians die too young." His dry chuckle might have seemed inappropriate had Raina not experienced the cruel irony firsthand. "They don't want to listen to us *old* Indians. They don't ask us how we keep livin' so long, 'cause they got their own ideas. They want to go live like white men. They say it's more fun for them."

Raina nodded. "Jared just worked too hard. Twelve, fifteen-hour days sometimes . . . His heart . . ."

"Was he too busy to make babies?"

"No." Curiously, she did not find his question intrusive, nor did she mind answering it. "We did try. It just didn't work out for us until...until Jared found out about Peter."

The old man grunted. "I told my girl it wasn't right, giving her baby away. She told me he was going to an Indian home, so I just let it go. She always had to do things her own way. Then she told me the name—that Defender that got to be a big-time lawyer down in Minneapolis. I knew he was probably giving her money, but I didn't say anything."

"Well, we *offered,* but..." She didn't like the turn the conversation was taking. "Maybe some for expenses. I'm not sure. Jared handled all the details of the adoption, but it wasn't like...like we *bought* Peter or anything." Whatever the arrangements had been, Raina felt that she owed Tomasina Skinner a debt of unending gratitude, regardless of whether her father approved.

She braced her hand on the edge of the table, leaned closer and entrusted him with the simple heart of her cause. "I've been Peter's mother since he was six days old, Mr. Skinner. I love him very much."

He nodded and pointed toward the end of the table. "Hand me that pail of water there. This bark has to be soaked."

She jumped at the chance to accommodate him and to talk about something else. "What are you making? Will this be—"

"Who wants coffee?" Gideon appeared at the door, steam rising from the melamine cups he carried, one in each hand.

Peter came next. With his free hand he held the door for Gideon, who served Raina one of the cups and kept the other for himself. Peter's cup was for his grandfather.

"Don't hardly keep any pop around." Arlen nodded his thanks, then sipped noisily, his grimace a sign that the coffee was especially hot. "Mmm, good and strong. Next time you come, I'll have some pop for you, *ninaoshishan*. What kind do you like?"

"Any kind." A long, narrow, bark-covered bowl on the table caught Peter's attention. He touched one of the clothespins that held the lining in place. "What're you making?"

"Winnowing baskets," Arlen said. "Good birch-bark baskets. That one's drying."

"They're for ricing," Gideon put in.

Arlen set his cup down. "You like wild rice?" he asked Peter as he gathered several pieces of bark for the pail Raina had set next to him.

"It's okay. We don't have it much."

"I do make wild-rice stuffing sometimes," Raina put in quickly.

"We're going to teach her how to bait her own hooks next. We'll get her trained." Gideon slid Raina a teasing smile, then nodded toward Peter. "This guy's gonna make a hell of a good fisherman. He caught a nice walleye the other day." He held up his hands to show Arlen, measuring generously. "That sucker was two pounds, easy."

"Bigger than that," Peter insisted, moving Gideon's left hand another inch. He grinned, ignoring the dubious look on Gideon's face. "More like that, yeah."

"Born fisherman," the boy's grandfather said.

As Arlen demonstrated the basket-making process, he described how the baskets would be used during the early autumn wild-rice harvest, when the Chippewa would exercise another of their treaty rights. It was an important source of income for him and for many others. He lamented the competition from the new cultivated varieties of wild rice, which was not rice at all, but truly a lake-grass grain, and he noted that the "farm stuff" was not to be mistaken for the real thing.

"That stuff has to be labeled 'cultivated,'" Gideon pointed out. "Real wild rice is longer, lighter in color, tastes better, and it's gathered in baskets like these by real Indians in real canoes. Right, Arlen?"

"Big difference. Big, big difference." He wagged a gnarled finger and gave Raina the hint of a smile. "You remember this when you make your stuffing next time."

When it was almost time to go, Peter helped Raina clear away cups and led the way inside. "I'll show you how we made the coffee, right on the stove. I didn't know you could do that. I thought if you didn't use a coffeemaker, you had to use instant. Remember how Dad hated instant?"

Gideon watched them disappear into the house, then turned to Arlen, who offered him a cigarette. Gideon told himself he didn't want to be rude. Besides, he'd been doing well, and he owed himself one. Arlen leaned forward in his chair as Gideon struck a match on his thumbnail and offered him first touch of the flame.

"What do you think of your grandson?" Gideon squinted past the smoke as he renewed his acquaintance with the gritty pleasure of the first long, deep drag from a good cigarette. "He seems like a pretty well-adjusted kid, doesn't he?"

"Adjusted to what?" Arlen's smoke mingled in the air with Gideon's. "He has some things to learn yet."

"Well, sure, he's not quite thirteen."

"Things about who he is and where he comes from."

"That's why they came up here, Arlen. Raina doesn't want to keep him away from us. She wants him to learn those things."

The old man gave the woman's purpose some thought as he smoked a little more. Finally he shook his head. "It's no good, Indians moving to the city."

Gideon studied his cigarette. He couldn't argue that point. It hadn't been that good for his brother, but it was all Jared had ever wanted. "The good life" meant different things to different people, and Indians were people, just like everyone else. They paid their money and took their chances, and they deserved the chance to choose.

"You've let well enough alone until now, Arlen. Why stir this up when the boy's almost grown?"

"Seeing him with her," the old man recalled. "No offense to your sister-in-law, but when I seen him with her, I knew it wasn't right."

Gideon understood how the old man must have felt, seeing the boy for the first time, and then having Marvin Strikes Many on hand with just the right goad. Something like, *Your grandson's being raised by a white woman, and Gideon Defender's the one to blame.*

"Now that you've met her, what do you think?"

"I think she's still white." Arlen appeared to be studying the toes of his moccasins. "Like I said, no offense, but I think you're forgetting, just because she's your sister-in-law."

"She's a good mother. You can see that."

"I can see that she cares for my grandson," he allowed. "But a boy his age needs a man to help raise him. And a Chippewa boy needs—"

"My father was dead by the time I was his age, and Peter's—" Gideon closed his eyes briefly. The taste of cigarette smoke turned acrid in his mouth. "Peter's is, too."

The door behind them opened, and Raina emerged, still praising Peter's first efforts at stove-top coffee making.

Arlen looked up as Peter stepped out behind her. "You would like wild rice the way I make it, *ninaoshishan*. The rice I have gathered myself."

Peter touched the unfinished edge of the basket on the table. "I wouldn't mind learning how to make these. They look pretty cool."

"It looks something like that basket you made for me for Mother's Day when you were about seven years old," Raina said proudly.

"That was just a grade-school project." He shrugged off his achievement as a pale comparison. "The teacher did half of it, and she was following directions out of a book."

"That's what schoolteachers do." Raina offered a maternal pat on the shoulder. "They get ideas from books. There's nothing wrong with that."

"Nothing wrong with learning the old ways, either," Gideon said. "Put the old ways together with a few new ideas, you never know. You might end up with the best of both worlds."

"Or you might lose out." After directing it first at Peter, Arlen deftly transferred his admonishment toward Gideon. "You might lose everything, just like we've *been* doing for the last hundred years. We've been compromising." The old man took a last puff on his cigarette, then spat the smoke in disgust as he pressed the butt into a jar lid on the table. He eyed Gideon dispassionately. "You're too young to be a tribal leader. That's why I never voted for you."

Gideon shook his head, chuckling. "No beatin' around the bush, this guy." He followed Arlen's example, putting out his cigarette in the jar lid. The end of a smoke signaled the end of a visit. "That's all right, Arlen. Man's gotta vote his conscience."

"Maybe you ought to think about teaching up here again," Arlen told Raina. "Maybe your brother-in-law could get you a job."

"I've always loved this place." She turned to her son. Reading him came less easily these days, but it was a mother's habit, and one she wasn't ready to break. "I don't think Peter wants to change schools."

Content to let the supposition stand, Peter tested the spring on one of the clothespins holding the bark to the basket frame, then eased it back into place.

"Next time you come back, we'll make a sweat," Arlen told Peter. "We'll smoke the pipe together."

Peter glanced at his mother, who was dead set against smoking, then his uncle, who was trying to quit, and finally his grandfather, who had offered him the forbidden right there in front of their faces. He'd never had a grandfather before, but he'd heard there could be interesting benefits.

He smiled. "That'd be cool."

"Good." The old man rose from the chair slowly, easing his stiff joints into motion. "I will give you something, then. A gift from your grandfather."

At Gideon's house that evening, Raina wasn't asked to stay for supper. She was simply included. But Peter had a place at Gideon's table and a towel in Gideon's bathroom. They showed Raina the room they had fixed up for Peter downstairs, next to the den, where the video games were now hooked up to the TV. Gideon had borrowed a roll-away from the lodge, and Peter had apparently acquired some fishing tackle. Raina didn't ask about it. Seeing it shelved in "Peter's room" near "Peter's bed" angered her a little, but it frightened her more.

Peter had a room elsewhere, she reminded herself. He *had* a bed—a bigger one than this, made up with the bedding she had chosen for it in the subtle colors he tended to choose for his clothes. He liked blue denim and brown corduroy, not the gaudy plaid that covered the rollaway. It hadn't been more than two weeks since Raina had pulled a plaid shirt off a rack in a department store, and Peter had said, "No way. I'm not wearin' *that*."

She was thinking of all those things as she helped Gideon put the last of the dishes away. She hadn't been much help, actually. Peter had taken out the trash, then bounded down the steps to use the TV in "his" den. Raina dried a few dishes and handed them to Gideon. She could have guessed where they might go, since the pine cupboards in the kitchen were few in number.

But whenever he had them open, she paid less attention to what was inside than to the unconscious ease with which Gideon took to such mundane chores. Gideon Defender putting his dishes away in his kitchen, filling the coffeepot with water, clamping an opener on a can and releasing the homey scent of fresh coffee. Remarkable, she thought as she watched the strong hand that was a natural at wood-chopping and paddle-wielding turn the crank on a kitchen device.

She'd never pictured him in *his* kitchen. She'd never imagined him in such domestic surroundings. In her mind, he was part of the wild life, both outdoors and, less frequently, in honky-tonks and poolrooms. She'd always been fascinated by the wildness she perceived to be intrinsic in him. Barely controlled, barely controllable, Gideon's very nature was like a curious passageway that lured her with the promise of something new and exciting at the end. She'd always approached excitement cautiously, one shoulder leaning in its direction, the other aimed for a last-minute escape.

But she remembered that, in the end, it was Gideon who had backed away. Maybe that was the way of wildness, she had decided. And in her mind she had consigned all wildness to a world quite different from hers, a world full of risk-taking and privation. She hadn't expected it to live in a place with dishes and cupboards, nor to make room in that place for her child. She should have felt comfortable with it, now that she could see for herself how unexpectedly familiar so much of it was. But she felt like an outsider. And that scared her.

"You've been pretty quiet," Gideon observed as he handed her a cup of the coffee he'd just made. "I thought some decaf might go down easy right about now."

She told herself it would be easier if she stopped letting his every move surprise her, and she murmured her thanks.

"Mii gwech," he said with a warm smile. "You remember. *Mii gwech?* Thanks?"

"Mii gwech," she repeated softly. They faced each other across the small kitchen, each with a countertop to lean against, each with cup in hand. "You speak Ojibwa fluently, don't you?"

"Mmm-hmm." He sipped his coffee. "I get stumped when people ask me to spell it, though. I speak it, but I don't write it."

"I don't think Jared knew much of the language at all."

"See, I'm one up on him. But don't tell Peter. I don't want to spoil anything for him." He glanced away. "The dad who knew everything. That was Jared. The man who could do no wrong."

"Was that the way you saw him, too?"

He glanced at her curiously, then dismissed the question by changing the subject entirely. "What did you think of

Arlen's suggestion? The one about coming back here to teach.''

"It's a little late in the year to start applying for teaching jobs.''

"There are still a couple of openings. I checked.''

"And you'd put in a good word for me?'' He nodded. "A few days ago you were discouraging an extended stay,'' she reminded him. "You said the political climate had rendered relations a bit—'' the pause was mostly for effect, because she did remember ''—*dicey* was the word you used.''

"That was then,'' he quipped, his tone suddenly as flat as hers was sharp. "This is now.''

"Yes.'' An outsider, she told herself, needed to be sharp. *Stay* sharp. Mix in a little sarcasm. "And what a difference a day makes, hmm? A little controversy over a few fish suddenly seems rather insignificant.''

"Not to me.'' He studied her with expressionless eyes. "Not to *us*.''

"And my son is now court-ordered to be one of *you*.''

"He always was.''

"I don't mean culturally. I never disputed that. I mean politically.''

"It's one and the same.'' He drew a deep breath, still watching her, waiting with less than his usual patience for her to stop skirting the issue.

"You haven't answered my question, Raina. I don't know what your lawyer told you, but *I'm* telling you there's a good possibility that Judge Half will rule that Arlen deserves *some* time with his grandson and vice versa. I don't know how much time, and I don't know how he'll suggest you work it. I just know that the precedent is pretty well established.''

Sharp, she told herself. Stay sharp. But she glanced away, the threat of too much truth blunting her will. "Yes, that's what my lawyer said."

"You won't lose him," he said.

The hope that he knew something she didn't brought her eyes back to his, wordlessly asking for a promise.

"No one's going to take him away from you." He couldn't stop himself. When she looked at him that way, he had to give her what she wanted. "That's not gonna happen. I won't—" He swallowed hard, looking elsewhere for help—the bright light above the sink, the shiny faucet, the dish drainer. "Well, the *judge* won't let that happen. He knows it's too late to take the boy back."

"You really think so?"

"Yeah." He nodded persuasively. "I can't see that happening now."

"I've thought about trying to get my old job back here." She offered a tentative smile. "I checked, too. They need a fourth-grade teacher. I just don't know whether it would be good for Peter. Jared didn't think much of the schools up here."

"He didn't think much of the *life* up here." Gideon stared into his cup. "But as it turned out, life in the fast lane didn't agree with him all that well, either."

"He used to say that *you* were the one looking for fast . . . oh, fast thrills or something."

"That's *cheap* thrills." His brow furrowed as he made a pretense of searching for the right words. "A fast buck and a faster woman. I think that about sums up my brother's favorite assessment of my basic needs."

"He never spoke unkindly of you, Gideon. Sometimes I thought he envied you your—" she shrugged, glancing around her as if some piece of it might be found in his kitchen "—your freewheeling life-style."

"My 'freewheeling life-style,'" Gideon repeated with a dry chuckle. "Right. Nothing about my life appealed to Jared. 'The good life'—that's what Jared wanted. The American dream, looming off in the distance at the end of that fast lane." He shook his head, raising his coffee cup as though he were toasting her. "I had nothing he envied. He had goals—I had needs. Big difference between the two."

"You don't think Jared had needs?"

"They were always met." His eyes conveyed the full weight of his meaning. "Always."

"And yours?"

He answered with a look, smoldering in silence.

"Gideon, I have to ask you something." But she had to glance away before she withered beneath the heat in his dark eyes. "Something I've thought about often over the years, but never—" She bit her lip, hesitating as she looked up at him again and sought his indulgence. "I never asked, even though I told myself there was a good chance the truth would ease my mind. But the prospect of opening a ruinous can of worms was always enough of a deterrent."

Before she went on, she stepped to the back of the kitchen and quietly closed the door at the top of the basement steps.

His eyes followed her every move.

She took a deep breath as she came back to him, speaking softly, steadily. "I have a feeling you know more about the circumstances of Peter's adoption than I do."

"What do you mean?"

"Specifically," she began carefully, "about Peter's biological father." She looked up, looked him straight in the eye. "Was it Jared?"

He was thunderstruck. "Jared?"

She squared her shoulders, preparing herself to hear the truth, whatever it was. "Did Jared have an affair with Tomasina Skinner?"

"That's a hell of a thing for you to ask me, Raina." He suddenly looked confused, even hurt. "My brother's dead. Why would you even...?" He shook his head, staring at her as though she'd just popped out of the floor. "Why would you think that?"

"Most people wait years for an adoption. Our was almost too easy." She wasn't going to let his reaction alter her course. "I said that to Jared once, just...just wondering how it came about. He said that being an Indian was an advantage for a change."

"That and being a lawyer."

"But it was all so—" Too good to be true, too wonderful to question. "One day he knew where we could get a baby, and the next day we had Peter."

"Didn't happen quite that fast."

"But Jared had had very little contact with the reservation since we left, as far as I knew. He seemed to go out of his way to avoid..."

"Avoid...what?" Gideon's smile did not reach his eyes. "Or should I say *who?*"

"All things Indian, I guess. Once he'd left it behind him, he kept saying he didn't want to look back."

"You guys wanted a baby," Gideon recalled for her, and she nodded, acknowledging that much. "Jared said he had a low sperm count. It was like he was confessing some terrible personal secret when he told me, like he'd found out he was missing—" For lack of acceptable words, he used those he once scoffed at. "'What separates the men from the boys,' I think he said. I thought he meant he couldn't get it—" His gesture, turning out to be as awkward as any word he could have chosen, ended in a frustrated slap to his own thigh. "You know, I thought he meant he couldn't perform."

"Perform?" She shook her head. "His sperm count was below average, but it wouldn't have been impossible for him to father a child . . . or for me, except for my . . ."

"He said you had a problem, too, but he didn't get—" *Personal* was the word that came to mind. The idea grated on him, but it had seemed as though once she'd become Jared's wife, nothing about Raina had been any of Gideon's damn business. He settled on "Technical."

"I have a tipped uterus," she told him. "Which isn't the end of the world, either, but with the combination of the two . . ."

"He couldn't *produce.* Couldn't get you pregnant."

Her eyes turned icy. "Sounds like you're talking about breeding stock instead of people."

He knew it did, just as he knew that the pleasure he took in making such a statement was of a pretty perverse nature. *Jared couldn't get the job done.* "So you're thinking he managed to get another woman pregnant."

"The thought did occur to me, yes."

"Are you jealous?"

"Jealous!" She scowled. "My husband is dead, for heaven's sake."

"They're both dead, *for heaven's sake.*" He lowered his voice and persisted. "Are you jealous?"

"No." She had the look of a woman who'd swallowed the first half of a dose of bitter medicine and was still determined to take the rest. "But I think I'm entitled to the truth. Did he confide in you?"

"I just told you what he confided."

"That's not what I'm asking." She sighed, then recited with exaggerated patience, "I know he's not here to defend himself, and I know you don't want to betray his memory in any way. Or his trust, or your sacred oath, or whatever." She laid her hand on his arm, found it rigid, and her touch turned to subtle stroking. "But it can't change anything now, can it?"

His throat went dry. "Not for him."

"Then tell me, Gideon." The pressure on his arm became insistent. "Did Jared have an affair with Peter's mother?"

His memory, his trust, a damned sacred oath? Did she imagine he had a suit of shining armor on, too?

Gideon shook his head and turned away.

Chapter 6

She followed him to the back porch, where she waited, watching him light up the second cigarette he'd had in as many months. The second in a single day. The red ash glowed steadily in the dark as he filled his lungs, seeking the insidious calm of an internal haze. Gideon held his breath, mixed with the smoke, willing it to do its damage the way it always had, the way so many things had. If it felt good now, it would hurt later. But he could take it. Hell, he was tough.

But Raina wasn't. She was a good woman, but she wasn't tough. Jared hadn't been tough, either. He'd been smart, but not tough. And Peter . . . well, Peter was still young yet. Soft and malleable. With any luck he would end up good and smart, loving and well loved, proud of his heritage and strong in every way. And with all that going for him, maybe he wouldn't have to be tough.

She stood behind him, waiting for her answer, and, damn his mean soul, he wanted to tell her *yes*. Yes, your husband was a sinner, too, and yes, he screwed up sometimes, and *yes,* Raina, you married the wrong man.

But he couldn't quite get the words out. He wasn't sure why. There was no one to dispute them, and they might have served him well.

For some equally mysterious reason, he couldn't tell her *no,* either.

"What difference does it make, Raina?"

There was no sound, and even though she had to be standing at least a foot away from him, he could feel her body stiffen. His first response to her question had seemed to confirm her suspicions, and she was wrestling with it. He could help her with that, he told himself. He could spare the living and let her think what she would of the dead. *I'm here for you,* he could say. He'd always known the truth would hurt, but whom would it hurt, and how?

"There's the chance that Jared's health problems might be hereditary," she suggested, almost timidly.

He stared through the screen into the night. The trees behind the house stood like dark, shadowy sentries, and in the distance, there were lights twinkling on the lake.

"Is that it?" he asked quietly. "Is that why you want to know whether Jared had an affair?"

"I'm asking you whether Jared was Peter's biological father."

"No, you're asking me whether Jared cheated on you." It was a question, Gideon realized, that a man had to answer for himself. All his brother could say was "If he did, it's history. It doesn't matter anymore."

"Then he *did.*"

"I didn't say that." *Yes, you did. To her, you did.* "Hell, I don't know," he admitted, giving in with a sigh. "I wasn't living with him. You were."

"I know he kept a lot inside," she said. "That's just the way he was. And I guess we buried it with him."

"Digging it up now might not change anything, but it could hurt somebody."

"Who?" Her motherly nose smelled a threat. "Peter?"

"First you. Then maybe Peter. Old ghosts ought to be left in the closet, where they can't hurt innocent people."

"I *am* Peter's real mother," she insisted, as though she believed he needed persuading now, too. "No matter what the circumstances of his conception or his birth were, *I'm* his true mother. And as his mother, I'm responsible for his health and his well-being, so if there's any possibility that he's inherited some kind of—"

"Jared was not Peter's father," Gideon said, his tone carefully controlled, utterly flat. "Not . . . biologically."

He took another pull on the cigarette, looking for heat. He could have sworn his skin was coated with ice. When she'd brought up the subject, he'd walked, but not far enough. The complications were piling up so damn fast he just wanted to walk out the door, jump in the lake and dive to the bottom.

Instead, there in the dark, he faced her.

"Look, I knew you guys wanted a baby," he said carefully, because now it was his turn to do some mental wrestling with all those damn pieces of the past. "And I knew that Tomasina Skinner planned to give hers up, so I told Jared about it. Simple as that. The fact that Jared was an Indian, along with him being a lawyer, *made* it as simple as that. No problem with the tribal court, and Jared handled the paperwork in the state court, smooth as still waters." He turned away and dragged deeply on his cigarette. On a trail of smoke he added, "Then he went and died on us."

"Gideon, you can't fault him for—"

"Don't *you?*" He wanted somebody else to, besides him. "Sometimes? Don't you ever say, 'Damn it, Jared, what did you have to go and *die* for?'"

"In the last week, sure. Well, I guess there've been a few other times," she admitted. "But I know it's selfish for me to think that way, as though he had a choice."

"Maybe. But I get mad at him, anyway, for checkin' out so soon, leaving some things unsettled between us." He reached for the empty coffee can he'd left on the porch, thinking it would come in handy for something. He hadn't expected it to be an ashtray.

Damn the complications, he told himself.

But a picture of his brother formed in his mind, and it made him smile. "Guess we're both human, huh? But if ol' Jared's earned his wings—and knowing him, he did it summa cum laude—then I don't believe he'll be wasting eternity looking for ways to use anything we say against us. I think he's above all that now."

"Yes, he is," she said with a sigh. "And I'm left with a predicament that wouldn't be a problem if he were here."

She sank into one of the wicker porch chairs and began deliberating aloud. "I could move up here. That really wouldn't be a problem. The sensible thing for me to do is to apply for a job here. That way, whatever happens, I can adjust."

The hand she lifted toward him was the color of moonlight. "Peter's all I have, Gideon. Everything else is superfluous. Is it possible . . . could I lose him entirely?"

"Not as long as he breathes."

As quickly as he reached out from the shadows, her small hand disappeared between his, which were larger and darker and much, much warmer than hers. "Peter is just as surely your son as you are his mother. He's never gonna forget that."

"But...say if this treaty thing turns out badly for you, and there's a lot of resentment over it, and the judge looks at me, and he sees a white woman who's your sister-in-law..."

"Don't be lookin' to buy trouble now," he warned, seating himself in the chair next to hers. "We've got enough to worry about. And I'm not going to let Peter become a political football. That I can promise you, Raina."

"Are you...on my side at all?"

"I am." He rubbed her hand, warming it between his. "Mostly because I'm on Peter's side." He cleared his throat of the bitter taste of having to qualify a promise that he wanted to give her outright. "He's lost Jared, too. I don't want to see him lose his mother."

"But the interests of the Pine Lake Band—"

"Are my responsibility." He felt her stiffen again, and he withdrew, leaning back into the shadows. "Make no mistake about that. I won't compromise the interests of the people. But Peter is one of the people. The fact that you're not isn't as important to me as the fact that he *is*."

"Is that supposed to be encouraging?"

"When you're talking to the chairman of our tribal band, yeah, it should be encouraging. I happen to think the judge will see it that way, too."

"What about Peter's uncle? What about my brother-in-law, my—" she gestured, searching, and her hand came to rest on his knee "—my old friend. I want to be able to talk to *him* without talking to the tribal chairman. Is that possible?"

"Depends on what you want to talk about."

"What I'm thinking. What I'm feeling. How worried I was the whole time I was gone, and how glad I am to be back." She paused. The way her hand stirred against his jeans was appealing in every sense he could imagine. "Can you take your chairman's hat off for a while and let me talk to Gideon?''

"I can take off anything you want," he told her. "Anything that's in your way."

"Shades of the Gideon Defender I used to know." There was an echo of relief in her laughter, a full range of appreciativeness in the way she patted his knee. "There must be a happy medium."

"Yeah." Gideon wasn't particularly amused. "His name was Jared."

Before she left, Raina went downstairs to say good-night to Peter. She found him asleep on the sofa in the den. She started to wake him, but Gideon was right behind her with a blanket.

"Let him sleep," he whispered as he covered the boy. "He's on vacation."

The only thing Gideon regretted was that Peter was too big for him to lift in his arms and carry into the bedroom without waking him. He could have done that the last time the boy had visited, when Peter was only six. He could have kissed him good-night then, too, the way Raina did.

And there had been a time before that when he would have kissed her good-night, a time when she would have expected him to. A time before the first time she'd said, *We can't let this happen.*

If she'd wanted him to kiss her this time, she might have lingered at the door. He knew she didn't feel right, leaving without her son. He could hear it in her voice. On the way to the front door, he'd kept his hands off the switches to avoid shining a rude light on her sadness, not because he hoped that in the dark she might reach out to him again, might turn and touch him somehow before she left for the night.

And she didn't, of course. He had something she wanted, but tonight it was not his kiss. She hardly paused at the threshold. She simply told him in passing that it would be her turn to make supper tomorrow, and she hurried out the door.

Gideon had changed a great deal in fifteen years. He wondered whether Raina realized that, and whether it mattered to her. He and Jared had never had much in common, but Gideon had respected his brother for what he'd made of himself. Even though he knew the feeling had not held true in reverse, he indulged himself in thinking that it might have, had Jared lived a little longer.

But what about Raina? With her back against the wall, she was talking about moving back onto his turf, and she wanted to know whose side he was on. He couldn't blame her for clinging to the notion that the world was made up of straight, rigid sides rather than curves that might bend and rebound, ebb and flow. They saw the world from different perspectives, just as he and Jared had.

Jared had clawed his way closer to Raina's vantage point, and Peter...well, Peter's parents had been handpicked, so that he might enjoy the advantages of having an Indian father who had made it in the white world and a mother who truly wanted a baby.

Whose side was he on? When it came right down to the bare bones, hadn't he always been on her side? Hadn't he taken her emphatic *no* for an answer? Hadn't he stepped aside and stayed out of their lives? Hadn't he given her what she'd wanted, always? Maybe she still didn't see it that way, didn't even realize it, because she'd never bothered to inventory her allies. But he had been on her side even when he doubted the existence of sides.

And if there were sides, they were all curved. There were surely no straight lines, nothing to keep Raina's path parallel to, but separate from, his. The great distance between them had gradually, inevitably closed in on them again, for all things in life were, after all, circular.

But he was on Peter's side of the circle now, too. He had been there at the beginning, and now the years had rolled around an inner curve and bumped the boy up against him again. That was the way of things. Gideon had learned the hard way. If Jared had lived a little longer, smart as he was, he would have come to recognize the circle, too.

Early the next morning Gideon went downstairs to wake Peter for breakfast. When he found only a rumpled blanket and a sofa pillow, he swore to himself that the next time the boy tried this, he wouldn't make it out of the house without running smack into Gideon, even if it meant *he* had to take up sleeping on the sofa.

"Hey, Uncle Gideon, is it okay if I put a nail in this wall?"

The voice coming from Peter's bedroom glided over Gideon's ruffled feathers. He kept a lid on his sigh of relief and followed the sound, ready with a smile by the time he reached the doorway. Apparently sometime during the night Peter had opted for more comfortable sleeping arrangements and moved to his bed.

"You got something you want nailed down?"

Peter handed Gideon a leather-wrapped circlet about the size of a small plate. "I tried a tack, but it fell on my head this morning. *Nimishoomis* gave it to me. He made it himself." It looked like a large spider's web woven of sinew on a willow hoop. Blue and white feathers and beads dangled from the bottom of the hoop, and there was a loop at the top. "He told me to hang it over my bed."

"It's a dreamcatcher." Gideon examined the fine workmanship of the webbing. Peter couldn't ask for a better artisan to teach him than his grandfather. "Do you know what this is for?"

"To catch dreams?"

"The bad ones get caught in the web." Gideon fingered a blue bead woven into the lower portion of the web. "You see, like this little rascal here. But the good ones slip on through—" he demonstrated with sinuous, undulating fingers that took a plunge behind Peter's ear "—and into your head."

The boy laughed. "It's a nice decoration, anyway. I needed something to hang on the wall."

"You don't think it'll work?"

Peter's face formed a get-real expression.

"You've never had to worry about bad dreams?"

"I've had a few." Reclaiming his gift, he rolled his thumb over the blue bead. "Sometimes I dream that my dad's still alive. The only bad part is waking up and realizing it was just a dream." He lifted his bony shoulders in an exaggerated, heartstring-tugging shrug. "Then sometimes I dream that he's not dead yet, but I, like, *know* something bad's about to happen, and I want to stop it, but I can't."

Abruptly those big, black eyes looked up at Gideon, their innocence completely unguarded. "It's pretty stupid, you know? But it seems real, even after I wake up, at least for a minute or two. I really hate it when that happens."

"I know what you mean."

"You do?"

"Sure." He wanted to hug the boy, to take comfort with him after the fact. But he held back, laying a hand on his shoulder instead. "Sure I do. I've had dreams about him, too."

Peter hung his head, ostensibly studying the intricacies of the dreamcatcher. "Sometimes I don't want to sleep at night."

"I know how that is, too. A guy gets to be your age, he starts feeling a little restless. Hungry for a little excitement." *That's when you go out and try to hunt up some kind of distraction.*

Peter tapped Gideon's arm with his fist. "I suppose when a guy gets to be *your* age, the excitement's pretty much over for him, so he turns into a killjoy for the rest of us."

"How did we go from me sympathizing with you to you pushing me over the hill prematurely?"

"We were talking about dreams, and how a guy can wake up—" Peter's short-lived smile faded "—feeling kinda weird."

"You mean weird *scared,* or weird *weird?*"

"Weird like you see something in your dream, like maybe a picture you saw in a magazine or something." He risked a brief glance at Gideon's poker face. Seeing no sign of comprehension, he took the further risk of elaborating. "A magazine that you didn't buy yourself, but another guy maybe found in his dad's workshop. You know what I mean?"

"I'm pretty sure I get the picture."

"Really. Pictures like you can hardly *believe.* You know, it *is* kinda fun to draw mustaches and glasses, tattoos and stuff like that, on *most* of 'em, but then—" he popped a quick shrug "—maybe you leave one or two without any touch-ups...you know, artistically speaking...just because you kinda like them the way they are."

"Some of them aren't half-bad without the tattoos," Gideon allowed, hanging on dearly to that poker face. "A guy might even be half-tempted to tear one of those pages out of the magazine and stick it in his drawer."

"Nah, my mom's always putting my clothes away, so I can't keep anything private." Peter's careless drop onto the bed stretched the wheezing springs to their limit. "I mean, if I *wanted* to keep something like that around. Which I wouldn't, because sometimes if you go to sleep thinking about, say something in a picture, and you dream that, like, something happens, and you wake up, and you realize it was only a dream..." His voice dropped to the confessional level. "But something really happened."

"And your bed's wet," Gideon kindly finished for him.

"I'm not a baby." Peter's cheeks flashed like neon apples. "I don't wet the bed. Something *else* happened. What, do you think I'm a *baby?*"

"I think you're becoming a man, and men—"

"Ejaculate, I know. I mean, hell, I'm not a little *kid.* I know all about sex and stuff, but—" his hands flopped helplessly against the bed "—I wasn't *doing* anything."

Gideon sat down on the bed beside him, bracing his elbows on his knees and wondering who'd ordered him up this baptism by fire before breakfast. He'd just barely had time to get his toes wet.

After a couple of false starts, he spread his hands in a commiserating gesture. "You don't have to be *doing* anything."

At the news, Peter looked grief-stricken. "You mean it can happen, like, *anytime?*"

"It can happen in your sleep. It happens to all of us." Gideon's nod affirmed their fellowship as two healthy, normal males. "Mostly when we're your age. Before the excitement's pretty much over for us."

"It happened to you?"

"Sure."

God help him, he didn't want to mess this up. He had to give the boy credit for having the nerve to broach the subject with an adult instead of another kid his age. By the time he was Peter's age, he'd managed to gather such an encyclopedia of misinformation that he'd gone to the mirror one morning expecting to find that his eyes were turning green.

Peter was visibly relieved to learn that he wasn't alone in his predicament. He toyed with the dreamcatcher, rolling it between his palms. "What did you do about . . . the bed?"

"I cleaned it up."

"My mom would get pretty suspicious if I washed my own sheets."

"Your mom knows all about sex, too."

"She doesn't know about—" Peter's eyes flashed in horror. "I told you, I wasn't *doing* anything."

"I know what you're saying." Anybody else's mom but yours. You don't want me to mention your mom and sex in the same sentence. "At least you've got a washing machine. We didn't. No dryer, either. So I just kinda cleaned up a little, left the bed—" He glanced over his shoulder at the rumpled sheets. "You're not still letting your mom make your bed, are you?"

"Well, yeah."

"There's your problem. See, I never had my own room. I had to share. And nobody ever cleaned up after me. But I think if you take care of your own bed, put your own clothes away, keep things kinda straightened up, you'll have more privacy."

Peter had to think that one over.

And another one, as well. "You really think she knows about stuff like this? My mom?"

"You mean, sex?" Gideon smiled benevolently. "It's hard to imagine, isn't it?"

"Kinda." Peter shrugged. "Hell, she doesn't know anything about what it's like to be a *guy.*"

"She knows what it's like to be a woman. That's pretty damned hard for *me* to imagine." Gideon gave a quick cross-check. "How about you?"

"Imagine being a woman? Who'd want to be a woman?" He rolled his eyes at the very thought. "Or a girl. I wouldn't want to be a girl. Geez, that would *really* suck."

"I think women have it hard in a lot of ways, but the old way teaches us that women have strong power, and they must be respected for that. They have life-giving medicine."

"You mean, they can have babies. Big deal. I'm glad *we* don't have to get pregnant and stuff." Peter's boyish laugh sounded, blessedly, as giddy as any twelve-year-old girl's. "Imagine a pregnant soccer goalie."

Gideon grinned. "Is that your position? Goalie?"

"Yeah."

"I'd like to see you play sometime."

Peter nodded. Then he remembered the catch. "Maybe I won't be playing this fall, huh? If I have to stay here?"

"How would you feel about changing schools?"

"I wouldn't like it much." He examined the dream-catcher, which seemed to have become a touchstone for serious consideration. "I guess one of my buddies is moving to Cleveland next month. His father got transferred."

"So you understand that it's a necessity sometimes?"

Without looking up, Peter nodded. "Is it going to be *this* time?"

"We'll try to take things as they come, okay? We'll work things out one step at a time."

"My mom's talking about applying for a job here."

"I know. You can be damn sure, whatever happens, she's gonna be right there with you."

"It was pretty nice of *nimishoomis* to make this for me." He lifted up the hoop and held it toward the window, letting the morning light flow through.

"You got that word down pretty good," Gideon allowed. "*Nimishoomis*. Do you take any languages in school?"

"I've had some French. I could learn Ojibwa easy." Peter closed one eye, sighting through the web. "So some dreams get caught in the web, huh? They just get stuck there, like, where everyone can see them?"

"Not *those* dreams. Only the bad ones." Gideon gave Peter's knee a playful sock with his knuckles. "The kind you were talking about? It lets those through. They're really not bad." He bounced the edge of his curled hand repeatedly on the boy's knee as he spoke. "Stuff happens to guys, stuff happens to girls. It evens out. It all works out pretty good in the end, you know, when you get older and you partner up with the right lady."

"So where's your lady?"

"We-ell, guess I must be doing something wrong. I've been dreaming about her since I was your age, but no partnership so far." Gideon shrugged. "Nothing lasting, anyway."

"Kind of a late bloomer, aren't you?" Peter offered the dreamcatcher as he elbowed Gideon's arm. "Maybe you'd better get *nimishoomis* to make you a few of these. Increase your odds before you *really* get too old."

"Trouble is, these only work when you're asleep. With my luck, I'll be meeting up with the ones that should have gotten caught in the web."

"Never know," Peter hinted, flashing an impish smile. "Maybe *you're* the one that got caught in *their* webs."

Chapter 7

Arlen wanted his grandson to spend a weekend with him. He'd been asked to judge more dance contests, and he was "kinda startin' to like the idea of pickin' the winners." He also liked the idea of an old man's grandson accompanying him to the powwow, listening closely to his words of wisdom, picking up a little Ojibwa language and a few dance steps along the way.

At first Gideon had been inclined to dismiss the idea, but he thought better of it after he'd put the suggestion to Peter, who was willing. By this time Peter had made friends with a couple of boys his age, including Marvin Strikes Many's son, Tom, who lived only a couple of miles from Arlen's cabin. It had been a few years since Arlen's own offspring had left home, and Gideon suspected that having a teenager around for a couple of days might be all it would take to convince Arlen to back off on his demands, to accept regular visits from his grandson rather than push for a change in Peter's custody. Arlen was also just the man to encourage Peter's burgeoning interest in Indian ways.

The trick would be to persuade Raina to give grandfather and grandson a little space without her supervision. In pursuit of that end—and maybe in the interest of getting away from any mention of the words *treaty rights* for a couple of days—he decided after supper one evening to ask her to share his own favorite space and a brief bit of time exclusively with him.

"Oh, it's been so long since I've been to the North Woods, Gideon, I'd love to go." Her smile was at once wishful and apologetic. "But I think Peter should go along with us. After all, he hardly knows Arlen. *I* hardly know Arlen."

Gideon handed her the after-supper cup of coffee that was becoming a nightly ritual, then took his seat beside her in what were becoming the his-and-hers chairs on the porch. "Would you consider leaving him with your own father for a couple of days?"

"Well, yes, but—"

"And your father lives where?"

"A retirement community in Arizona, which is why we haven't... which is why Peter doesn't—"

"Know *him* very well, either?" She nodded regretfully. He offered an accommodating comeback. "That's the way things are these days. People are free to find a climate that suits them, but the downside is that family members are scattered from hell to Texas."

Ease her into this, he told himself. He considered the various aspects of his plan as he sipped his coffee. He liked its prospects. It involved a fair amount of diplomacy, which was turning out to be one of his strong suits. If he played his cards right, he might be able to keep everyone happy.

"I think it might help your cause if you showed the judge that you're willing to let him have a relationship with his grandfather."

"I am," she insisted. "I want that, for Peter's sake. I've said so." She glanced away. "But I'm not sure we should..."

"What?" By *we*, he knew she meant the two of them. "What are you afraid of, Raina?" She stared out at the lake. "Are you still afraid of me?" he asked carefully, barely disturbing the weight of her silence.

"I was never afraid of you." Her voice trailed off on the tail of her flimsy fib. "I just don't think I should go traipsing off...."

"With me."

"Without Peter."

"Peter will do just fine with his grandfather for a couple of days, and you'll be okay with me." He laid a hand over his heart and offered his most endearing smile. "Will you trust me on this one?"

She held up two fingers.

"What does that mean? Peace? Victory?"

"Two," she informed him. "Two counts you're asking me to trust you on."

He slid his palm over the two fingers, folding them back into her hand, his eyes inviting her to give in to her own fancy for a change, to stop questioning and submit. Enveloping her small hand in his, he brought both to rest on his thigh.

"You remember that place I told you about way back when?" For him it was a once-upon-a-time. It had no name or number. "I told you I'd take you to a special place come spring, a place you'd never want to leave."

"I remember. You called it Hidden Falls. We never got there."

"Come with me now."

He waited, his eyes daring her to accept, even though he knew damn well he'd already lured her past her intent to refuse.

She drew her smile out slowly, but her answer glittered in her eyes.

Ordinarily it would have been next to impossible to get a permit to go into the wilderness area on such short notice, but having been a guide himself, Gideon had connections. All it took was a phone call to his old friend and former employer, camping outfitter Jim Collins, and everything was arranged. Jim had their canoe and supply packs ready. Gideon didn't need the detailed maps the outfitter also provided. Even Jim allowed that the "chief" of the Pine Lake Band of Chippewa knew the North Woods better than anyone.

But he did have one word of caution for Gideon. "There is one fishing party out there that... Well, maybe you'll just wanna keep an eye out and steer clear." The outfitter looked at Raina reflectively, then added an extra foam pad to the sleeping gear. "You wanna take special care when you're escorting a pretty lady, take a few extra precautions, add a little extra comfort."

"Keep 'em comin' back. Yeah, I remember." Gideon offered Raina her pick from the beef jerky jar on Jim's desk. When she declined, he helped himself. "So what's with this fishing party? What's their problem?"

Lean as a scarecrow, Jim gave a sardonic chuckle as he hitched up his ever-sagging jeans. "Nothing a little attitude adjustment wouldn't cure."

"Always give the client his due, Jim." Gideon tore into the strip of leathery meat with his back teeth. "Couple of weekend Daniel Boones who don't need a guide?"

"No, these two are regulars. Been coming up here for years. Chuck Taylor and Daryl Weist. Did you ever run into them when you were working for us?"

"I don't remember taking them out back then, but I know I've run across those names recently." It was important to remember the names. The same ones showed up repeatedly on letters and petitions. He made a point of remembering the names of his adversaries, but he didn't want the faces fixed in his mind. The smug and incensed faces of people who showed up at public information meetings and state-house-step rallies. "Those guys belong to a group called the North Woods Anglers Club," he told Jim. "Real vocal about their commitment to saving *the state's* natural resources."

"They also know everything there is to know about Indians." Jim slanted his friend a look that mixed amusement with disgust. "Why, they were telling me just yesterday how a compromise with the Pine Lake Band would be just like making a pact with the devil, since Indian fish and wildlife managers never bother to enforce the tribal regulations and quotas in the first place, and since they don't know, uh—" He grinned. "Don't know diddly-squat about wildlife management, anyway."

"Yeah, right," Gideon sneered. "Did they really say 'diddly-squat'?"

"Well, words that smelled the same." Jim tossed Gideon a waterproof fanny pack emblazoned with the outfitting company's logo. "Compliments of the house."

"Thanks." Gideon opened the bag and started transferring the contents of his pockets.

"Besides," Jim went on, "these guys have read their history books, and they know damn well Indians don't really believe in civilized law. According to them, that's why the tribal courts routinely dismiss most of the cases that come before them."

"Can I count on that?" The irony of the claim almost made Raina laugh.

"You can count on not being tried in tribal court," Gideon told her. "Their jurisdiction doesn't cover you." He raised a warning hand. They had an agreement. "End of discussion."

"For now."

"So these guys gave you quite an earful." Gideon tucked his billfold into the self-sealing pack. "Where do you stand on the treaty issue, Jim?"

"On the side of good sense. The way I see it, you guys decide to go to court, you're gonna win. You *should* win. Just out of curiosity, I read a copy of the treaty. I'm no lawyer, but it looks to me like you could end up with half the fish and game harvest in that couple-million-acre—whaddyacallit?—ceded territory area if you take this thing to court. I think you oughta hang in there and go for the brass ring, man." With a shrug, Jim acknowledged that it was no risk to him to talk big. "'Course, my business is outside of that ceded territory."

"Yeah, well, if we could compromise, we might be able to keep the peace." Gideon sealed the pouch, then nodded toward Raina. "Doesn't she get one of these, too?"

"Sure." Absently, Jim turned his attention to the supply shelves. The seat of his jeans drooped like an empty feedbag. "Besides—" for a moment he forgot what he was looking for, and his hand was still busy helping him expound "—there ain't enough of you to make a dent in that kind of haul. What've you got down there? A couple thousand Pine Lake Chippewa?"

"Twenty-five hundred, and most of the members are living off the reservation." Gideon noted with some amusement that Jim, all wound up in his discourse, had just given Raina two of the complimentary fanny packs.

"Okay, so every man, woman and child goes out hunting and fishing three hundred and sixty-five days a year, these guys still got nothing to worry about."

"They're worried about Indians getting something they don't have themselves, which would be a real turnabout, wouldn't it?" Gideon helped himself to another stick of beef jerky, using it as a pointer. "I'm worried about the threat of violence. Like you say, our numbers are small."

"The thing to remember is, these two guys didn't talk real nice."

Gideon opened his mouth, then closed it, the meat forgotten as he eyed Jim. "Did you have anything to say to them?"

"I told them I didn't think the settlement would hurt anything." Jim shrugged, flashing Gideon a look of apology. "Hell, those guys and their buddies are paying customers, Gideon. You know how that is. I ain't gonna argue with them *too* much."

"You can't change their minds, either. No point in trying."

"Just so you know they're out there." Jim took a sparring stance and playfully cuffed Gideon on the shoulder. "Hell, they mess with you, they'll learn a little something about Indians they probably ain't figured out yet. Like you don't wanna back Gideon Defender into no damn corner, that's for sure."

"Sounds like there's a story there," Raina said.

"Hot damn, you should have seen this guy." Jim hitched his jeans up on his skinny hips. He didn't seem to notice that the effort was wasted. "Playing pool down at the Duck's Tail, and some jerk tries to bad-mouth this ol' warrior for

dancin' with the wrong, uh. . . ." Jim flashed Gideon a que-
rying glance.

"Don't tell me the whole thing blow-by-blow," Raina
said, settling the question. "Just tell me exactly how many
of his own teeth this man has left in his head."

"Never seen Gideon on the losin' end," Jim said. "But
I'm sure he's sent a few dentists some business."

"Well, as my buddy Clint Eastwood said…" Gideon went
snake-eyed, and his voice dropped to a husky whisper. "'I
ain't like that no more.'"

Shoreline trees bowed close to the lapping lake, some
dipping their leaves like women washing their hair. The
morning sun cast its bright gems into tranquil waters as the
canoe approached a family of loons, the two babies bob-
bing along behind their parents. The distinctive yodeling call
carried across the water, answered in the distance by a similar song.

"Can you tell the male from the female?" Gideon asked,
as though he was giving a test. The question was posed to
her back, for it was Gideon's powerful paddling that provided most of the propulsion and steered the canoe, as well.

Raina got to play at paddling while she enjoyed the ever-
changing view. "They look the same."

"Only the male does the yodeling. He's letting his neighbors know he's out strolling in his own backyard." Even as
Gideon spoke, the loon changed its tune from the haunting
yodel to a quavering tremolo. Abruptly it drew itself up-
right on the water, coiling its neck and stretching the full-
ness of its five-foot wingspan.

"My God, he's big." Raina's paddle froze in midair.
"Gideon, I think he's angry."

"He's charging," Gideon said with a chuckle. "And
we're paddling on past, Papa, so just relax."

"I had no idea they were that big. Boy, is he mad." She swiveled in her seat, amazed by the bird's ability to pull itself up in the water like a 747 taking to the air. "And their call always sounds so peaceful." The loon gave out another warning. "On tape."

"On tape?"

"'Sounds of Nature' tapes. I use them to help me sleep." The loon's angry cry echoed across the water. "Whoa, I think they edited that one out."

"He's just letting us know he's there to protect his family. He helped incubate those chicks. Earlier in the season, he carried the little guys on his back a lot when Mama wanted to go diving."

"Diving?"

"Best diver there is." Gideon's paddle dripped across the canoe as he switched it to the other side. "We call him the *mahng.* Legend has it that once the world was all water. And *Chimaunido,* who is God, asked for a volunteer to dive to the bottom and bring up some mud, so that He could create the land. Otter, Beaver and Muskrat each tried and failed. *Mahng* was the only one who could hold his breath long enough and dive deep enough to get the job done. His bones are solid, so he's a much heavier bird than, say, the mallard. The air sacs under the loon's skin keep him afloat. When he wants to make a dive, he just lets the air out."

"What does he do with all that weight when he wants to fly?"

"He needs a good stretch of water for his runway. It takes some heavy-duty paddling and wing-flapping for him to get airborne, but once he's up, he can cruise over a hundred miles an hour."

The deep chuckle at Raina's back sent a shiver sluicing through her. Gideon always told his stories, even the fables, as though they explained some truth, great or small.

Some truth about him, she thought. Some simple truth about the enigma that was Gideon Defender.

"Of course, he's in serious trouble on the ground. On land he can't take off and can't walk worth a damn, 'cause his legs are stuck way back on his body for diving." He stopped paddling, and she followed suit, letting the canoe drift. "So here's this creature who thrives only in water or in the air—land is his nemesis—but when *Chimaunido* says, 'Who'll help me make the land?' *mahng* turns out to be the right man for the job."

In the distance, the loon yodeled peacefully again.

"*Mahng* was given the dentalium shell necklace as a reward," Gideon concluded. "It's a sign of leadership. Only a leader may wear the *megis* necklace."

Raina turned, squinting into the sun. "So where's yours?"

"I have one."

"Really?"

"Would it surprise you to see me wear a necklace?" He smiled. "Feathers and beaded buckskins? Would it surprise you to hear me sing Indian? To see me dance in the traditional way?"

"No, of course not."

"I have the *megis* necklace, and the responsibility that goes with it. *Mahng* is like my brother."

Raina laughed softly. "You'd never guess that from the kind of welcome he just gave you."

"Guess I'm kinda like the prodigal brother." He dipped his paddle into the water again, but his eyes held hers. "Like I said, he was just protecting his wife and kids."

"Maybe *I'm* the threat," she muttered as she turned, facing forward. Maybe the bird could tell that she'd come from the city. Maybe she smelled of engine emissions, fluorocarbons and oil spills.

"I've read that acid rain and mercury might, umm...that they're a terrible threat to the loon." *Might do them in,* she'd almost said, but she didn't want to be an alarmist. Something could be done to reverse the threat. Something could *always* be done. "I can't imagine these woods without that sound."

"Without *mahng?*"

She felt his eyes on her, questioning her common sense. Without the loon, the North Woods would be desolate, but to Gideon, it was more than that.

"Without the diver, we'd have no place to lay our heads," he said. "No earth at all. Some might doubt that, but what they will tell you is that there is nothing to prove it. The stories mean nothing. They aren't scientific."

Another tremolo reverberated somewhere on the otherwise quiet waterway ahead of them.

"Doesn't that warning call sound like laughter to you? Kind of wild and desperate, like, 'Look around you, brother! Wake up and smell the rain!'"

Suddenly she could feel his breath against the back of her neck. She shivered, and he gave a deep, throaty chuckle. "The rain should smell like Raina," he said. "Clean and sweet. What would you do if I kissed you now?"

She closed her eyes and drew a deep, sharp breath. "Tip the canoe."

He chuckled again. "That's what I thought."

She heard him tuck his paddle in the rack. "Are we just going to drift?" she asked, her small voice floating on the water like the crystal notes from a music box. Every sound seemed to gain volume, in contrast with the quiet woods along the shore. It was midsummer, and birdsong had decreased with the season.

"I'm going to drop a line and catch us some lunch. What would you like with your mercury, honey? Bass? A little trout, perhaps?"

"Gideon!" She racked her paddle, stretched her legs and brushed her hands over her jeans. "Since I'm wearing plenty of sunblock, all I want is fresh sunshine with my lunch."

"Sure you don't wanna order up a little purified air-conditioning, maybe some bottled water?"

"No, but I do wish I'd thought of putting on a swimsuit under my jeans—even though I'd have to slather on the sunblock—but I was afraid of causing a stir—" she eyed him pointedly "—among the mosquitoes."

He made a pretense of taking a look around as he prepared his fishing gear. "Nothin' astir so far, except the damselflies."

Noting that the water's edge was alive with the black-winged creatures that looked like flying metallic green sticks, Raina almost missed Gideon's lazy appraisal of her casual, ordinary, hardly provocative man-tailored shirt and jeans.

His smile was both slow and appreciative. "And me."

Gideon didn't yet have lunch on the stringer, but he was in no hurry until another canoe appeared, disturbing their floating idyll. He cursed under his breath as he reeled in his line. A twelve-hundred-mile maze of waterways—interconnecting lakes and streams that the Park Service called canoe area wilderness, no motors allowed—and he had to run into two north-country good ol' boys. He knew damn well who they were. The hair standing up on the back of his neck told him that much.

They grinned and leered as they paddled closer. Whatever these boys had been drinking for breakfast wasn't part of Jim's supply pack. Regular clients of Jim's should have known better. Getting tanked on a canoe trip was a sure way to end up floating home facedown.

But it wasn't any of Gideon's business.

The interlopers slid off to the side, keeping their distance, but their voices carried well enough.

"Looky here, Chuck, these Indians do know something about angling. All this time they had us thinkin' they couldn't catch nothin' without a spear or a net."

Gideon watched the tip of his own rod as he reeled in his line. The man in the front of the other canoe pulled in his paddle, laying it across his thighs.

"Hey, how's it goin' there, Chief? What are they bitin' on?"

"Frybread," Gideon quipped. He set his fishing rod down and picked up his paddle.

"No kidding?"

"Don't you recognize him, Daryl?"

The question had the man in front rubber-necking for clues while the bigger man wielded the rudder paddle, bending the course of the intruding canoe.

"He really is their chief," the big one called Chuck said. "He's the one they interviewed on TV. You know, when they talked about this settlement the politicians have cooked up."

"Sorry, boys, I'm unavailable for comment." Gideon sliced into the water with his paddle, and his canoe surged forward. "Enjoy the fishing."

"We will. Right, Daryl?"

"Damn straight. We always do, and we ain't gonna let nothin' change that."

"You might wanna put your life vests on," Gideon called out. Then he muttered, "Call yourselves sportsmen, you damn fools?"

"Don't worry about them, Gideon." Raina glanced back at him as she reached for her paddle.

"Force of habit. I'll paddle," he told her. "You just kinda casually keep an eye on those two turkeys over your shoulder. They make any sudden moves, you hit the deck."

She did a double take. "Sudden moves? Like what?"

"Like they're reaching for something." His deft, powerful strokes had them skimming over the water. "You never know how hot under the collar those red necks of theirs are liable to get."

The watch she kept over her shoulder was anything but casual. Her eyes widened. "Oh, my God."

"What the—?" He reached for her even faster than he ducked. "I told you to—"

"It's just a cigarette." She stayed his hand on her shoulder. "He took out a cigarette. It's okay."

"The idea was to get down, not wait to find out what…" He shook his head as he switched his paddle from one side to the other. "Some of these guys are fanatics, Raina, which means you don't trust them when your back is turned."

"Okay, I'm watching your back, and they're—" her eyes shifted to his face, and she gave a snappy smile "—out of sight now."

Gideon kept paddling. They slipped through the water, both silent for a time. She didn't understand, and he didn't want her to. Bigotry didn't scare him much, except for her sake. He'd lived with it all his life. Usually it was more subtle. It was that all-knowing stare.

You're an Indian. We expect certain things.

People used to notice when he ordered shots with a beer chaser. Now they noticed when he ordered pop. Either way, he could almost hear what they were thinking. It wasn't so much that being noticed bothered him, but getting stares did. It was so damned disrespectful. But it had generally been a subtle kind of disrespect. Until lately. Until the Pine Lake Band of Chippewa had pointed out that the state had no jurisdiction over their treaty rights. Since then, he'd started to wonder whatever had happened to good, old-fashioned *subtle* prejudice.

No, it didn't scare him, except for *her* sake. But it did embarrass him. Taunts from two jackasses who were probably too stupid to go on living should have meant no more to him than a little static on the radio. He congratulated himself for not launching himself at them headlong. They were bound to topple out before the day was over, and with no help from him.

But Raina had seen it. Raina had heard what they'd said. It was *their* disgrace, not his, but it chafed a raw place deep inside him, where a remnant of unearned shame had tied a terrible knot in his gut.

"I don't think they'll bother us now, do you?" Raina said finally.

"Probably not." He eased up on his paddling. "Likely the only shot they had in mind was verbal."

"Right." She tucked her knees and spun on her bottom, reversing herself on the canoe seat so that she could offer a face-to-face, glad-we-got-past-that-one smile. "Just a couple of pigheaded jerks, right?"

"Probably perfectly nice guys, as long as nobody mentions Indians or fishing rights." God, she was pretty. Her hair, cinched down by her billed cap, was poufed around her small ears and glistened in the sun like a counter display of gold jewelry. Her smile just naturally made *him* want to smile. "But I'll never witness that firsthand unless I do something about this Indian-looking face of mine."

"Don't you dare."

"What?"

"Change—" she leaned toward him, reaching for his smooth cheek "—anything."

"You like my face the way it is?"

"Yes." She nodded. "I always have."

"Oh yeah?" In one fluid motion he slid off his seat and moved toward her, balanced on the balls of his feet. The canoe drifted, its balance unaffected. "I've always liked yours, too." Smiling, he laid his hands on her knees as he knelt before her. "Which is something you've always known."

He slipped between her legs, bracing the insides of her knees against his hips. Thus bracketed, he took her chin in his hand. Her lips parted, and he covered her mouth with his. Her head fell back, and he deepened the kiss, making quick little stabs with his tongue. He felt her wind her hands into the loose front of his chambray shirt, brushing against his flat nipples and making them pucker, as though he'd gotten a blast of cool wind. He lowered his own hand, tracing the arch of her throat with his fingers as he withdrew his tongue to the corner of her mouth, then traced the slack seam of her lips with the tip.

"I like your mouth, Raina," he whispered against it. "Always have."

She clutched his shirt. "If those guys were to creep up on us now, they'd probably..."

"Probably what?" His mouth curved in a sly smile. "String me up to a tree?"

She gulped. "Say things."

"You've got that right. In this neck of the woods, they would 'say things' if they thought I might be messing with the wrong woman. But taking a walleye with a spear might just get me shot."

"It's not that I care what they have to say." She closed her eyes. "It's just that..."

"Whenever I get too close, it makes you nervous." He gave her lower lip a brief nibble. "Did my brother make you nervous?"

"You move so much more..." Pushing her fists against his chest, she gave her head a quick shake. He made a silent vow not to ask for any more comparisons between brothers.

She looked up at him. "Do you always cut right to the chase?"

"That was a kiss, honey. Nobody's chasing anybody." With a tip of his head, he reminded her of their surroundings. "You wanna run? You'll have to get wet first."

"You'd never catch me in the water. I'm the one who taught Peter to swim." She braced her hands on his brawny shoulders and taunted him with a coy smile. "I'm beginning to wonder whether you can even catch our lunch."

"A direct challenge to a man's rod—" he gave a naughty wink "—cannot be ignored. Consider yourself off the hook—for the time being."

Chapter 8

For lunch there was pan-fried lake trout. The aroma, wafting beneath their noses on wood smoke and pine-scented air, was so mouth-watering that when Gideon flopped the first fish on Raina's plate she pounced on it like a ravenous cat. It took some fast tongue-juggling to keep from getting burned. Oh, but the flavor was fresh and delicate. Even the bit of meat she dropped in her lap was too good to waste, and Gideon laughed when she snatched it up and popped it into her mouth.

"There's more," he offered.

"But not enough." Seated cross-legged on a slab of granite, she held out her plate for another serving. "I can't remember the last time I had fish this fresh."

"You should have married a fisherman."

"No fisherman ever proposed." It was an innocent remark, and true enough, considering she'd really known only one superlative fisherman in her life. And Gideon well knew who that was. She shrugged and added blithely, "I guess I should have become a fisherman myself, but I'd rather go along for the ride and let someone else do the actual hooking."

"Not being much of a hooker yourself."

"I'm better at procuring." She pulled a small fish bone from between her lips, the urge to smile brightening her eyes. "I'm hell on wheels with a shopping cart," she added finally, "but, mmm, this is really my favorite kind of eating."

"Mine too."

"Thank you for providing fire and food." She reached for his empty plate.

"Mind if I thump my chest and sound the call?"

"What call?"

"Mission accomplished. The male bragging call." He slipped his hands beneath his hair, laced his fingers together at his nape and leaned back against the trunk of a white birch. "As opposed to the mating call, which is sort of a 'heads up' warning."

"Heads—" she arched one eyebrow in disbelief "—up?"

"We're talking about mating calls." His eyes were alight with the pleasure he was taking in the natural way she played the game.

"You said *warning,* and you said—"

"Is it possible that behind this prim exterior lurks a naughty mind? I'm talking about the natural world here. I'm comparing me, man—fire and food provider—to—"

"Me, woman." She shifted the plates to her left hand and offered a handshake with the right. "Hearth tender and food preparer. Glad to meet you."

"You comedian," he said with a chuckle. "Me whipped. I wish you could paddle as well as you can joke around, you woman."

"No you don't. You hardly gave me a chance to do any serious paddling." This was turning out to be a traditional division of labor. He'd taught her to use sand, then water, on the plates for cleanup, which she did. But it was his turn to sit back and relax. She waggled a finger at him as she re-packed the camp kitchen. "You're a one-man crew, Gideon Defender. A real loner."

"You think so?" He smiled as she approached. She stood over him, a shapely shadow blocking only half the sun. Still smiling, he squinted against the glare. "I've been told that I'm a people-pleaser. Always trying to be somebody's champion."

"Who told you that?"

"I don't know. Some counselor."

From where he sat, she appeared to drop from the sky and land beside him, perching on the incline of another slab of rock. "What counselor?"

Her curiosity bore the seed of caring. He could hear it in her voice. All he had to do was water it.

"The one who helped me get off the bottle." It had been a long time since he'd given any thought to talking with her about it. Suddenly he was thinking the time might be right, if he could just keep it light.

"When was this?"

"A while back." He wouldn't have expected her to re-member dates, but she looked as though she were hearing about his infamous bout with the devil's brew for the first time. And for some probably very pathetic reason, he liked that cloud of concern in her eyes. "You didn't know?"

"No."

"Jared knew."

"He kept your confidence, then. He never told me."

"I don't know whose secret it was." He shrugged as he eased his spine a few inches up the tree trunk. "It wasn't mine. I never told him not to tell you."

"Maybe he thought you wanted it that way."

"Maybe he thought he'd have to come to the center for family week." He glanced away from the puzzled look in her eyes. "Like I asked him to. He said he didn't want to expose you to any truth-or-dare sessions."

"I would have gone," she assured him. "Or not. Whatever would have helped more."

"In the end I finally decided to help myself. Getting treatment only started the process." He rubbed the back of his neck and noted that she was hanging on his every word. His brother was dead, and here he was telling on him, when he had no right to lay blame at anyone else's door. "Jared was right, you know. Who knows what I would have said back then if I'd gotten the chance?"

"You can say whatever needs saying, Gideon. I'm no china doll. I can always talk back."

He chuckled. "Yeah, you've got a mouth on you, all right."

"Was that why you were living in the Cities?"

"No." *Damn you, Defender, a* yes *would be a whole lot simpler.* "Well, partly. I went down there to find a better-paying job, but I was..." *See how complicated it gets?* He jerked at an innocent blade of grass. "It was a long time ago. So now I'm doin' okay. I'm doin' *good,* actually. I'm trying to..."

Somehow he'd missed any sound of movement, but when he lifted his chin, she was there. His heart tripped over the soft light in her eyes and landed quivering at the mercy of her moist lips touching his. Her kiss was deliciously delicate, like a touch of morning dew, or a close encounter with a hummingbird's wing, hovering for a moment, then drifting away.

He half expected her to vanish with the blink of his startled eyes.

"What was that for?"

"For you." She sat back on her heels and braced her hands on her thighs, looking at him as though he were a bowl of flowers she'd just arranged. "For the man you are."

"You think you know who that is?"

"I think I'm learning. You have more patience than you used to have. More self-control. But you're still..." She reached out tentatively and plucked at his shirtsleeve. "You always had a very strong presence, Gideon. Very masterful. I think Jared found it a bit intimidating."

The incredible words stacked up one right behind the other, whap whap whap, like dominoes. He tumbled them with a laugh.

"You've gotta be kidding."

"Jared was older, but you were stronger," she insisted. "And I don't mean just physically. You were the one who took care of your mother when she was ill. Jared wanted to pay someone else to do it."

Gideon shrugged. Like he'd had a choice when the woman was *dying.* "She wanted to be home."

"I know she did. You're a very caring man, Gideon Defender." She sat down next to him, stretching her legs out beside his. Had she waggled her feet side to side, they would have touched him midcalf. "And you're a born leader."

As much as he enjoyed her praise, he still had to groan at the thought of him being a born anything. Hell-raiser, maybe. "Sometimes I think I'm just bluffing my way along as chairman. To hear Arlen Skinner and Marvin Strikes Many tell it, I got elected by default. My critics didn't bother to vote."

"You've made a lot of improvements," she pointed out, as though she'd taken inventory.

He told himself that he would have to remember how much credit this kicking-the-habit talk could earn him.

"How important is this treaty compromise to your program?"

"The compromise would be just that. A settlement. We'd gain a little land and some investment capital, and we'd return to some of our traditional practices without any interference from the state, which is what most of us want. In return, we'd give up some of our off-reservation treaty rights, which is what the state wants."

He'd told himself that he wanted to get away from this for a while, but he found that he didn't mind sorting it out for the umpteenth time with her as a sounding board.

"It's important because it might keep the peace. And it's important for our self-respect. Guys like those two we ran into this morning have been calling the shots long enough. It's a sport for them, and that whole scene this morning was part of the game. It's all about who's in control."

"They weren't." She sounded disgusted. "They were totally out of control, like those men at the dock the first time you took us out on Pine Lake."

"We've always fished and hunted for the same reason we gather rice and maple sap. For food. Traditionally, we fished with nets and spears. Those are the ways we were given to feed ourselves, and we value those ways. The reservations haven't changed that. The casinos haven't changed it, either." His gesture dismissed both would-be agents of change. "The reservations took away most of the land. The casinos bring in money. Big deal."

"Losing the land was no big deal?"

"We never owned it. We used it. And the treaty says we can still use it. We are who we are because of what Arlen called our Indian ways." He looked to her for acknowledgment. "Remember? He told Peter he would need his Indian ways. Not just fishing or smoking the pipe, but *the way* things are done. And the way we use what we've been given. Does that make sense to you?"

"Yes. So far."

He couldn't blame her for reserving judgment. The jury was still out on how all this might affect her and Peter.

But he wanted her to understand that there was a lot to consider. "The only thing that changes is that sometimes people forget. You forget who you are, you start thinkin' you're nobody." He searched her eyes for some sign that she could imagine what it was like. *I'm talking about myself now, Raina. I'm talking about myself at twelve, and I'm talking about Peter at thirty-eight.* "Sometimes you lose sight of what's important. Then you lose your way."

"I can't imagine you losing your way." She laid her small hand on his thigh.

Incredibly, it weighed heavily on him.

She smiled. "I'll bet you know exactly where we are right now."

"You will, huh?" Relieved by the sudden switch in tone, he bobbed his chin, challengingly. "How much?"

"I'm betting on *you.*"

"I know." He arched an eyebrow. "How much?"

"If you looked at a map, you would know exactly where we are right now. You could put your finger right on the exact spot." He raised both eyebrows. She lowered hers. "Couldn't you?"

He laughed. "Why do you think I told Jim to forget the map? Wouldn't do me a damn bit of good."

"Are we lost?"

Grinning, he tapped a fist on her knee. "We're on our way to Hidden Falls, which is not on the map." He gave her a flirty wink. "I know *the way* there, and I know *the way* back."

"That's a relief."

"I haven't guided anyone astray up here yet." He nudged her shoulder with his. "'Course, there's always a first time."

"Oh, look!" She pointed to the lake. "Another loon." Her finger became an airbrush, tracing the big bird's graceful progress in the water.

Gideon watched, too. "See the white necklace? The stray shells scattered across his back?"

"You really have a necklace like that?"

"Sure do," he said proudly.

She studied him briefly, then shook her head. "Nah, you're not gonna get us lost. Not even as a joke. It would be too embarrassing for you."

He smiled mischievously. "But leading us astray is an altogether different matter."

Not a trace of their visit was left on the shore when Raina climbed into the canoe. Gideon lifted the bow, gave it a push and hopped aboard without even getting his feet wet. They paddled close to the shore, carried the canoe across a portage, then slipped into a rapid stream. The current eddied, and paddling was mostly a matter of controlling the canoe's direction. Gideon handled the craft so skillfully that all Raina had to do was enjoy the swift ride.

Another portage took them back into glassy water. Reflections of the pines stretched across the lake like long fingers. A beaver's cruising head blazed a trail through the lily pads close to shore, slipping through the water with a stick in its mouth. The white water lilies bobbed in the beaver's gently rippling wake.

They followed a stream that grew so narrow, it seemed to hold no promise as a passage. But the next portage enabled them to bypass the stream's bottleneck, which was, in fact, the hidden falls he'd promised her. The water tumbled over a six-foot drop, splashing into a clear-water cove surrounded by massive red and white pine. The pine scent, the soothing sound of falling water, the choir of crickets, the occasional call of a loon blended into a lovely island of serenity.

Gideon set the canoe down near the water's edge. Most of the portage work had been his. Those brawny shoulders had been shaped in part by years of carrying a canoe over his head, and his height allowed few paddling partners to measure up to the task of assisting. He flexed his shoulders as he surveyed the spot he'd cherished in recent years only as a memory. Maybe his mind had improved on it a little.

"Not much of a falls, huh?"

"I wasn't expecting Niagara." Raina released the straps on the pack she'd been toting and lowered it to the ground. "It's a beautiful spot."

"I don't know whether Jim routes people this way now, but he didn't use to. Neither did I." He stretched, then used his fingers to iron the kinks out of his back. "We wanted it to stay like this."

"I'm the first?"

"Paddlers probably stumble on it once in a while. I haven't been here since…" He considered for a moment. "I don't know when. And you're the first person I've brought here."

"Can you believe it? A truly natural place." She lifted her arms, spun like a pinwheel, then faced him, exhilarated as she walked backward toward the water's edge. "It was like this a hundred years ago, and two hundred years ago, and back, back, back…."

"Whoa." His arm shot out, and he grabbed her hand. "You're about to back into the ice age."

"It's not that cold, is it?"

"Right now the water's about as warm as it ever gets."

"Can we go swimming?" Her face lit up, giving him a rare peek at the little girl in her. She lifted his hand toward the sky and danced under their arms, then ducked back and turned, drawing his arm around her waist as she backed up to him. "Do-si-do your partner," she sang merrily. "Can we have a campfire?"

"I can make it *feel* like we have a campfire."

She flashed a twinkling smile over her shoulder. "Hmm, yes, if memory serves—"

"I mean with a camp stove, which isn't as intrusive on the…" She looked a little disappointed, like a kid poised for a race and getting no takers. "Forget the memories, Raina." Close to her ear, his voice dropped for another husky imitation of his favorite Eastwood line. "'I ain't like that no more.'"

"Not at all?"

She turned slowly, and their eyes were suddenly locked in a heated stare. He wasn't going to chase her. He'd made that mistake before. He could run her down easy. He could give her a head start and still beat her, hands down, but he would end up losing.

He tucked his thumbs in the front pockets of his jeans and shrugged. "We can go swimming if you want. Like I said, the water's as warm right now as it ever gets, but I guarantee you won't last long."

"How about you?"

A smile tickled the corner of his mouth. "I can outlast you."

"You sure about that?"

"Try me."

She stared at him for a moment, as though she were trying to decide just how she might interpret his challenge to her advantage. Her sigh sounded like a concession to his staying power. "But no campfire?"

"I'll build you a fire." He looked into her eyes and touched the yellow-gold hair that swept her shoulder. "What else do you want?"

"I want to be exhausted." She closed her eyes. "I want to be able to sleep."

Gideon wasn't interested in doing any fishing once Raina had made her wishes crystal clear. Supper consisted of the meal packs supplied by the outfitter. Over campfire coffee they watched the setting sun spill a purple wash across a tall cloud's lumpy belly. Above their heads a spray of pine needles made a dark etching against the salmon-pink sky.

He set up the yellow igloo-shaped tent, tossed the sleeping bags inside, then stripped down to his black briefs.

Raina took the hint, again wishing she'd thought to wear a swimsuit under her clothes. But her underwear would serve. Her bra and panties always matched, and neither was ever skimpy. By the time she had folded the rest of her clothes and set them on a rock, he was already in the water. Which was cold. Smooth and clear as glass, but *cold*.

She waded in, carefully negotiating the slick, round rocks as she splashed a handful of cold water over the back of her neck to, as her mother had always said, acclimate her "cold receptors." She was almost ready to submerge gracefully when a soggy mop of black hair sprang from the water, laughing like a distressed loon. The monster clamped cold hands on her warm arms and dragged her, yelping and flailing like a dog on an ice slick, into the depths.

Once the monstrous laughing and distressed shrieking toned down, they bobbed like two corks, face-to-face, chins skimming the water, circling each other, taunting and giggling like children. Below the surface they were locked together, hands to elbows, hands to waist, now drifting at arm's length, now easing closer, knee sliding against thigh, thigh against hip.

"Told you it was cold."

"You said it was as warm as it gets."

He pushed his hair back. She did the same.

He grinned. "Told you it was cold."

Her teeth chattered. "I'm not cold."

"Is that purple lipstick you're wearing?"

Eyes, charcoal brown and crystal blue, glistened in the half-light of evening. Lips drew back in tight, waterproof smiles. "You know what?"

"What?"

"I learned this at a cosmetics demonstration once. 'Always remember—warm water plumps, cold water shrivels.'"

"Shrivels what?"

"Skin."

"You're tellin' me."

"On the other hand, some movie stars soak theirs in ice water every day."

"Their what?"

"Skin."

"Hmm." He shot a mouthful of water at her. "You don't play fair. You know that, don't you?"

"It can become a permanent condition."

"What?"

She shot water back at him. "Shrivelment."

"At least it won't show." His return volley hit its mark. "Like those purple lips."

They splashed around until it was almost dark, but in the end the shivering got to her first, and she waded ashore. Gideon used his hands to sluice the water off his arms and legs as he hurried to retrieve his T-shirt, jeans and flannel shirt. Raina huddled next to the dying campfire, dripping and poking at the embers with a stick. He helped her ef-forts along by adding a few pinecones, which went up like Roman candles, torching the log he threw on for good measure.

"Don't stand too close to the fire." He rubbed her briskly with his T-shirt. "I outlasted you, didn't I?" She gave him a tight-lipped stare, but he persisted. "Didn't I?"

Shivering, she nodded. "It k-kind of felt okay until we g-got out."

"Here, put this on." He handed her his flannel shirt, which looked voluminous hanging from her small hand.

She slipped it on, buttoned it, then executed the bra-removal-under-the-shirt trick, right before his very eyes.

"Slick," he said, his voice replete with genuine admira-tion. He tossed a loosely folded sleeping bag on the ground close to the fire and, with a gracious gesture, offered her a seat. Then he stepped away from the firelight. He kept his back to her while he peeled off the wet briefs.

Raina was soon mesmerized by the play of shadows over his perfectly taut buttocks. She was fascinated by the smooth, easy way he stepped into his jeans, pulled them up powerful legs and settled them at the base of his long, ta-pered back. He zipped them as he returned to the fire.

And he caught the look in her eye, just before she glanced away.

She could hear the smile in his voice. "You didn't peek, did you?"

She lifted her hair off the back of her neck and gave her head a little shake. "I didn't mean to."

"Right." He chuckled, thoroughly gratified. "I don't have your finesse at stripping off wet underwear."

"You don't need it. Doing what comes naturally is easy for you." She used her fingers as a comb. "For me, there are so many ifs, ands and buts. They're all in my head, I know.

But—'' She smiled wistfully. "See, there it is. That pesky old 'but.'''

"The hell, you say." He sat beside her, cross-legged on the sleeping bag, and extended his hands toward the fire. "You knew there would only be one tent. Which means we're going to sleep close to each other, unless you want to kick me outside in the cold."

"Oh, no, of course not. We're roughing it."

"You know what?" He turned to her and plunged his fingers into her hair, lifting it toward the heat of the fire. "All roughing it aside, I could make love to you so easy. If I started kissing you and touching you, it would come naturally. And I could make you forget all the ifs, ands and pesky buts." He looked into her eyes and smiled confidently. "But I won't."

"You won't?"

"No." He scooted closer, his knees touching hers as he ruffled her hair. "I've thought about it, and I've decided not to."

"Really." She stared, partly amused, partly incredulous. "Just like that, *you've* decided—"

"Not to." He watched her hair slide through his fingers, smiling complacently as though he had given it some style. "There, now, isn't that a relief? You can just put it out of your head."

"It wasn't *in* my head. It was in *your* head."

"Well—" his bare shoulders rolled in a shrug "—now it's not. Are you exhausted yet?"

"Exhausted?"

"We could take a run through the woods, and you could pretend I'm chasing you."

"Gideon!" Her quick laugh betrayed barely curbed anticipation warring with inbred hesitancy. She laid a finger against his chin. "You're teasing me, aren't you?"

"It's up to you to figure that out." He tucked his chin and caught her finger with his lips for an impetuous nibble, grazing the tip with his teeth. He smiled, satisfied. "While I'm trying to figure out whether you're teasing me."

"I'm not sure I like this game."

"I'm not sure I do, either, but we seem to be playing it." With a forefinger he traced the arrowing neckline of his shirt until he hit the buttoned juncture in the shallow valley between her breasts. "How 'bout if we just sit by this fire you wanted me to build for you and swap hungry looks?"

"You're being difficult."

His deep chuckle sounded ominous with the darkness so close about them. "It comes naturally."

She mirrored his move, tracing the thong he wore around his neck until her finger reached the small leather pouch that hung to the middle of his chest. "What's this?"

"Just a . . ." He glanced down, as if he'd forgotten. "It's my medicine bundle."

"Is the contents a secret?"

"The contents is personal." He slid his hand over hers as he raised his brow. "Can I ask a favor? How good are you at massaging away an awful ache?" He ignored her wide-eyed double-take. "Do you know how long it's been since I did this much paddling? If you plan to go back the way you came, you need to give your workhorse a good rubdown."

"Oh. Oh, certainly. Why didn't I think of that?" She scooted around behind him and started thumping his shoulders with tension-busting karate chops. "Actually, I'm quite good at this. I took a course. Would you rather lie down?"

"I think it's better if I stay semivertical." His chin dropped to his chest. He closed his eyes and briskly ruffled his own wet hair. "If I fall asleep, there's no tellin' what I might miss out on."

"Try to relax, then, and give me the high sign when I hit on something that needs extra attention."

"The high sign it is," he said with a chuckle.

Her hands were more skilled than he'd anticipated. Her ministrations lulled him into total witlessness, and the sounds he made as the tension drained out of his neck, his shoulders, then his back, were unintelligible groans of pleasure. When she was done, she let him drift euphorically, his forehead pillowed on his knees. After a while he turned his head to the side and watched the mesmerizing dance of the remaining gold flames, listening to the pine wood crackle and the crickets chirp.

A sudden, long, drawn-out canine call brought his head up slowly. Even in the North Woods, this was a rare treat.

"Coyote?" she asked.

He inclined his head toward the sound, then shook it only slightly. "Timber wolf. Listen." The lone howl started low and rose slowly, stretching skyward. Then others joined in, and the distant darkness came alive with the woeful chorus.

"Are they far away?" she whispered, peering into the blackness beyond the orange flames.

"Can't tell." He bounced a playful fist against her flannel-covered thigh. "What, do you think I'm a bat?"

"No, but…" The wolf song filled the night. "There must be dozens of them."

"Half a dozen, tops. No two hitting the same note." He listened for a moment, letting the performers demonstrate. "See? If they do, one changes to a different pitch, so they sound like a huge pack."

"But they do sort of harmonize." She let the sound have its way with her body, and her shoulders did the hoochie-coochie. "It sends shivers up my spine."

"Damn. I wanted to do that." His hands claimed her shoulders, and he turned her away from him. "Let me give it a try. You did a little paddling. I'll give you a little massage."

"I guess I am a *little* sore."

He leaned close to her ear and whispered, "You were great, by the way."

"Really?" She rolled her head from side to side in response to the muscle-kneading he was doing at the base of her neck. "It was good for me, too."

They hardly spoke as they arranged their sleeping bags side by side in the little tent. The slow, easy way they'd approached each other in the warm glow of the fire had been good and right, and now she wondered when and how he would make his move. For, of course, it *was* his move. He'd planned it. She hadn't. It would take her *almost* by surprise, and she would find it impossible to resist.

The sound of a zipper brought her head up quickly. He was opening the rain flaps, admitting the moonlight through the tent's mesh screens.

"Too much air?" he wondered.

"Oh, no," she said quickly.

"Your hair's dry, isn't it?"

She nodded.

He undid another zipper. "I get claustrophobic in these things. I hate it when it rains and you have to close them up."

"Me too." Actually, she'd never given it a thought.

He went to his bed. She slipped her legs into hers. He turned to her, slid his fingers into her hair and touched his forehead to hers. "Nice and dry," he muttered. "Still warm from the fire."

She returned the gesture. "Yours, too." Warm, long, thick and wonderful, she thought.

"You've got 'Sounds of Nature' all around you tonight." He turned his head slightly, rubbing the high part of his cheek up and down, over her temple, her eyelid, her cheek. He drew a deep breath, full of her scent. "Live, not recorded."

"Mmm, yes."

"You'll sleep like a baby," he promised, his voice deliciously husky. "Good night, Raina."

Unreasonably miffed, baffled by her own disappointment, she followed her sinking heart into the pocket of her bed, tossing him a whispered "Good night." She closed her eyes and listened to the night sounds. They were better than a tape, of course. The crickets, the owl, the loon, all blended their clear, soft calls, bidding her to rest. She felt peaceful. The intimate sound of Gideon's slow, shallow breathing made her feel safe. And warm. And more. Waiting for sleep, she inadvertently kept it at bay.

Gideon lay on top of his sleeping bag, slumbering blissfully. Then something in his dreams must have disturbed him, for he groaned and flung one arm above his head, nestling his face in the crook of his elbow. His hair looked longer now. It spilled away from his face and neck like a pool of black ink. Moonlight skated over the contours of his muscular chest and puddled in the shallow saucer of his belly. His jeans rode low on his hips, the waistband slack, the snap undone.

Raina closed her eyes. She could almost feel his warm, satiny skin against her palms again. She flexed her fingers and recalled the firm flesh, the hard muscle. So close. Close enough to hear the change in the tempo of his breathing. He groaned again, almost painfully. What was he dreaming about? she wondered. Or whom? She imagined him calling to her, saying her name in his sleep. It was a fanciful notion, of course, but it excited her. Almost as much as the bulge that had risen beneath the fly of his jeans.

Dear Gideon, in sleep your body betrays you. Your "high sign" refuses to lie dormant.

Her thighs tingled. A wicked urge sprouted deep within her and grew undeniably strong. Lying on her side, she scooted closer, braced herself on her elbow and slid her hand over his belly. It felt wonderfully hard and warm. Pleasure, she thought. It pleasured her simply to touch him, and it was a pleasure she longed to share.

Perhaps her touch alone would bring more pleasure to his secret dream. She found herself coveting his secrets, determined to become part of them, to insinuate herself into his dream. The contents of the pouch that lay against his chest was personal. The contents of the pouch in his jeans was personal, too. But while he slept, it revealed itself to her, beckoning, entreating. She told herself that she might do him another service. She might relieve this intensely personal tension, as she had relieved his other tension earlier.

Ah, he looked so beautiful, stretched out so that he filled the tent. Even in repose his body teemed with dangerous, alluring potential. Her hand stirred, her fingertips inched toward the unsnapped tab, searching first for the dimple in his belly. Her thumb found it, followed the rim, filled the depression, then moved on. The zipper gave way, a fraction of a fraction of an inch. Somehow his belly dipped away even farther, giving her hand more room to explore. What she sought was easy to find. The slick tip, the hard ridge, the oddly enticing thickness that filled her hand.

He held his breath for fear of scaring her away. He could understand the plight of a woman two years a widow, but did *she,* he wondered, understand his? In dreams she had touched him, but never, in his most compelling fantasy, had he been gloved this tightly in her small hand. He felt the light touch of her lips on his shoulder, and then her hand slid away. His whole body followed its retreat, turning to her, reaching for her, pulling her into his arms.

Her eyes were filled with moonlight and awkward surprise. His eyes demanded an explanation. Not why she'd touched him—he wasn't one to question such bittersweet serendipity—but why she'd stopped.

"You looked so...so beautiful. I..." Her breathy excuse got caught in her throat.

"Me?" He would indulge himself no further than a smile. "You've gone without too long."

"It's not that. It's..." *It's you.*

He didn't need to know what it was. Didn't even want to know. It was bound to make everything more complicated when he was doing his damnedest to keep from jumping the gun with her. But those eyes, those big blue eyes, were brimming with complications.

His hand skimmed the length of his flannel shirt, following the S-curve that filled it out. At the end of the road, her thigh emerged. He gripped it and drew it toward him. "Just tell me what you need, Raina."

"Gideon..."

"Gideon?" He nuzzled her neck and whispered into its hollows, "Gideon's what?"

"Gideon's everything."

With a throaty chuckle, he cradled her in one arm while his free hand slipped the shirt buttons loose, his moist lips marking her skin at each interval.

"What would you do with 'Gideon's everything'?" he muttered when he reached her belly.

"I would...I would...."

"Toy with it?" Reversing his direction, he nibbled a path to the soft underside of her breast, where he nuzzled and nose-butted, like a calf coaxing its mother to let the milk down. "The way you started to a minute ago?"

She started to reach for him again, but he stopped her and tucked her arm behind her back. His supporting arm lurked beneath her, and his hand was a ready clamp, putting her seeking hand out of action. Another time, he told himself as he lowered his mouth over her thrusting breast. He flicked his tongue over her erect nipple, then nibbled and suckled until she moaned, almost, but not quite, pitiably.

He slid his hand over her hip, rotating it away from him as he moved down the outside, then up the inside of her thigh. Her legs clamped together instinctively, despite her erratic breathing, despite her needy groan.

"Open your legs for me, sweetheart." He closed his eyes and rubbed his face in the vale between her breasts, tasting her salty-sweetness with the tip of his tongue. "Let me give you what you need."

"No, let me," she pleaded. "Let me show you...what I started to...what you want me to..."

"No, let *me*." His fingertips arrowed into the juncture he sought, gaining access, fingers spreading, prying reluctant thighs apart. He drew dizzying circles around her nipple with the tip of his nose, distracting her from the two fingers he slipped between moist folds. "Relax and let me be your baby," he whispered.

He suckled, and he stroked deeper, ever deeper. His tongue flicked, and his thumb did likewise, tuning her, then playing sweet, excruciatingly sweet notes. High notes. High, higher notes until there was only one note left, and she hit it like a bottle rocket.

Morning came veiled in blue-gray mist. Gideon had coffee ready. They sat side by side on a fallen log, scorching one another with stolen glances, scalding one another with every accidentally-on-purpose touch. Each had tried to relieve tension for the other. Both wondered why it was still there, thicker and heavier than ever.

"We should get a move on. This is the best time to be out on the water." Gideon heaved himself off the rustic sofa. He nodded toward the bright green head of a mallard gliding through the mist. "Everybody's out feeding."

Raina sighed as she followed his lead. "I hate to leave this place now."

"It wasn't easy to get you to come here." They looked at each other. She gave the first shy smile. He shook his head, then permitted himself to laugh. "I never know what to expect with you, Raina."

She walked away, dragging her feet against the grass. "It's just that it's so beautiful here."

She had called him beautiful, too. He remembered it clearly. He wondered if she'd meant it. Any of it. "You roused the sleeping dragon, Raina."

"I know."

"Did it help?" She stood still, her back to him. Gently, he rephrased the question. "Did you sleep better?"

"Did you?"

Questions, questions, questions. Why couldn't she just answer him? Tell him yes. Just say, *Yes, Gideon, you gave me what I wanted. Thank you very much.*

No, he had not slept better, partly because he didn't know where to go from here. He snatched his white T-shirt off the rock where he'd left it and pulled it over his head. It was damp and cold, and wearing it made him feel both good and miserable.

"It's beautiful out there, too," he told her gruffly. "We'll have our breakfast on the water."

He strapped the main camp pack to his back, hoisted the red canoe above his head and took the portage with determined stride. Raina followed in contemplative silence. Once they were out on the water, there was a certain freedom of motion that pulled their focus from each other, releasing mental suction in a way that produced an almost audible pop.

They slipped past a female moose feeding in the shallows. She lifted her shovel nose out of the water, grinding her dripping breakfast with powerful jaws as her eyes followed them with minimal interest. They both laughed when she shook her head, noisily flapping her big ears. Indifferent and absolutely unthreatened, she swung her head away, then dunked her nose for more juicy grazing.

As the morning wore on, low clouds kept the sun from burning the mist off the water. The fishing would have been great, Gideon thought. But he wasn't in the right mood. "I think we're in for some rain," he said absently as his paddle sliced the water. Slip-slide, slip-slide, slip-slide.

Raina looked straight up. "It's not supposed to do that." But an errant raindrop hit her nose. More drops pattered softly, scattering circles across the water in the pattern of a wedding-band quilt.

"Well, it's doing it anyway," Gideon said.

By the time they put in to shore it was coming down steadily. Thunder started rumbling as they set up the tent. Birch leaves rattled in the wind, and the water dripped from the pines, intensifying the evergreen scent. They tossed the packs into the tent and scrambled in after them.

"You're soaking wet." It was the only thing Gideon could think of to say. At least the stuff inside the packs was dry. He took out the two requisite towels, which, laid end-to-end, didn't add up to half a bath towel.

But at the prospect of spending a rainy afternoon inside the tent, he had it in his mind to be gallant. He tossed her a towel, which she used on her hair, while he did the same.

Then their eyes met. She looked incredibly sexy with tousled hair and wet clothes.

He tried to clear the gravel from his throat. "Let me help you get dry."

It was an offer that entailed removing clothes. All it took was their shirts—skinning the cat with his, then peeling hers away with a bit more care and a thoughtful smoothing back of her hair after the shirt came away—and he was lost. He had the towel in his hand again, and he meant to use it, but his good intentions turned to mush at the mere sight of a drop of water on the swell of her breast. He dipped his head to claim it with his tongue.

The taste was pure ambrosia. He glanced up and saw the quick approval in her eyes. He unhooked the fastener between her breasts and stripped the wet fabric away. "So pretty," he murmured, but in daylight her pale breasts seemed to want covering. So he cupped them in his dark hands.

The thunder grumbled overhead. The rain pelted all around them. Gideon lifted his gaze slowly from the place between her breasts where his thumbs lay side by side, to the little hollow at the base of her throat where her pulse throbbed, to her lower lip as she quickly sucked it and left it moist for him.

The motion drew him like a hawk descending for prey. His lips claimed hers. His tongue darted in search of hers, and hers met him at the door. His hands slid to her waist and made short work of the fastenings on her pants.

"Would you say we're going to need a bed?"

She nodded.

His eyes never left hers as he reached for a sleeping bag, dragged it close, undid the bands and flipped it open, all with one hand. In another moment her wet clothes were gone. His were chafing him something fierce. He lowered her to the pallet and went hungering after her, pulling her hand down between the legs of his soggy jeans. He closed his eyes and caught his breath when she flexed her fingers, pressing, stroking.

He groaned. "It would be a damn shame if Gideon's everything caught a chill."

Her small laugh was sensuously deep. She helped him peel off the wet jeans. Then, in the gray light of a rainy afternoon, they admired one another with unabashed eyes and unrestrained hands, with openmouthed kisses and bold tongues. Dampness turned steamy as they rubbed skin against skin, driving one another to the brink again and again, just to see how close they could come. But close would not suffice this time.

"Tell me what you want," he exhorted gruffly as he rose above her, poised for a swift strike.

"This is what I want," she whispered, caressing him between his legs. "All of this inside me."

He prepared himself. All for her, he thought, properly gift-wrapped. But someday, maybe...

On that hope, he slipped himself inside her with long, strong, deep strokes. She gasped and cried out his name. He backed off only slightly as he slid his hands beneath her bottom. She locked her legs around his waist. His hips took the lead, tagging their tempo to the steady tapping of the rain, which picked up gradually until the heavens finally broke wide open and the deluge washed over them.

They dozed in each other's arms, reveling in timeless, weightless peace. The easy time. The afterglow. The distant thunder was a soothing sound, as was the soft rain. They drifted, awash in unspoken love words.

But the drifting eventually stopped, and the words slipped away, still unspoken. They were two separate entities again.

And they found themselves purposely not looking at each other for fear of detecting something in a look—some kind of disappointment, some sign of rejection—that would make them feel chillingly naked.

It was she who broke the silence, because well enough wasn't well enough if it had to be left alone.

"This complicates things, doesn't it?"

"How so?" *Damn,* he *had* to ask. And then he couldn't help dipping the damn question in cold brass. "What do you want to make of it, Raina?"

"Nothing," she said tightly.

Nothing at all? Have it your way, then. "It's as simple or as complicated as you want it to be."

"What about you?"

He stared at the curve of the tent roof. "I'm flexible."

"Really." She covered herself with a corner of the sleeping bag. "Then I certainly appreciate the use of the condom."

"There's no other way these days, right?"

"Right." She turned her face toward the wall. Her throat felt scratchy, lined with sand. "Funny. I got used to thinking none of that pertained to me, but now..." She swallowed hard against the encroachment of awful heartache. "Now I guess it does."

"I guess so." He jammed his hands beneath his head and stared hard at the nylon ceiling. "Some women buy their own now. Dutch treat."

She shut her eyes tightly. "I'll keep that in mind."

Chapter 9

There was a part of Gideon's brain that was fully aware of the fact that sex was one of life's great wild cards. It was the great complicater. The gate to heaven, the road to hell. He didn't know how many times he had to prove that to the other part of his brain. One look at the woman sitting as far away from him as the pickup's bench seat would allow should have been all the proof necessary. If you wanted to get somewhere with a woman, leave sex out of it, at least until the trapdoor to hell was safely frozen over.

Things had changed between Raina and him, and the reason was clear. Raina had broken her own rules.

He'd never been quite sure what the rules were. He'd learned one or two hard lessons during his tougher years, and he'd taken those into account. Otherwise, he thought he'd read all the signals right. But, damn, for a while there she'd turned into a wounded bird. After the rain, they'd paddled back to Jim's place, with her in retreat and him walking on eggs. Her conversation had been soft and thready. She'd admired every bird, every bee, every bend in the waterway, like someone taking her last look at the world. When they got back to Pine Lake he half expected her to ask him to drop her off at a convent, or maybe a tomb, where she was ready to inscribe the epitaph herself: *Gideon Defender loved me to death.*

But she'd mended her own wings by the time they'd reached his house. The melancholy clouds disappeared from her eyes, replaced by distant, clear-day blue. *Distant* was the key word. Things had definitely changed.

Most women were hard to figure, but this one was a doozy.

When they pulled up to the house, Gideon was surprised to find his driveway blocked by a Jeep bearing the official seal of the Pine Lake Chippewa Band. This must have been a piece of the plan he'd forgotten.

"Wonder what Carl's doing here." He said it casually, but Raina's eyes turned anxious. "He's not a cop," Gideon hastened to assure her as he set the pickup's parking brake. "He's one of our game wardens. He gets out to the Skinner place pretty often, so I asked him to kinda discreetly make sure things were going okay with Peter."

She flung the pickup door open. "I knew it was a mistake to leave him with—"

"Hold on now." Gideon hurried up the driveway to catch up with her. "Let's not jump to any conclusions. Peter must be here, too. Otherwise Carl couldn't have gotten in the house."

They walked in on what appeared to be nothing more than a friendly card game, with Peter hosting his grandfather and Carl Earlie at the kitchen table. All three looked up when Gideon and Raina came in, but the greetings were ominously guarded.

"We figured we'd save you a trip out to Arlen's," Carl explained as he threw in his poker hand. "I'm gonna give Arlen a ride home."

Peter looked at his watch. "It's Sunday night. You said you'd be back Sunday afternoon. These guys have been waiting here for two hours for you to get back."

"We got caught in the rain." Gideon turned a chair away from the table and straddled it, bracing his forearms on the backrest. This was a switch. A kid watching the time on his parents.

Parent. Parent and guardian. Whatever. The damn complications came in battalions.

"Did you wear your grandfather out?" Raina asked as she stepped close behind her son's chair.

He looked up at her and shrugged. "We did a lot of stuff. Spent a lot of time at the powwow. I learned how to do a dance."

The chin jerk he made toward his grandfather was a new mannerism for Peter. It seemed perfectly natural to everyone in the room but Raina, who knew him better than he knew himself and noticed every change in him lately with a mother's mixed feelings. He was growing up. He was forging new connections. He was slipping away.

"What was that dance, *nimishoomis?*" Peter asked.

"Traditional grass dance." Arlen shared his nod of approval with Peter, then Gideon. "He did pretty good. We started making him a bustle."

"And the other thing I'm supposed to tell you is that I—" Peter cast a quick glance Carl's way, checking to see whether the man had changed his mind about the requirement. Clearly he hadn't. "Well, Tom and Oscar and me went out kinda late, and we had a couple beers."

Raina's response was automatic. "Oh, Peter, you *didn't.*"

"No big deal," Peter complained. "Nobody got drunk or anything."

"I was in bed sleepin'," Arlen reported. "I told him not to be sneakin' out. He didn't listen. Looks like he wants to learn some things the hard way."

"This isn't going to work, Peter." Raina laid her hands on Peter's wiry shoulders, while he hung his head, staring at the five cards he would never play.

Carl shoved his chair back from the table and rose to his feet. "Listen, I'm gonna get out of the way here and take Arlen on back." He turned to Gideon. "The other thing is, Rosie said to tell you that Judge Half wants to see everybody over at the court tomorrow afternoon."

The news hit Raina like a wrecking ball. "That hardly gives me time to get hold of my attorney." She wanted it over, but she wasn't ready. She noticed the ace in Peter's hand, and she wondered where hers was. She had no cards to play, in fact. Nothing but a mother's commitment to her child.

Gideon spoke quietly, avoiding her eyes. "All he'll be able to do is advise you, Raina."

"You mean I won't be represented?"

"You'll be heard," he said impatiently, as though she were speaking out of turn and in front of the wrong people.

But a rising sense of desperation kept her going. "I don't like the way that sounds."

"Call your attorney." His curt gesture smacked of resentment, even though his tone was utterly controlled. "You're right. You should have an expert around to advise you."

"There's something else," Carl announced officiously. He straightened his uniform, tucking his shirt into the back of his pants. "Arlen here says there's been some kind of secret meetings going on between the Strikes Manys and some of them big-shot sportsmen. They're all hot against the settlement, so they're talking about finding ways to defeat it so the treaty ends up in court.''

"Where the sportsmen are betting we'll lose, and the Strikes Manys are betting we'll win. Makes for a strange alliance, doesn't it?'' Gideon shook his head. "Why are you telling us this, Arlen? I thought you didn't approve of the settlement.''

"I don't. But the Strikes Manys are fooling themselves real bad, talking with those guys about working together. We picked our leaders, even though some of us never voted for certain ones.'' He gave Gideon the loaded eye. "But they're who we've got, and they're Indians, at least.''

"Those damn rednecks just wanna use the Strikes Manys to make it look like they're not against Indians,'' Carl said. With a sardonic chuckle, he added, "Hell, they *love* Indians. Some of their very favorite people are Indians. Like those guys who play for Cleveland and Atlanta.''

The tension eased with the three men sharing in the bitter humor over one of their least favorite institutionalized insults to Indians.

"Dealing with those guys is gonna mean trouble for all of us. You need to read up on Red Cloud and Spotted Tail,'' Arlen told Gideon in passing as he angled toward the door.

"What for?'' Gideon challenged kiddingly as he saw the guests out. "They were ornery Sioux.''

"They were Indians. And they spent a lot of years trying to compromise with the white government.'' Arlen summed up his parting bit of wisdom with a solemn nod. "Some things change, some things don't.''

After Arlen had left with Carl, Gideon figured it was time for a serious family-type powwow—the kind he'd rarely experienced, up until this summer. Raina and Peter were the ones who knew the ropes with this family business, but she was on edge, and he was sulking.

"How about some sandwiches?" Gideon suggested when he joined them in the kitchen.

"Not hungry," Peter mumbled, awaiting the inevitable cave-in with studied apathy.

"No, thank you." His mother folded her arms tightly under her bosom, her prestorm stance equally well rehearsed.

"All right, then, let's all—" Gideon glanced back and forth between them "—have a seat."

"Let's just get it over with," Peter suggested.

Gideon shook his head. "I don't know about your mom, but I'm not gonna lay into you over this sneaking out, Peter. Things are a little up in the air right now, and you took advantage of the situation. I don't feel real good about that, do you?"

"It was no big deal," the boy reiterated stubbornly. "If Carl hadn't come along, nobody woulda had to know."

"Listen, if this all goes okay tomorrow—and I really don't think we'll be looking at any big upsets—you and me are gonna have a little talk about some of the ruts along the road to manhood."

Peter rolled his eyes and sighed dramatically. "Not *this* again."

"Yeah, *this* again." Gideon's hand was allowed to rest on the boy's shoulder only briefly before Peter shrugged it away. "You don't need to be drinking now, Peter. You've got too much goin' for you. Booze can only get in the way."

"You got another false tooth to scare me with?" He indicated Gideon's lower half by way of the chin jerk he was quickly perfecting. "Maybe a wooden leg or something?"

"No, but I can bar the window and sleep outside your door, if that's what it takes."

"You'd be a fire hazard." Peter saw the chance to play both ends against the middle and, like any normal kid, he used it readily. "Anyway, with any luck, we'll be goin' back home. Right, Mom?"

The question took Raina by surprise. Suddenly she had her little boy back. Her prodigal son was ready to be taken home. And, just for a moment, all that mattered was that he was ready, and that he had turned to her.

Tears scalded the back of her throat. If she spoke, they would surely surge upward and reduce her to an emotional wreck. She had no answers, anyway, but she gave a quick nod and opened her arms to him.

That he permitted a hug—even returned it—felt like something of a victory, particularly when Gideon's pat on the shoulder had been turned away. Oh, God, she was a poor excuse for a woman of character! But Raina was willing to take her small triumphs however they presented themselves these days.

The next morning Peter was up earlier than Gideon expected. He himself was up earlier than he wanted to be, after last night. He would have given anything to have been able to take Raina to bed and make the world—mostly *his* world—go away for her. But, of course, he was dreaming with his eyes wide open on that score.

Peter was helping himself to a bowl of the Lucky Charms he'd asked Gideon to stock for him. "Mom's downstairs, sleeping on the sofa in the den," he reported.

Gideon headed for the coffee fixings. "Let's try to be real quiet. She hasn't been sleeping very long. Couple of hours, tops."

"She's been up all night?"

Gideon nodded solemnly.

"Did she think I might run off or what?"

"She just wanted to stay close by." Gideon shoved the pot under the faucet and ran some water. "She's a strong woman, your mother. She's worried about how all this is affecting you. You need to give some thought to what it would be like to be in her shoes right now."

"And not cause any trouble."

"That would help." For a kid Peter's age, it was probably a lot to ask, considering the circumstances. "It's gonna work out."

"You think so?" It was a rhetorical question, quickly followed by the real concern. "Yeah, but how?"

"We'll know soon enough." Gideon turned the coffeepot on, then turned to watch Peter slurp spoonfuls of tiny pink and blue marshmallows into his mouth. "Your grandfather didn't have a chance to make a sweat with you?"

Cheeks puffed out like a foraging squirrel's, the boy grunted, "Uh-uh."

"That's maybe what we should've done this weekend. Might have kept us all out of trouble."

"You guys haff any twouble up in the Noth Wooz?" Two big gulps slid audibly down Peter's throat. "Run into any bears?"

"No bears."

"Too bad." The spoon clattered in Peter's bowl. "How come you don't have a beard?"

"What?" From bears to beards? Gideon rubbed his chin as if there had been some hair there just a minute ago, then pulled a dubious scowl.

"I was just thinking—my dad didn't have much of a beard, either." On his way to the sink, Peter stopped to check out the reflection of his profile in the toaster. "Do you think I'm ever gonna get a beard?"

"Why? You wanna be shavin' every day?"

"I was kinda wondering when I might start."

Gideon shrugged. "I maybe shave once a week."

"I noticed my grandfather doesn't have much of a beard, either." Peter gave his cereal bowl a hasty rinsing.

"Indian men usually don't. It works out pretty good. We don't have to go around with little pieces of toilet paper stuck to our faces."

"Huh?"

Gideon chuckled. "I hear some of those muscle-bound pinup boys shave their chests, too. So if you ever wanna be a muscle-bound pinup boy, you've got the Chippewa advantage."

"I don't care about chests. It's just that some of my friends are starting to shave—" Peter did a double-take and let out a belated hoot. "You gotta be kidding. They *shave* their *chests?*"

"Strange world, isn't it?" Gideon smiled, pleased with the lead-in he'd inadvertently given himself. "A guy needs the old tried-and-true ways just to help him keep his head straight."

"We did smoke the pipe together."

"You and your grandfather?"

"He said I shouldn't smoke cigarettes, like he does, but that the pipe isn't like smoking. It's like a holy thing. I didn't understand all the prayers, but it felt..." A grunt conveyed his frustration with the puniness of mere words. "I liked the way it felt. Like someone was listening."

Gideon affirmed the feeling with a nod. "I know what you mean. You try to hang on to that, okay? Don't let anything make you forget."

That goes without saying, Peter's big, brown, twelve-year-old eyes said. The look was all innocence, total trust.

Gideon suddenly felt like a very old man.

"I want you to know something, Peter. You and your mother are both very important to me. You're family, and that means everything." He stood next to the boy, their backsides resting against the counter, arms identically folded, one ankle crossed over the other, each contemplating his own bare toes. "I know we haven't been close, but if you're willing, I'd like to see that change."

Raina appeared in the doorway, her sleepy eyes underscored by gray smudges of fatigue. By the look she gave him, Gideon knew she'd heard what he'd said. He saw no sign of approval, and none of disapproval. Only weariness.

"You look like you could use some coffee," he said, straightening as though somebody had said, *Hop to it*.

"I could, thanks."

"I could make you some toast, Mom," Peter offered, following Gideon's swift lead. "We've got English muffins, too, and raspberry jam."

"Just..."

Gideon looked up from the coffeepot. Peter turned from the refrigerator. Both pairs of beautiful brown eyes anxiously awaited her command.

She smiled. "Actually, I think I could go for an English muffin, too."

Peter smiled, too. "I'll make it for you."

Despite Gideon's efforts to pave the way for a friendly, open-and-shut hearing, the group that gathered in the lobby outside Judge Half's chambers could well have been an assembly of strangers from different parts of the globe. And they might well have been gathered for a wake, unhappily scheduled for a still, sticky, sluggish summer afternoon. The air was cloying, the silence deafening, the eyes politely blind.

In reality, the only new face belonged to Raina's attorney, Jeffrey Metz, who met her at the courthouse. He shook hands all around, then sidled up to Raina and quietly assured her that he had done his research and that he was "on top of the issues." The judge had acted in accordance with state and federal law so far. "But we'll see," he concluded as the judge opened his office door and announced that he was ready to discuss the Defender case.

They flowed toward the voice like molasses. First Arlen, then Metz, then Peter filed in. "Sorry about the air-conditioning," the man who was waiting for them was saying. "It broke down yesterday."

The judge's voice sounded prophetic. Gideon dragged his feet, reluctant to heed the call. And so did Raina. Just before they reached the office door, she tugged on his arm, suddenly desperate to draw him away from the others for a quick word. She looked up at him plaintively, as though ultimately he were the one she trusted.

"Gideon, I'm scared."

He wanted to hold her in his arms, then and there. He glanced at the plain round clock that hung on the wall just above her head, but he didn't see the time. What he saw was two people holding on to each other for dear life. What he felt was her silky hair against his cheek, and what he heard was his voice promising her that she had nothing to worry about because he would take care of everything, and the hell with Mr. Jeffrey Metz.

He looked down at her again and smiled. In her long-sleeved yellow blouse and navy skirt, she looked the perfect image of the fourth-grade teacher of every nine-year-old boy's dreams. Bad things should never happen to a woman like this, he told himself. He cast about for some magic words, but he drew a blank.

"You're doin' fine, Raina." *Yeah, right. Some pitiful imitation of a hero you turn out to be, Defender.*

Raina closed her eyes and shook her head. Her lips were so pale they were almost translucent. "No, I'm not. They're going to take my son away."

He put his hand on her shoulder and slid it slowly down the back of her arm. "I don't think so."

"What if they do?" She glanced at the office door, which stood open, waiting. Her chest heaved on a quick, panicky breath. "There must be something I can do. Something *you* can do. Isn't there?"

"Arlen's not going to press this thing much further, Raina. After what happened this past weekend?" With a cluck of his tongue he shook his head. "It's not gonna happen."

"What if it does?"

He squeezed her hand, her frantic question echoing in his head. As far as he was concerned, there was only one ultimate answer. "You're his mother. Nothing's ever gonna change that."

The judge's voice shot through their circuits like a power surge.

"You two coming?"

Judge Half made the session feel more like a meeting than a hearing. Everyone sat around in a circle. Each face in the room glowed with its own sweaty sheen. Arlen sat near the window and smoked. Gideon rested his ankle on his knee and waggled his booted foot. Peter had his knees going up and down like pistons as he bounced his heels on the floor. Raina's hands were knotted in her lap.

But everyone had a say. As promised, Judge Half was interested in hearing from almost everyone present. Jeffrey Metz simply took notes. The judge said he'd heard a rumor that Raina had inquired about a teaching position with the Pine Lake School.

"We're getting a new facility pretty soon, right, Chairman? Casino profits are goin' for a good cause." At Gideon's affirming nod, the judge turned to Raina. "If you really want to teach here again, I hope you get the job."

"I enjoyed teaching here before," she said.

Playing his role like an orchestra leader, the judge swung his seat toward Peter. "I see you're getting along with your grandfather pretty good."

"We spent the weekend together." Peter gripped his knees, trying to force them to be still for a moment, but they kept popping up at odd intervals, as though they had a mind of their own. "We went to the powwow and stuff."

"That's good." The judge cued Arlen. "How did that go, then?"

"Good, good."

"I did sorta screw up on curfew times and stuff," Peter admitted. "But, you know, if *nimishoomis* is still willing to let me come and visit once in a while, I'll behave myself a lot better."

"*Nimishoomis*, huh? That's very good." Judge Half reflected for a moment. "What would 'once in a while' be, do you think?"

"I don't know." The knees started bouncing furiously again. "I get pretty busy once school starts. But we can come back next summer." Peter lifted one shoulder. "Or spring. I'd like to learn how to spear fish when Uncle Gideon gets us our treaty settlement."

"You've been getting to know your uncle pretty well, too, I see. These are interesting times for all of us, Peter." Without missing a beat in his lecture, Judge Half swept a handful of papers off the desk top just behind him. "It's good to be Chippewa. We are a small minority in this big American country, but we have much to be proud of. And these are interesting times for us. We know who we are, and we will let our neighbors learn who we are. And learn *from* us, if they will." He eyed Peter pointedly. "But we need every Chippewa we have."

"Well, I'm Chippewa, Judge. I know that. I've always known that."

"Good, good. Mrs. Defender has done well by you." He spared Raina a deferential nod. "I encourage you to follow up on the teaching job. We need teachers. Don't we, Gideon?"

"We do."

"So I just want to encourage that." Turning to his papers, the judge gave the top one a cursory glance, then set it aside and scanned the next as he spoke.

"Now, I've gone over all the records. There is one glaring piece of information that is missing, and that, of course, is the identity of Peter's biological father. In fact, the court records contain an affidavit requesting his mother's anonymity, so that information was not available to the social worker, or to Mrs. Defender. But Arlen knew, because his daughter told him. And Jared Defender knew, because he had contact with her. According to the records, Jared made all the legal arrangements." When he finally looked up, he directed his attention to Raina. "I found that interesting."

"Jared was able to make the arrangements because he was a lawyer," Raina explained quickly. "And Gideon told him that he knew—" she glanced at Arlen and said the next words softly, gently, seemingly for his benefit "—a woman who was looking for...adoptive parents for..."

It was as though another piece of the puzzle had dropped into the judge's handful of papers. He looked up at Gideon. "You knew."

"Yes."

"I see." Ostensibly deep in thought, the judge set aside another page. "You realize that since Arlen is Peter's closest blood relative, and since every case of this kind affects not only a child and a family, but also the interests and the future of the Pine Lake Band of Chippewa, I'm inclined to declare that the boy's biological grandfather—"

Gideon leaned forward. "Judge, my brother was an enrolled member of this band, and he was legally—"

"You're interrupting me, Mr. Chairman. And I am presiding here."

There was a brief stare-down. Eyes smoldering, Gideon glanced away.

Having made his point, the judge continued, his imperious tone never wavering. "Now, I'm willing to recognize Mrs. Defender as Peter's mother in every sense but the biological sense. And the biological sense is what establishes Peter's degree of Indian blood, his right to tribal enrollment, and his right to call himself Pine Lake Chippewa. So I hope that Mrs. Defender will continue to take part in Peter's upbringing—in fact, I intend to stipulate with Mr. Skinner, who, as primary custodial—"

"No!" Gideon shot out of his chair, instinctively putting himself between Peter and the judge.

The move stunned everyone. Gideon could feel the eyes boring holes in him from all sides. He had but one ace, and it took him a moment to drag it up from its deep, dark, well-guarded hole.

With it came an icy exterior and a calm, steady voice. "Excuse me, Judge Half, I meant to say no, Arlen is not Peter's closest blood relative. I am."

The judge didn't look too surprised. "I guess a simple blood test is all it will take to clear up this whole thing—"

"What are you talkin' about?" Peter demanded.

Gideon steeled himself against the voice until it came pounding on his ear. The boy's rising confusion speared Gideon right between the shoulder blades.

"Uncle...*Uncle* Gideon, what the *hell* are you talkin' about?"

Turning slowly, Gideon struggled with a thick tongue and a dearth of words. "Jared raised you, Peter. He was your father. I've got no right to make that claim." He forced himself to look the boy in the eye. "But I . . ."

"Gave me away?"

Gideon rubbed his forehead with unsteady fingertips, then muttered an expletive into his palm. The room seemed to be tipping and swaying like the deck of a big fishing boat, and somewhere on the periphery, seesawing at odds with him right now, sat Tomasina's father and Peter's mother. He wished one of them would just blast him and get it over with.

But it was Peter who demanded, "Why?"

"All I can tell you right here and right now is that it wasn't because I didn't want to be your father." Gideon turned unseeing eyes on Judge Half. "In a million years, I never thought you'd take the boy from the mother who raised him and give primary custody to . . ."

"An old man?" Arlen put in. "At least I know my duty to the boy."

"You see it differently is all."

Judge Half sat back in his chair. "Gideon, I guess you and me should have had a little heart-to-heart before we got everybody together for this. You know what's at stake here. We suffered the wholesale removal of Indian children from their tribes and families for longer than either one of us can remember, longer than Arlen can remember, and he's older than both of us put together."

When his nickel's worth of humor fell flat, the judge turned his lecture back on Gideon. "We've been through this before, in this court. And you stood with the tribe. If you hadn't been personally involved this time—"

"Yeah, well, I *am* personally involved. And I thought some kind of a compromise could be worked out, so that

Peter could have his grandfather as a *grandfather*. And his mother... and his father, Jared was his..." Suddenly the words wouldn't go together in the right order. Jared was his real, legal, undisputed... "Hell, I've been Peter's uncle all these years. I'm not... I promised—" He closed his eyes, and his voice drifted in frustration. "I promised not to interfere."

"I'll order the blood tests. Soon as we have some results, we'll be able to make a decision." For Gideon's benefit, Judge Half added a footnote. "I don't know who you made this promise to, but I suspect he's dead."

He motioned Peter closer. "I'd like to talk with you just a little bit more, son, but the rest of them can listen in if they want. I have a feeling there's going to be some heated discussion after this little set-to breaks up, and I just want to give you a little background." He glanced at each of the adults as he expounded. "'Cause I get 'em in here every day. Domestic entanglements. I deal with 'em every day. It's hard for people to get along. Gettin' harder all the time, seems like.

"See, the old way, we didn't have judges. We had people who were a little older, a little wiser, who tried to mediate disputes. And the old way, if something happened that made it impossible for parents to raise a child—say, some kind of trouble—"

"I could see if somebody died or got killed," Peter said bitterly.

"Well, there's all kinds of bad trouble, son. Anyway, something happened, like, okay, maybe the baby's mother died."

"Yeah, but she didn't die until way later," the boy reminded him.

"I'm talking about an example here." Judge Half's reproach was followed by a pregnant pause, a silencing look.

"If the baby's mother died, then it would have been a natural thing for a man to give his son to his married brother to raise, it being pretty hard for a man to raise a baby alone. Now, none of this probably would've been kept a big secret. In fact, the old way, a child's uncles were like his father, too. And his aunties were like his mother. No questions, no problems."

He shrugged, backed off on the romanticism and opted for honesty. "Well, that's not true. People are people, and they bicker and complain and make problems for themselves, but they work it out if they can. Maybe sooner, maybe later, but they do the best they can.

"And that's what we're gonna do here. We're gonna work this out. You've got people here who love you. You're probably a little mad at 'em right now, so I just wanted to point that out. I heard a lot of good things you had going amongst you when you all first came in and sat down. Things were a little strained, but everybody's been willing, deep down."

The judge wagged a finger. "So you go ahead and be mad, but don't be too hard on these people, son. They're all family. *Your* family."

"That's easy for *you* to say, Judge."

"You think my job's easy?" He snorted. "Maybe I'll turn it over to you one day."

"Don't bet on it." Peter scowled briefly at Gideon, then at the judge. "Do I have to stay with *him?*"

"Where do you want to stay?" the judge asked.

"He can stay with me." Arlen, too, glanced at Gideon. But there was no judgment in his eyes, and he spoke kindly. "We'll make a sweat tomorrow night. Maybe you'd wanna come."

"You think you're gonna make me get into some little tent with *him* and—"

Arlen rose from his chair slowly, his old knees cracking into place. "No one is ever forced into a sweat. You can try it out first with me if you want to. If you don't, that's up to you."

Raina was shell-shocked. Her heart hammered wildly, her pulse rang in her ears, but her senses were as dull as mud. She wasn't sure she had form or substance. Maybe she'd become invisible. When she turned to her attorney, she was surprised to find she still had a voice.

"Isn't *anything* up to *me?*"

"Well, the state's jurisdiction is limited where the child is an enrolled tribal member, but I intend to pursue some research along several possible lines." Metz scanned his notes. "Maybe there's some kind of a damage suit here against somebody. I mean, mental, emotional—"

"Damage suit?" The words sounded absurd. Dazed, Raina shook her head. "I want my son."

"Well, we don't have a ruling yet, but I'm just trying to get one jump ahead—"

Tell him to jump off a bridge, Gideon thought, his heart breaking as he stood there, angrily watching her seek out an ally other than himself.

"I want to know exactly where I stand," she said.

"In my opinion—" Metz edged her toward the door "—no matter what those blood tests show, your prospects are rather dismal. Except, as I said, if we can find an angle for a civil suit."

"Thank you." Miraculously the starch had returned to Raina's voice. "You've been no help whatsoever, but thank you for making the drive up here, Jeff."

She finally turned to Gideon. "I want to talk to you."

He was glad *somebody* did.

Chapter 10

She waited until they were alone, and then she didn't know where to start. Let *him* start, she decided. The ball was in his court. Unbeknownst to her, it had actually been there all along. So let him finally put it into play. Let him put forth some combination of words that didn't add up to craziness. She was all ears, which was appropriate. It surely made her look as foolish as she felt.

But they went to his house, ate his ham-and-cheese sandwiches, drank his coffee and sat on his porch, all without speaking more than a dozen words.

So it was up to her, and she went right to the sore spot. "Why didn't you tell me?"

"That I was Peter's biological father?" His voice was quietly strained, as though he had to pull it back through the sieve of his memories. "I didn't see how it would do anybody any good. I figured somewhere down the road, when Peter was older—after he'd gotten to know me a little better—I'd tell him about some of my past mistakes." He stared into the mug of coffee he held cradled in both hands. "And I'd tell him how he was the only good thing that ever came of those mistakes."

"What I'm asking you is . . ." She waited until he looked up. "Why didn't you tell *me?*"

"God, Raina. Tell *you?*" He glanced at the plank ceiling, shaking his head over a mirthless chuckle. "When do you think would have been the best time?"

"In the very beginning."

"Jared figured total anonymity was the best way to go."

"He did, did he? Except that *he* knew, so I don't see how the term *total* applies."

"Jared agreed to be Peter's father. That made me his uncle. The more people who knew otherwise, the harder it would have been to keep it that cut-and-dried." Gideon offered a wistful, self-conscious smile. "I knew I'd done wrong. I wanted to find a way to make it right, and I went to Jared. We were just trying to keep it simple, I guess."

"You could have told me."

"Jared thought—"

"Jared thought, Jared thought, Jared thought." She'd fallen back on the same crutch enough times herself, but she wasn't about to let him borrow it. Not now. "As the judge rightly pointed out, Jared is dead. *You* could have told me."

"I thought about it once or twice, but, hell, as little contact as we've had?" He avoided her eyes. "What would be the point? After all this time, it seemed like it would create more problems we didn't need."

She wanted to shake him and shout right in his ear. *We've had some pretty big contact in the last few days, Gideon. Am I the only one who's noticed?*

But, of course, she didn't. Instead, she calmly quizzed him about things that touched her only indirectly. It seemed important to make him turn over everything that had been hidden from her, as though her knowing every detail might somehow undo the damage.

"Why did you give him... I mean, why didn't you and Tomasina—"

"See, that's why." His rigid hand leveled a curt karate chop on her questions. "That's why I didn't want to tell you. Because then you'd start asking why, and none of the reasons are gonna sound very good to you. It's all over and done with. The whys don't matter anymore. What mattered then and what matters now is that Peter got a good home out of the deal."

"What about his mother?"

"What about...?" His eyes filled with a tenderness that transformed the tone of his voice. "What about her?"

"Did you love her?"

"Did I love... Tomasina?"

The intensity in his eyes turned hers away.

"I'm sorry," she muttered. "I shouldn't have asked you that."

"Why? What answer did you hope to hear? That I did?" He paused, and her heartbeat stalled in the interim. "Or that I didn't?"

"It's none of my business."

Then why was she asking? And why was she still waiting for an answer, *the* answer?

And why did he feel a need to tell her in the bluntest way possible?

"We had sex, and I got her pregnant." He looked her straight in the eye, daring her to judge him more harshly than he judged himself. "That was what was between us.

Neither one of us liked the idea of getting married—at least, not to each other. She didn't want a baby, didn't want an abortion, didn't especially like the idea of giving him up for adoption until after Jared talked to her. But ol' Jared was always pretty persuasive.''

"Did he support her financially?"

"I supported her, mostly. We lived together in St. Paul for six months, which was why I was surprised to learn that Arlen knew anything about it. I didn't think she talked to him much. Hell, she didn't talk to *me* much."

"Didn't Arlen even know that you were the man she was seeing?"

"You never knew any more about that woman than she wanted you to know. Especially how she felt about anything. She never let anything show." He gave a dry laugh. "I guess *I* should talk, you know, thinking back on what I was like in those days. But, anyway, she said it was none of her father's damn business."

"But she told him she was pregnant."

"Yeah, I guess she did. And that was the kicker, wasn't it?" He sipped his coffee, offering her a sheepish glance over the rim of his cup. Then he shrugged. "Surprised the hell out of me. Maybe it was her way of thumbing her nose at the ol' man. She liked to let people know that she was gonna live her life exactly the way she damn well pleased.

"But at least she kept her word," he allowed. "She said she'd carry the baby to term if I'd help her get away from home. She'd always wanted to live in the Cities. And, hell, she took to city life like a pigeon. But me, I hated it. I worked a lot of different jobs—construction, assembly lines, fast food. Tommy took some classes, played bingo, did pretty much whatever she wanted."

It was the first time he'd used a nickname for the woman with whom he'd conceived a child. He'd schooled himself to manage his memories carefully, and the only other person who had heard the story was an uninvolved counselor. Now, here he was, telling the whole damn thing to Raina. Raina *was* involved. She was practically sitting on the edge of her chair, and the look in her eyes—her intense, vicarious involvement in the whole sordid mess—was killing him.

"Except party," he noted quickly, grasping for any uplifting straw he might offer. "We agreed on that much. We stayed out of the bars while she was pregnant. Hell of a long six months, but..." He turned to look out the window. His voice drifted as the memories turned from bad to worse. "After Peter was born, she split. And I told myself I was nursing a big heartache. Aching for what, I didn't know, but it served as a nice, slick slide to the edge of nowhere. I ended up in detox."

"Which was not an alcohol treatment center," Raina recalled.

"No. It's a place where—" A place her experience wouldn't allow her to imagine, which was just fine, because he didn't want her be able to imagine what it had been like for him there. Four days in hell had convinced him he wasn't going any lower. "It was a place where they were putting too many Indians. Later on, I was part of the group of community activists and Indian leaders that got the Health and Human Services Department to take a look at what was going on there. We forced them to shut the place down."

Her eyes brightened. "I remember. It was in the news. But I didn't know you were part of—"

"There were quite a few of us," he said, minimizing his contribution with a dismissive gesture. "But that came a whole lot later. After I dried out, I asked Jared to help get me into a treatment center. He did. And I'm grateful to him for that.''

"Do you need connections to get into treatment?''

"Depends.'' He smiled indulgently. "You need a health insurance card, a bank account, a social worker...*something*. I had a brother who was embarrassed to be related to me.'' He anticipated her objections and waved them away with an easy smile. "Anyway, I met this old Indian guy who was working as a janitor there. He'd been a tribal councilman. He'd also been through the program. I'd never thought about getting into politics, but I sure liked ol' Everett. I learned a lot from him. And I actually talked to him, told him things I never told anyone else.''

He remembered telling Everett about Raina and about Peter. Everett had suggested that Gideon trusted his brother with what he loved most because somewhere along the line he'd decided he couldn't trust himself. He'd always thought it a strange observation, since he knew damn well he'd resented Jared, and for no good reason. Jared had always done everything right, for God's sake. Where was the crime in that?

"Everett must have been almost like a father to you,'' she said. "I've never heard much about your father. Not from Jared, and not from you.''

Gideon shrugged. "My ol' man never had the time of day for us. But Everett told me that he'd missed out with his own kids, too. He said that's what drunks usually do.'' And when the time had come, Gideon told himself, he had done the same. Like father, like son.

Damn, it had been so much easier being an uncle.

"I knew Jared would make a good father. I knew you'd be the best mother a kid could—'' Elbows braced on his knees, he spread his hands wide. "When do you think I should have told you, Raina?"

"I guess it doesn't matter now. I can see how it became more difficult, the more time that passed and the more distant we became."

"You were always the one who sent the Christmas cards with all your family news and the school pictures." He thanked her now with a wistful smile. "God, he's growing up so fast."

She glanced away, then swallowed hard. He could see her putting words together in her head and gathering the courage to say them. Her breast quivered with her next long, deep breath.

She looked him in the eye. "Are you going to take him from me, Gideon?"

"No." He shook his head. "No, I can't—"

"You don't want him, and I can't have him—is that—"

"Don't want him!" The accusation drove him to his feet. "You think I don't want—" Old memories and new emotions swirled around them as she stood up to him. He grabbed her shoulders. "I want, Raina. I've wanted—" he closed his eyes and savored a quick, deep dose of her delicate scent "—so bad sometimes I could hardly..." He dropped his hands to his sides and turned away. "That's what happens when you stop anesthetizing yourself. The feelings catch up to you." And speaking of bad, God help him, he had it bad.

"Peter has feelings, too."

"Once he cools off, you're the one he'll talk feelings with. You're his mother." He glanced at her quickly, then away. "And obviously he'll still see Jared as his father."

"My parental rights have been stripped away. Abruptly. Unexpectedly." She grabbed his arm and made him look at her. *"Unfairly,"* she insisted, as though she thought she would get an argument out of him on that score.

When she didn't, she sighed. "And the most frustrating part is that I can't do anything about it. Peter's always been able to count on me." Her grip on his arm tightened for a moment, then fell away. The vigor in her voice withered. "I feel powerless, and I hate it."

"You've already taken steps. You've said you're willing to move back up here." He shoved his hands into the pockets of his jeans and stood for a moment like a diver mentally setting himself up to spring. "You know, there's an obvious solution to this," he said finally.

"What?"

Their eyes met, hers guileless, his guarded. "We could get married."

"Married?"

She said it as though she were unfamiliar with the concept. He felt like a guy who had somehow managed to get clobbered by the ton of bricks he had just dropped. It wasn't easy to shove the damn things off, but with a cavalier shrug he gave it a try. "Why not?"

"Surely," she said, sounding a little dazed herself, "the real question is *why?*"

"Because..." *I want you to be my wife* probably wouldn't cut it. "Because I want to marry my son's mother. Isn't that a good enough reason?"

She glared at him. "It may well be that the last person Peter wants his mother to marry is his father."

"Well, it's not up to him. We're his..." When he realized he'd placed his hand on his chest, he smiled ruefully and included her with an openhanded gesture. "We're the adults. It's up to us."

"This is absolutely ridiculous." She backed away, as though his outstretched hand threatened her somehow. "No, this is *outrageous*. I can't.... We stayed together out there in a beautiful, beautiful...and we..." She waved her hand vaguely toward the outdoors, and her voice suddenly teetered on a hurt-filled pitch. The misty glimmer in her eyes accused him of some cryptic crime. "But you didn't even...because it meant absolutely nothing. Nothing but...but what you said about..."

She made a cutoff gesture with two very shaky hands. "I have to go now."

Still stinging, he was a little slow on the uptake, but the sound of her heels on the wood floor incited his whoa-there reflex. He caught up to her before she got to the front door.

"Raina—" Now that he had her by the arm, he didn't know what to say. She'd called his proposal absurd, but she was hardly laughing.

"No. Don't touch me, Gideon." She shook him off and plowed her fingers through her hair, squaring herself up for a revised, more composed exit. "I guess I need to cool off, too. Peter and I both. We don't understand—"

"Let me drive you," he said gently, working hard to keep his twice-rejected hand from reaching for a third rebuff.

"No. I'll be fine." She took a deep breath. "There. I'm fine. It's important never never to lose your head, you see." She smiled weakly. "I'll be fine."

"I'm not letting you go like this."

"How *will* you let me go, then? The last time it was to your brother."

"He turned out to be the right man for you."

"And when did you decide that?" She wrapped her arms around her middle, steadying herself, setting her chin.

She was winding up to tell him off, he thought. He could feel it coming.

"You found a wife for your brother, and then you gave us a child," she clipped. "Quite a remarkable piece of work, Gideon. And now that you're a tribal leader, you're making big changes around here. If you can get this treaty thing through, I think a movie would be in order." Bolstered by an infusion of flippancy, she managed a stiff-lipped smile. "With somebody like Charlton Heston playing you. Gideon Defender, the leader, the prophet, the right hand of God."

"Cut it out, Raina." His befuddled gaze sharpened. "I'm just trying to get by, that's all. To work things out the best way I—"

"*Your* way. Which is to avoid making commitments."

"That's a damn lie!"

"You 'work things out' for everyone around you, while you manage to—"

"What do you mean, avoid commitments?" He grabbed her shoulders. "I just asked you to marry me, for God's sake."

She lifted her pretty, aristocratic chin. "You proposed an *arrangement,* not a marriage."

"I offered a solution to a problem. I knew damn well what kind of a response I'd get." Gradually he drew her closer, noting an unmistakable flicker in her eyes as he slid first one arm around her, then the other. His lips were a scant inch from hers, and his eyes glowed with a complacent smile. "But I know how to get a different kind of response from you, don't I?"

"Gideon, this isn't—" She closed her eyes. He splayed his hands over the swell of her hips and pressed her firmly against him. Her complaint turned soft, and he used it, molded her to his hardness. "It isn't fair."

"It isn't a game. There are no referees to decide what's fair—"

"And what's foul?" she challenged breathlessly, her chest heaving involuntarily against him.

He nuzzled her hair back from her temple and whispered, "It's up to us."

"We have to be sensible." It sounded like the hazy echo of some old, dusty advice.

"Why?" he breathed against the side of her neck. "I got a lousy response to my proposal, but how about this?" He took her earlobe between his teeth, gently sawing on it, tormenting her with his flickering tongue as he deftly unzipped the back of her skirt. He tucked his hand into her cotton panties and stroked her bottom, drawing her up to him and holding her tight against his hard member. "How will you respond to this, hmm?"

She whispered his name so softly that it felt like a caress, and he hungered after her mouth, demanding more of the same. Her lips parted on a jagged sigh, welcoming his questing tongue. It was a hot, wet, seductive kiss, at once promising and postulating. His lips nipped, then sipped, then devoured, while his tongue made love to her mouth. He rubbed his hands teasingly over the warm curve of her hips, pushing her clothing down, but just a little.

"Yes or no?" He licked her lower lip, then nipped it as he rocked his hips against hers, whispering hotly, "Yes or no, Raina?"

"Yes." Her body listed, yearning for his. She gripped his shoulders. "Yes, yes."

"Yes, what?"

She loosened the first two buttons on her blouse, then looked up at him shyly. "Yes, make love to me."

"Yes, who?" he demanded, finishing the job she'd started as he lowered one knee to the floor. "Who do you want to—"

He tasted her nipple, tonguing and suckling until it hardened. She slid her fingers into his hair and cuddled him at her breast, whispering, "Gideon. I want you, Gideon."

The magic words. The words that turned him from mere man into hunter, warrior, prince, king. Words that compelled him to sweep her into his arms and carry her to his bed, to finish undressing her and to worship every sensitive part of her body with coddling hands and adoring lips. She pulled his shirt open and lifted her head, straining to touch the small nubbin of his nipple with the tip of her tongue. He played a little keep-away, enjoying the sweet shiver it gave him to let her touch and glide away.

Her teeth grazed him as she fumbled with his belt buckle, and he groaned. "How long will you respond this way, Raina?" He eased his thigh between hers, prodding her to ride it. When she did, he whispered, "Is this a yes?"

The buckle came loose with a soft clink. She tore at the snap on his jeans. "Yessss . . ."

He lowered his pants, lowered his hips, applied his rigid, needy probe to the private entrance to her body. He found her moist and ready for him. "And this? Is this a yes?"

"Yes, Gideon, yes."

He took pains to protect her, just as he took care to prepare her. She filled her hands with his hard, warm buttocks and urged him to come to her, arched to receive the full measure of his initial thrust and draw him deep, deep down into her inner self. He drew back slowly, like a bowman taking scrupulous aim at a very small target. But he was loath to let fly his arrow now that it was so sweetly notched. He set a slow, undulating rhythm, reaching ever closer to the target, attuning himself to her gradual need for a quicker pace.

"How long?" he whispered, then flicked his tongue over her temple, sipping her saltiness. "How long can you stay with me? I can keep this up all night."

"Then do it!" She pressed her cheek against his shoulder and wrapped him with arms and legs and earnest desire. "Oh, Gideon, yes, do it...do it."

He had no choice but to oblige with all his considerable skill, not to mention his heart and soul.

And later, when again she said, "Oh, Gideon," he knew he'd done it right. Her soft sigh poured over him like warm, cleansing water, and her intimate touch convinced him that he belonged to her and always would, whether she stayed or left him.

"You'll have to play yourself in the movie," she decided out of the clear blue.

"Why?"

"Because there's no one else like you." She propped herself up on her elbows and looked down at him. The shift gave him a nice view of her lovely bare breasts, but it took her hand away from him. "You're beautiful," she said, her voice filled with wonder.

"Don't stop touching me, Raina." He drew her back into the cradle of his arm, in one fluid move reclaiming her hand and placing it low on his flat belly. "Please. I've never..."

"Never what?"

"Felt this good." He'd dreamed of making love to her, and the dream was always good. But he'd never dreamed that she would come willingly to his bed. He closed his eyes, turned his lips to her hair and whispered, "I always knew we'd be good together."

She sighed. For a long, quiet moment neither of them moved. But when he nuzzled the fine wisp of hair at her temple, something cool and wet slid over the tip of his nose. It felt suspiciously like a tear—a tender, frightening, feminine thing with which he had precious little experience.

He whispered her name.

She stiffened. "I have to go."

"Go where?" He caught her and held her, searching her eyes for some explanation. All he found was a troubling semblance of the evening shadows that surrounded them. "This is the only place you need to be right now," he told her solemnly. "Stay with me."

"Gideon, I can't think." She took a quick swipe at the corner of her eye with the heel of her hand. "I have to go back to my room and try to sort things out. Try to—"

"You need sleep, Raina."

She closed her eyes, but she said, "I can't sleep."

"What is it?" He caught her face in his hands. "Tell me what's wrong."

She was trying, albeit feebly, to push herself away from him, but he was having none of it. He massaged her temples with his thumbs until, muscle by muscle, she relaxed her body against his, giving in, letting him take the pressure away. "Even when I'm exhausted, it's very hard for me to fall asleep."

"That's because you're trying too hard. You think too much. You always did." He stuffed an extra pillow behind his neck and settled her in his arms, pressing her head into the pocket of his shoulder. "I can help you sleep."

"Gideon—"

"Shhh, Raina. Which sounds of nature would you like to hear? I can do loons if you like. Or wolves, or..."

He started humming. She tipped her chin up, and he saw the surprise in her eyes. He touched his finger to his lips, then with one hand stroked her brow, gently coaxing her eyelids closed as he sang to her softly in Chippewa, words he remembered from his boyhood when *nookomis*, his grandmother, had sung them to him. Shortest boyhood on record, as he recalled. And it had been such a long, long time ago.

She slept well in Gideon's arms that night. She slept soundly, even when he slipped away early in the morning. It was when he phoned from the office that she finally woke. He told her that he'd checked on the status of her application for a teaching position, and she was in. Despite the bright lilt in the voice that delivered the news, and even though it was the answer she'd hoped for, the news was somehow disquieting.

It was decided, then. All the staid, comfortable, routine aspects of her life were about to change. It occurred to her that if she examined the great changes in her life too closely, she would find that one man had somehow played a major role in many of them. And she was lying in his bed right now, between sheets that smelled deliciously of his body. In bed, *where he'd always known they would be good together*. And that was not enough.

"Why so quiet?" asked the voice on the phone. The same voice she'd heard in the dark last night. The same voice that had sent shivers scurrying down her spine. "Isn't that what you wanted to hear?"

"Yes," she said, but her tone was flat. "It really is. I'll need a place to live. Any suggestions?"

"How fancy?"

"Two bedrooms. Beyond that, the basics would be nice."

Seated at his desk, Gideon tapped the eraser end of a pencil on a pile of letters, many of them written essentially to curse him and all his ancestors. He shoved the tedious rancor aside.

Two bedrooms, plus the basics. Hell, he could offer her that much. In fact, he had offered her that and more. But he wasn't going to beg.

"What are you going to do with your house?" he asked.

"Sell it. It's too much house for the two of us, anyway. It's time I unloaded it. I have a friend who sells real estate. I'll call her today." She paused, then added quietly, "It's time I made some changes."

"Right." Choose your own time, choose your own brand, sweetheart. "Well, you don't qualify for tribal housing, but there are always a few winterized lake cabins available for rent in the off-season."

"I'll start looking into that today." She sighed. "This is going to be so hard for Peter."

"We're remodeling the high school," he reported buoyantly. "Adding a swimming pool and a bunch of space for new programs. Putting the casino profits to good use, just like the judge said. And if things keep going the way they are, we'll be able to pay for college for any of our kids who want to go."

"*Our* kids?"

"Pine Lake Chippewa kids." Elbow propped on the desk, he rested his brow in one large hand and rubbed his temples. "Raina...somehow I think Peter's going to be our kid—yours and mine. Maybe if you'd try to look at it that way..."

"Like joint custody? Isn't that the usual fallout from a divorce?" She gave a little tsk. "The pain of a divorce without the legalities. How ironic."

"Yeah." He lifted his face to the morning sun and the breeze wafting through an open window. "Ironic as hell."

"It's going to be hard for Peter to look at it the way you're suggesting."

"I have a feeling Arlen's going to help us out with that. I mean, I think he's willing to let me, uh . . ."

"Take your rightful place?"

"They're concerned about Peter's place, not mine. They want him to be part of the tribe."

Absently he moved an official-looking piece of paper from one side of his desk to the other. "I was served with a court order for a paternity test this morning. The judge walked across the street and handed it to me personally." He gave a dry chuckle as he snatched a pencil from the howling coyote mug that Rosie had given him in honor of some holiday he'd hardly known existed. "As if he thought I might try to duck out on it or something. So I'm going over to the clinic before I head up to Arlen's this afternoon. I want the three of us to do a sweat, like Arlen said."

"What about me?"

"You're his mooring, Raina. He was already straining against the bonds before any of this other stuff cropped up. Now he's got a whole new cause, but he was gonna test out the big waters, anyway."

"He's too young."

"No, he's not." With one hand he snapped the pencil in half. "Look, he thinks he hates my guts right now. That's something we need to deal with."

"*Thinks?*"

"Okay, so maybe he does," he admitted, his exasperation level rising. "Maybe he always will. Maybe he'll let it fester and eat away at his insides until—"

"Gideon, please." Her voice sounded thready and distant. "It's just that I'm feeling rather shut out of all this."

"All his life you've been his safe harbor." And *I've* been shut out. I shut *myself* out. "Don't worry, Raina. He'll come back to you. It's part of the circle. Don't you see that?"

"Bring him home—*here*—as soon as you can. Will you do that, Gideon?"

"I will." He closed his eyes and swallowed back the sand in his throat. "Will you be there? At home, when I get back?"

"I can't stay here like this, like . . . Gideon, I feel so—" The space between them sounded long, hollow and empty. "If I'm not here, I'll be at the lodge. I really have nowhere else to go until . . ."

"I'll find you."

Chapter 11

Peter wasn't ready to go back to anyone. Far from it. Gideon found him sitting on the porch with his grandfather, both of them working on his dance bustle. Peter was preparing the vanes of the synthetic feathers that Arlen was working into a creation that would eventually become a dancer's fan-shaped tail feathers.

Gideon greeted Arlen with a handshake. Then grandfather reminded grandson of his manners, just as uncle had once done. The boy dutifully, if grudgingly, obliged Gideon with the requisite handshake.

"That cop came and got me again," Peter said as he went back to carving the end of a feather with his grandfather's penknife. "Took me to a clinic. I had to have a stupid blood test."

"I know." Gideon hiked one booted foot up to the porch and braced his hand on his knee. "I did, too."

"So, what if they don't match?"

Gideon hadn't given that possibility much thought. Maybe he was flattering himself, but he could see more of himself in Peter every day. "None of this changes anything as far as your mom and . . . and your dad are concerned."

"My dad?" Peter's dark eyes challenged Gideon to try to apply that designation to himself. Just *try*. But when Gideon wouldn't take the bait, the boy shrugged it off. "My dad's not concerned about anything anymore. He's dead. You can bet if *he* was here—"

"He's not." Gideon traded a hiked brow for Peter's glare. "So, you wanna do a sweat with your grandfather and me or not?"

The muscles in Peter's jaw were working just as vigorously as his hands. Gideon waited patiently for his answer. Finally the boy glanced up from his task. "I wouldn't have to be too mad at you if you wouldn't have to mention anything about being, you know . . . my father or anything."

"It's a deal." Gideon scraped the sole of his boot against the edge of the porch as he lowered his foot to the ground. "We go into the sweat simply as three men. Different generations, different experiences, all living in the same world."

Arlen flashed Gideon a glance that sparkled with approval. "Next time you go up for chairman, I might just vote for you."

In the close, dark heat of the sweat lodge, Peter learned new ways to pray. They were ways that were almost as old as the red-hot rocks that were used to make the steam, but they were new to him. He took the heat and the smoke in stride and contributed what prayerful thoughts he could come up with on the spot without giving too much of himself away. He'd already been given away once, and now that he knew who'd done it, he wasn't sure he could trust him again. After all, a guy had ideas, and then he had *thoughts*.

He'd told his uncle Gideon some stuff, but that was before he knew he wasn't really *Uncle* Gideon. Well, he was, but he wasn't. Either way, things could never again be the way they were. Which was okay. He wasn't a kid anymore, and he didn't like it when people treated him like one.

The trouble was, he felt like a kid sometimes. Not often, but *some*times. And when those times came, whose kid was he going to be?

Since nobody was anxious to force anything on him, he'd been spending a lot of time with his new friends. He talked about Tom and Oscar during the sweat, about how he was teaching them how to head a soccer ball and they were showing him how to do the men's fancy dance. He told his grandfather and Gideon that they were pretty cool dudes.

What Gideon didn't realize was that Tom Strikes Many had also given Peter a few political lectures. Tom had spent long hours listening to his father bemoan the prospect of limiting some of the treaty rights through what Marvin called "Defender's sellout." The Strikes Many clan had threatened to file a legal suit, claiming that the Pine Lake Tribal Council and its chairman couldn't speak for them. The federal court had denied their claim.

But there were new ideas being discussed now. Secret challenges were being issued by another group opposed to the settlement. Challenges like, *If you've got the guts to defend your so-called treaty rights in a real court of law, why not start out in criminal court? Why not do what you say you have the right to do—what the state says no one can do—and that's hunt and fish out of season or by illegal methods off the reservation in the ceded territory?*

It had been done, of course. But not blatantly. And now, with the settlement in the works, the tribal fish and game wardens were guarding their jurisdiction closely. But there were other jurisdictions. And there were many ways to skin a cat.

The sweat had been good for Gideon. There had been no talk of politics, for such was not the purpose of a sweat. With their tangled relationships off-limits for discussion, they'd spoken of other things, and they'd spoken candidly, for in the dark, close, warm womb of the sweat, there was no other way to speak. They had shared cares and concerns for those close to them, for friends and family and the Indian community. They had made prayers for wisdom and clear vision.

Gideon knew that Raina would not be happy to learn that Peter had not come home with him. The boy had said he'd made plans with his friends, and Gideon chose to respect that. But he hoped she would take what communication they'd had as a positive sign. Gideon certainly did.

Now if he could only figure out how to communicate with Raina. He called her at the lodge and asked her to have dinner with him. "Like a date," he said hopefully. "Like two people who just want to get to know each other."

"What's it going to take for us to get to know each other?"

"I don't know." Something like a sweat would have been good. Except traditionally, men and women didn't go in together. He could see why. Damn, it was hard to keep sex out of it. "I figured I'd get dressed up, though."

She laughed. "Oh, great. And me sitting here with nothing to wear."

"Wear the dress you had on the first time I saw you this summer. You looked all sunshine and flowers."

"That one isn't very dressy."

"Wear the hat, too. I loved the hat."

She was ready at the appointed time, and she was listening for the knock on the door. But when it came, her body had to jump up pretty fast to keep pace with her heart. Silly to be nervous, she told herself. Or overly eager. She'd just been with him in the most intimate way possible. For her, anyway. For him, well, maybe *that* was a date, and maybe conversation over dinner was an intimacy. Who could tell about men?

There would be none of *that* tonight. Nothing too personal. She'd already decided that she wasn't going to keep him waiting. She didn't want to have to invite him in, to have him sit on the bed and watch her comb her hair or put on her shoes. This was a date.

But the doorknob proved to be a tricky mechanism for an unsteady hand, and when she opened the door, the man who stood before her startled her even more than his quick knock. He was physically breathtaking. His hair seemed thicker and darker, more luxuriant, than ever, his eyes more penetrating, his lips fuller, his shoulders broader. And when had she ever seen him dressed in a sport jacket?

"Hi."

His smile lit a matching spark in his eyes. "Hi, yourself."

She smiled, too. She couldn't help it. Her senses were instantly, giddily glutted with all things Gideon.

"This is as fancy as I get," he said, sounding almost apologetic. Along with the brown jacket, he wore a blue chambray shirt, blue jeans and a wide brown belt. Very understated. Very handsome. The dentalium choker added a touch of true distinction. She reached up to touch it, forgetting all about her plan to remain impersonal.

"The loon's necklace." Her smile turned wistful as she traced a row of tubular shells with an admiring forefinger. "The sign of a chief."

"Sign of leadership," he corrected. "And the loon would have to fight me for it. I might as well admit right off, I wore it to impress you."

"I'm impressed."

"So am I." He braced his shoulder against the door-frame and gave her an appreciative head-to-toe appraisal. She'd worn the dress he'd said he liked, along with a silver bracelet that Peter had given her for Mother's Day. She fanned her skirt demurely, fluttering the soft cotton like a little girl with a brand-new full-circle skirt.

"You look great. Do I get a kiss?" He pushed himself away from the door and took her shoulders in his hands. "Isn't that what people do on dates? Give each other a kiss at the door?"

"That comes at the end," she said, smiling. Lord, he looked good enough to eat. "Like dessert."

"I like to start with dessert." He lowered his head, and her lips sank into his for a long, slow, wet, glad-to-be-together kiss. Their mouths parted reluctantly, their lower lips lingering to touch a little longer, tongues reaching for one more tiny taste. And their eyes held court together beyond that, acclaiming the dessert cum appetizer with a silent *mmm*.

Finally Gideon glanced at the top of her head and gave a lopsided smile. "Where's the hat?"

"It's kind of a *sun* hat."

"I'm kind of a sucker for sun hats."

With a light, feminine laugh she took the hat down from the closet shelf and let him put it on for her. It was just a hat, she told herself. Nothing too personal. Neither was the way he winked at her and flipped the petals on the big sunflower that was tacked to the hat band.

He'd made reservations at the most exclusive restaurant on the lake, one that was not on tribal land. They were seated at a table near the fireplace. Not far away, the dining room's huge windows overlooked the lake, its blue waters glistening in the summer's evening sunlight.

They talked about the day each of them had had in the comfortable conversational tones of two people who were more than friends, who shared more than a backyard fence or acquaintances in common. She was pleased to hear about the reception he'd gotten at Arlen's. Even though he couldn't tell her what was said in the sweat, he was able to convey the sense of renewal that had pervaded. He knew he had a long way to go with Peter and that it would take time to regain the boy's trust. But he believed he'd made a start.

Then he learned that in a single day she had been promised a teaching contract, put her house on the market and looked at several houses that would be available for rent when school started.

"Nothing I'm crazy about," she said with a shrug. "But who knows? Once the house sells, I might just decide to buy something here and fix it up to my liking."

"That's what I did. 'Course, I don't know much about stuff like decorating."

She planted her elbow at the edge of the table, rested her chin on the back of her hand and smiled warmly. "Your house is very comfortable. It suits you perfectly."

"What would you do to it, if you were going to, say, fix it up to your liking?"

"I might add on so I could open up the kitchen more. Do that whole great room thing. The fireplace would be a real focal point. I like the woodwork and the stone. I like the North Woods feel." She glanced at the rafters and considered more possibilities as she reached for her water glass. "I'd put some flower beds in, maybe a deck. I love the porch."

He caught her hand in his and turned her wrist slowly, inspecting her bracelet. It had a single silver charm attached. "What does this say?" He tilted the small, shiny cutout toward the flame that flickered within the amber votive cup in the middle of the table. It took a moment to decipher the words in the dim light, but finally he looked up, smiling. "So you're 'Number One Mom.'"

"My last Mother's Day present." She glanced away, her cheeks flushing. "I mean, most recent."

"There'll be more." He pressed her hand between his, massaging palm to palm. "I've never thanked you, Raina. Seeing him now, seeing the fine, healthy young man you're raising...I want to thank you."

"I'm his mother." Her tone was as level as the look she gave him. "I think...I hope I've done what good mothers do. Thanks aren't—"

"Necessary, I know." He rubbed his thumb over the links of the bracelet. "He thanked you with this. And I'm thanking you." He shook his head, chuckling as he tore his eyes from the bracelet. "I gotta tell you, you know what I thought?"

"What?"

"I thought this was probably something Jared had given you, and maybe it said 'I love you' or something, and I thought..." He looked into her eyes, lingering uncertainty muting his voice. "I thought, this woman's trying to tell me something."

"I do have gifts from Jared. Keepsakes and memories." But it was Gideon's hands that warmed hers now, his thumb caressing the soft side of her wrist. "He did love me, you know."

"I know."

"And I loved him."

"I know that, too."

"So did Peter."

Gideon nodded. They sat there for a long, quiet moment, holding hands across the table. There was such an aura about them that the waiter bypassed them twice, reluctant to offer menus until the mood at the table changed.

"Raina," Gideon began finally. "What you said about the way this is shaping up to be like a custody battle in a divorce..." He lifted his eyes to hers, probing deeply, earnestly. "It shouldn't be like that. I mean, why should Peter be part of that kind of tug-of-war when there's been no divorce?" With gentle urgency he squeezed her hand. "You know, we...when we put ourselves into it, we really get along fine. What I mean to say is, if we—"

A restive murmur spreading from table to table drew their attention from their own little world. Around the room other curious heads were popping up the same way. One of the waiters was hastily drawing the drapes, while a couple of people stood half out of their chairs, trying to get a peek before the view was cut off. A tide of noise seemed to be building outside. The buzz level in the dining room was also on the rise, along with growing disquiet.

Gideon signaled the waiter who had been patiently waiting for a break in their tête-à-tête. "What's going on?"

The young man handed Raina an open menu. "Just a little commotion at the boat landing."

Distracted, Gideon ignored the menu he was offered. "What kind of commotion?"

The dining room supervisor paused on his way back from the window. "We'll do our best to see that the disturbance doesn't interfere with your dinner, sir."

Gideon rose from his chair as the white-haired man in charge hurried away. He turned to the young waiter, who had already assumed the proper pose—hands clasped behind his back—for his presentation of the evening specials. "What's going on out there?"

The waiter chafed at the question. "I don't exactly know how to say this without, uh... What it looks like is some kind of a protest or something. Some Indians and, you know, some... other guys sort of yelling—"

"Don't go away," Gideon told Raina. He dropped his cloth napkin on top of the silverware next to his plate. "I'll check it out, and I'll be right back."

Raina tried to wait. She knew the best course was to stay out of the way. The voices sounded angry, and they were getting angrier by the second. She heard one of the waiters say that the police had been called. Then she heard another one mention that there were teenagers involved. "Just a bunch of Indian kids, got caught using spears." Someone else laughed and added, "They probably didn't even catch anything."

Raina was out the door in a heartbeat. She walked quickly, homing in on the shouting.

At first all she saw was a crowd of fuming people, mostly men wearing baseball caps, some carrying placards, and some brandishing what looked like bumper stickers. She saw a few red-slashed circles containing images of nets and spears. Great form of expression, she thought. What happened to the peace sign? She didn't see any "I-heart-Indians."

The bend in the shoreline suddenly afforded her a view of the far end of the boat landing. Her stride went from a walk to a trot when she got her first glimpse of the little group the protestors had surrounded. It wasn't just teenagers. Marvin Strikes Many and four other men had landed at the big public dock in two boats. But among the younger faces Raina recognized were Peter and his friends, Oscar and Tom.

The confrontation was quickly escalating toward violence. Each side was doing its best to shout the other down, and Gideon was trying to muscle his way into the center of it all.

"Get back on the boats," Gideon shouted. Then, to the sign-carriers, "Listen, you people, the police have been called. Why don't you just back off and—"

The answers came from the crowd, which had become a single entity, a mindless animal with numerous mouths.

"We're staying right here until somebody gets here to investigate."

"Nobody gets off this dock now!"

"Did somebody call the game wardens, too? Tell 'em to come see for themselves what these people are up to."

"We got a treaty that says your state wardens got no say," Marvin Strikes Many shouted.

"And we've also got a right to use the public landing," his son put in.

Gideon waved his arm as he pushed his way to the fore. "Would you guys just settle down—"

"We got a right to see what you *think* you got a right to take out of this lake," one of the bumper-sticker wavers said.

"Yeah, and what methods you're using." The crowd surged like an inchworm, its body gaining a few planks' worth of dock space. "Look, they've got spears!"

"They got spears, and they got nets!"

"Where's the media when they could do some good?"

"They'll be here."

"This isn't Wisconsin. Damn Indians took over on the fishing there, but nobody's gettin' away with that here."

"Hell, you know what they say over there," one of the mouths shouted. "Save a walleye, spear a squaw!"

"Hey, spear a pregnant squaw, save two walleye!"

The threat stabbed Raina in the stomach. Real, physical pain. She felt sick. She was close enough now to see the fear in Peter's eyes. He'd suffered some stares, some thoughtless, ignorant remarks in his young life, but nothing like this. And Raina had felt a mother's pain at cruelties perpetrated on her child, but this, *this* was insufferable. Her rage was bigger than she was, and she about to leave some claw marks on somebody.

All she could see was Peter, and all she sought was a way to get to him. He was scared, but he wasn't cowed by the threats. And when he saw her running up the wooden steps, he was afraid only for his mother.

"Mom! Stay back! I'll be okay, we're just—"

"Mom?" The animal's myriad eyes shifted her way, and one of its mouths laughed. "How'd you whelp anything that dark, lady? You oughta be—"

The anger welled deep in her throat as she clawed her way through the belly of the animal. She saw no faces. She had no interest in names. She had blood in her eye and bile in her throat. She was going to reach her son, and the hairy arms and knobby knees were *going* to get out of her way.

The calm summer evening was no more. The clear sky was ugly with murky bedlam. The air crackled with explosive charges. Raina had no sense of herself anymore. She was a she-wolf, and her pup was behind a wall of cruel, sweaty bodies. The shouts came fast and furious now, but only a few penetrated her red rage.

"Raina, don't!"

"Mom!"

"That kid's got some kind of spear!"

The violence erupted so suddenly that it was hard to recount the incident later. No one was supposed to be armed. There was not supposed to be any physical contact. The protesters had all agreed. Even the man who drew the pistol claimed later that he didn't even realize it was in his hand. There was a lot of pushing and shoving, a boy with a weapon, and everybody was mad. Everybody was just plain damn mad.

And madness reigned.

Raina saw it all in bleary, smeary slow motion. Peter was on one side. A gun appeared on the other. The din turned into background noise for her scream when Gideon lunged for the gun. It sounded like a car backfiring, startling but unremarkable until Gideon's big body fell across the gunman, like a defensive tackle flattening the opposing quarterback. Both sides shrank back as the two men came thudding down on the wooden planking.

Shouts of "Look out! They're shooting!" and "Somebody's shot!" threw the mob into a panic. Raina's wrath and fear injected her with the physical strength to push her way past the jostling bodies.

"Somebody call the police!"

"Somebody call an ambulance!"

"Somebody call 911!"

But the shriek of sirens already filled the air.

Raina reached Gideon just as Marvin Strikes Many went down on his knees next to him, calling his name.

Pinned beneath his victim, the gunman was wild-eyed, blood vessels bulging in his forehead. "Get him up! The gun went off! The gun just went off on me!"

Marvin helped Raina pull Gideon onto her lap. His eyes were closed, but she could feel the pulse in his neck. His arm slid away from his body, pulling his jacket open. The front of his shirt was soaked with blood.

"Oh, God, get some help! Please!"

"Open his shirt up," Marvin ordered. He pulled his own T-shirt over his head and wadded it into a compress.

Raina tore at the front of Gideon's shirt, crooning to him as her fingers flew about their task. "Gideon, can you hear me? It's going to be all right."

Her eyes met Marvin's as he pressed the cloth against Gideon's side. The eyes of an ally. The caring hands of a friend. "Hold it tight," she pleaded.

"You hold *him* tight," Marvin advised hoarsely. "He saved that boy. Don't you let him go."

She leaned over him protectively, cradling his head in her arm, rubbing her lips over his forehead. "I won't," she whispered. "I'm staying with you, Gideon. I'm holding on. You hold on, too, okay?"

The gunman scrambled away, but he was met by a policeman before he reached the end of the dock. The gun lay close by. Raina's peripheral vision clouded. Shock dimmed her awareness of people milling around, closing in, moving away. Shock permeated the crowd. It was tangible, heavy, stupefying. The hot scene had suddenly shattered, and the mob had broken into jagged shards. The people who came with the sirens seemed to flow into the cracks, rounding up the pieces.

"Mom! He's not gonna die, is he?"

Raina blinked back the tears as she reached for her son's arm. "Peter, are you all right?"

"That guy was gonna shoot me. We'd been praying on our way over with... All I had was this." Peter knelt near Gideon's head. The object in his outstretched hand was a small ceremonial pipe. "Oh, God, there wasn't supposed to be any fighting," he said as he touched Gideon's cheek. "Mom, that gun was aimed at me. He saved my life, and now he's hurt bad."

Raina understood the plea in her son's voice. *Do something, Mom.* And because her hands were busy doing what they could, she leaned across Gideon's face, touched her forehead to Peter's and whispered, "I'm praying for him. How about you?" She felt his nod.

"Who is he?" a bystander asked.

"Is that Gideon Defender?"

"Defender? Isn't he the tribal chief?"

The white dentalium shells lay against the ridge of his collar bone in stark contrast with his skin.

"The ambulance is here." A uniformed policeman knelt beside Marvin. "The paramedics will be able to help him."

"I'm staying with him," Raina told the next pair of shoes. They were black. Her eyes traveled up the black pants, over the paramedic's sleeve patch, to a woman's sympathetic eyes. "He needs me," Raina said. "I have to be with him."

"That's fine." The paramedic started checking vital signs. "You did fine. You slowed the bleeding. We'll help him now."

A stretcher appeared, along with more uniforms and the hands of people trying to take Gideon from her.

"You can ride with him," one of them told her. "Are you his—"

"Peter!" He was gone. Raina turned to the woman with the kind eyes. "Get my son. Please. I can't leave my son."

"The police are taking care of—"

"No, you don't understand. He's only twelve. He—"

"I'll look after Peter," Marvin promised. He stepped back as Gideon's large, limp body was moved to the stretcher. "You go with the chairman. You see they take care of him."

Chapter 12

Raina climbed into the ambulance behind the stretcher. Someone told her to keep talking to him, which she did. He was going to be all right, she promised quietly. The doctors would take care of him. She stroked his hair. The sirens, the flashing lights and the measures taken by the paramedics all dimmed for her when he turned his head toward the sound of her voice.

"Raina?" He struggled against the strap that immobilized his arm. "Where's Peter? Is he okay?"

"Peter's fine." She ran her hand along the length of his arm, found his hand and held it tight. "You took the bullet that was meant for him."

"*Chimau...ni...do*," he muttered, drifting. "Thank God."

"We're going to have to get that necklace off him," one of the paramedics said. "Does it matter if we cut it?"

"Yes, it matters," Raina said. She slid her hand under the

back of his neck, found the leather tie and pulled it loose. "I'll take care of this for you, Gideon. Okay?"

He groaned.

She closed her eyes and brushed her lips against his temple, whispering, "Can you hear me, darling?" No response. "Please know that I love you."

At the local clinic a yawning garage door admitted the ambulance, and several people dressed in white were there to meet them. Gideon's stretcher soon disappeared behind double doors. Carl Earlie came running down the hall just as the doors swung shut.

"How is he?"

"He's been shot."

"I heard."

"He's terribly hurt. His side—" Raina gripped her own side and noticed the blood on her skirt for the first time. Gideon's precious blood, spilled in such large drops over the yards of soft pastel field flowers he'd asked her to wear for him. She looked up at his friend, whose eyes matched hers for near panic. "I don't know."

"Is he conscious?"

"He was for a minute. He asked about Peter."

"I got there when they were rounding people up. I took charge of the boy."

"Rounding people up? You mean the man with the gun?"

"They got him, yeah. And some other arrests were made."

"Peter?"

"Marvin and some other guys, but I've got Peter. And I sent somebody out to Arlen's place to get the old man. He's family."

One of the women in white came barreling through the doors again. "Mrs. Defender?"

"Yes." She glanced meaningfully at Carl. "I'm Raina Defender."

"He needs surgery, and we don't have the facilities. We've got him stabilized, but something's still bleeding. The bus leaves *right now*," the woman recited, as though she anticipated some dawdling. "We'll take next of kin, but we're moving fast."

So was Raina. She clutched the shell necklace to her breast. It was all she carried. "My purse is at the restaurant, but Peter has a key to Gideon's house. I should—"

"You should be with the chief. We'll be along, too, but you—" He lifted his hand beseechingly. "You stay right with him."

"Bring Peter," she said over her shoulder, and she followed the woman in white.

Gideon's condition was critical. He was flown by helicopter to the nearest hospital of any size, which was in Duluth. Raina waited, taking the calls that came from Gideon's secretary, Judge Half and others. No word yet. She would let them know. Tell everyone to stay calm.

Carl called from Gideon's house. Before he put Peter on the phone, he told her that Arlen had just gotten there, and they would be on their way soon. Peter said he could just see the sun coming up, and it made him think everything would be okay. Raina permitted herself a hopeful smile. She'd lost all track of time. She wasn't even sure how far Duluth was from Pine Lake, or how long it might take anyone to drive there. But it was good to hear her son's voice telling her that he believed in the sunrise.

When Gideon was brought from the recovery room to ICU, Raina was waiting for him. She was determined to be there when he woke up. There were moments when she thought he was lucid—when he looked at her and called her

by name—but he was just as likely to call her Rosie and ask
her to get someone on the phone. The someone's name was
usually garbled. Raina had to give him credit for some kind
of subconscious control, for he never called her Tomasina.
At least, not in English. She didn't know what he was saying in Ojibwa.

But there were other things that he could not control,
mainly his rebellious stomach. The nurses assured Raina
that it was all part of the normal response to the anesthe-
sia. But for a while he was a very sick man, and she was glad
he was oblivious to it all.

She was also glad when Arlen and Carl finally brought
Peter to the hospital. He was only allowed to see Gideon for
a few minutes, which was just as well. The monitors, the
tubes and bottles, and the sight of one so strong and vigor-
ous now lying helpless, were distressing to a twelve-year-old
boy. Especially when, as he said, "It could have been me."

Arlen was given permission to perform a pipe ceremony
and burn sweet grass for purification. Raina found the scent
a bit cloying, but it definitely had a soothing effect on Gideon. While he rested and Carl kept vigil outside ICU, Raina
had supper with Peter and Arlen in the hospital cafeteria.
She couldn't remember what she'd eaten in the last twenty-
four hours. Not much. The last normal, sensible moment
she remembered seemed part of a distant past, another life.
She and Gideon had gone out for dinner together. But
they'd never gotten around to ordering any food.

"I guess I broke the law, Mom." Peter's hamburger was
fast disappearing into his stomach without being chewed. "I
couldn't hit anything with a spear, but we did use a net, and
we did catch some fish. And that's against Minnesota law.
But it's a Chippewa treaty right."

Raina nodded, then quietly asked, "Why did you let him go with them, Arlen?"

Peter was quick to defend his grandfather. "*Nimishoomis* didn't know. I didn't ask. See, it was kind of a civil disobedience thing, like Martin Luther King, you know? It was, like, to make a statement about our rights and stuff." The boy shook his head. "Nobody thought it would turn out the way it did."

"Strikes Manys were talking to the wrong people." Arlen stirred two teaspoons of sugar into his coffee. "That anglers' club, or whatever they call themselves. They have no respect. It's no good to listen to people who don't know the meaning of respect."

"Respect for what?" Peter asked.

"Respect for any way that isn't *their* way. They see only this much of the world." The old man bracketed his eyes with leathery hands, demonstrating blinders. "They see only their own straight line. The rest of the circle is invisible to them."

"But Marvin says that we have to stand up for our rights in court."

"And maybe we do." Arlen glanced at a fluorescent ceiling light. "But the man who's lying up in that room, bad hurt, that's the man who was chosen to speak for us. To go behind his back and make plans with people who shout in our faces and call our women 'squaws' and threaten to spear them—"

Raina grimaced. "You don't think they *mean* that, do you?"

"Is it supposed to be a joke? Is that what makes them laugh?" The old man shook his head in amazement. "No wonder they don't understand Indian humor." Then he tested her with, "Do you think they *meant* to shoot the chairman?"

"I think that guy meant to shoot *me*," Peter said around a mouthful of sesame-seed bun.

Raina recalled the scene on the boat dock—the rising heat, the growing tension, the words shooting like missiles. "It was a mob. It was terrible, totally irrational. It felt like...something inhuman. Evil, maybe." And she remembered Gideon's mission. "This is what the attempt to reach a settlement is all about. This is what Gideon hoped to avoid by offering to compromise."

Arlen ignored her observation. "What do the doctors say?"

"That he's a very strong man. That 'barring any unforeseen complications,' he should pull through." Raina touched Peter's arm. "He's going to be all right. I'm sure of it."

"That bossy secretary of his wants you to call her as soon as he's well enough to talk about tribal business," Arlen said. "She seems to think the Pine Lake Chippewa will be on hold until their chairman speaks. Since they don't want us in his room too much, I'm going to stay with my grandson at Pine Lake, if that's all right with you. There's a telephone at his...at Gideon's house."

"Of course."

Arlen smiled gently. "When he speaks, you must call us, too."

Raina nodded, as she struggled to recall the right phrase. "My brain's turned to mush. How do you say 'thank you' in Ojibwa?"

With a nod Arlen deferred to Peter.

"*Mii gwech*," the boy told his mother. She repeated the words to Arlen.

* * *

She lowered the guard rail and rested her head in her arms on the side of Gideon's bed, her face near his hand. It was the familiar heads-down-on-your-desks posture. She had given the command many times, but it had been a long time since she'd assumed the position herself. She only wanted to close her eyes for a few minutes, and this was as good a way as any. The IV was stuck in his other arm. This arm was free. She could stay close to it. If it moved the slightest bit, she would know.

But when it did, she was dozing, drifting on a cloud-white sheet draped over a wooden lift-top desk in her first-grade classroom. She was only half listening to Mrs. Wrist's reading of a story called "The Loon's Necklace." Oddly, her teacher called the loon *mahng*. She could feel Mrs. Wrist's fingers combing through her hair, and she could hear her watch going beep-beep-beep. But she wanted to keep her eyes closed. She really didn't want to answer when her name was called.

"Raina?"

The voice was deep and painfully raspy. It hardly sounded like the voice of Mrs....

Her hair sifted through his fingers as she raised her head. He couldn't seem to lift his own head off the pillow, but he knew she was there. He knew her by touch and by smell. He knew he was alive, and he knew she was there. Somewhere. He heard her call his name, felt her lips pressed against the backs of his fingers. He was alive, and she was there beside him.

Her face rose over him like a sleepy morning sun. She smiled and brushed her hair back after he'd mussed it up, waking her. He had news for her. She'd never looked more beautiful. In fact, he would have done some more mussing if his arm hadn't felt so heavy.

So did his tongue. Thick and heavy. He started small. "Hi."

"Hi, yourself, sleepyhead."

"You're the one—" Muzzy-headed, he didn't have much voice, wasn't sure where he was except that he was down and she was up. "You must be the one . . . sleeping on my bed, Goldilocks."

She smiled at him exultantly, as though he'd just said something remarkable. "Sorry."

"You're welcome to my bed . . . anytime." He needed to do something about the needles in his throat, but swallowing didn't seem to be one of his options. "Could use a shot of water."

"I'll have to ask. You've really been sick to your stomach." She laid her hand there comfortingly. He could almost feel her rubbing his abdomen, sort of off to one side. "I'll bet you're sore from it."

He felt as though he were probably on the verge of a lot of pain all over. But mostly he felt mummified. "Feel like I've been on a six-day binge. How many has it been?"

"Not to worry. Less than two."

"Where's Peter?"

"He's safe, thanks to you. He's with Arlen." She closed her eyes, leaned down and snuggled her face against the side of his neck. "He's fine, darling. He's fine, he's fine."

"Darling? That's a . . . first." Articulating his elbow was a matter of foggy mind over heavy matter, but he managed to bring his hand up to her face. He found a damp cheek. "Hey, what's this?" He felt a shudder slide through her. "Hmm? What's this? Am I in for some bad—" His word kept getting sanded off at the end. "Throat's killing me, honey. Please. A little water."

"It's probably from the tubes." She sat up and stroked his hair back from his face. "You've had tubes everywhere. Mouth, nose—" He started to test out his other arm—to see if he could do something about sitting up—but she stopped him. "Careful. You've still got one in your arm. And, um...other places."

"Question is, am I—" The details were fuzzy, but he remembered hearing gunfire, then feeling a flash of fire somewhere in his gut. "Am I missing any parts?" He meant to be funny. Sort of. But she wasn't smiling. "What?"

"Your right kidney."

"My—"

"It'll be fine," she told him quickly, but the way her voice was trembling, he wasn't so sure she was giving it to him straight. "The doctor says you'll be perfectly, perfectly fine. People donate kidneys every day. They wouldn't take a kidney from a healthy person and put it into someone else if a person couldn't live a normal, healthy life with just—"

He lifted the arm that seemed to be the only part of him he could get working and tried to touch her chin. The back of his hand slid over her breast. She grabbed it before it retreated ignominiously back to the bed and held it close to her heart. Her dress felt smooth and soft. The same one she'd worn to the restaurant. Two days, he was thinking, same dress? How un-Raina of her.

But he asked, "What else?"

"That's all. That's enough." She squeezed his hand tight and tucked it possessively between her breasts. Just where it wanted to be. "We almost lost you."

"We?" *You almost lost me?* You and... "We almost lost...Peter." Now he remembered where the gun had been pointed. He remembered his own insides freezing up in that horrifying, endless moment before the gun had been fired.

"He was here earlier. They wouldn't let him stay long, and anyway, kids... You know? He got a little..." She scanned the small room, which was crammed with equipment. "All this is a little scary. Especially after he saw you get..." She pressed her lips together tightly and blinked furiously.

"He's not hurt?"

She shook her head.

"Then what's to cry about?" He managed a wan smile. "You haven't been cryin' like this ever since—"

She shook her head even more vigorously, half laughing as she lifted her hand to her face. But his, energized by her emotion, got there first. His weary eyes held hers as he caught a tear, then licked it like cake frosting from his finger.

"Thirstier 'n hell," he said in his hoarse voice, and she gave a teary laugh. "Sure nothing important's missing?" Lips pressed together, she nodded, her eyes glistening merrily through her tears.

"Did you check?"

"Not yet," she whispered.

"Later, then." He closed his eyes. "They got me on some kind of fairy dust, don't they?"

"Mmm-hmm." Her soft, sweet voice came closer. "So you don't hurt so much."

"Don't feel much except tired."

"Sleep, then."

"Don't want to. Not while you're... still here."

"I'll be here when you wake up." She was toying with his hair again. He liked it when she did that. "Before you go back to sleep, I have one more thing to say."

"Better...hurry."

"*Mii gwech,* Gideon Defender."

Eyes still closed, he did his best to smile.

She felt as though he were slipping away again, and it scared her. *Stay with me another moment, just to make sure.* "Did I say it right?"

"Not quite." His lips hardly moved. "Supposed to end with a kiss."

She licked her lips, then used them to moisten his in a tender, loving way.

"*Mii gwech,*" he said.

In the next two days there were a flood of flowers and a barrage of phone calls. The governor, legislators, congressmen—Gideon had no shortage of well-wishers. His doctor told him that the less he rested, the longer it would take him to recover, so he agreed to keep the visitors to a minimum. But he had to let his people know that he was going to be all right. He asked to see Carl, Arlen and Rosie as soon as he was able to sit up.

"One TV camera, one reporter, one microphone," he told Rosie. "I want to let people see that I'm still kickin'."

"We've got some guys who are all set to go on the warpath, Gideon. They're fightin' mad."

"What guys? Anybody starts talking like that, you tell them to keep a lid on it. We can have our day in court without taking any of our kids spearfishing just to see if we can get somebody to take a potshot at one of them." He knew he didn't have to tell that to Carl or Rosie, but he wanted them to relay his message to anyone who would listen. "I know, I know. It wasn't supposed to be like that. Hell, it's *never* supposed to be like that. But it doesn't take much of a spark to light a fuse."

He turned to the old man, whose approval he had re cently come to covet. "I've done my reading, Arlen. I know all about Red Cloud's compromises to try to save the Grea Sioux Reserve and the Black Hills. And I know the Siou have been in court over it off and on for nearly a hundre years."

"The Sioux have been offered money," Arlen reminde him. "They turned it down."

"They want the land. And that's what we're trying to ge Some of the land back. A part of the lake where we can tak the fish our own way. The way our more traditional peopl still remember."

"The treaty promises more than that. But either way there's going to be a fight. Promises are like river water fo them. An endless flow." Arlen eyed Gideon and gave hi that mischievous look that put a youthful sparkle in his eye "Do like the beaver. Find a way to build a dam."

"Not like the other night. I don't make a very good dam." Gideon touched his side, which was bandaged beneath th cotton hospital robe. "They put a hole in me real easy."

"And like Judge Half says, there are too few Indians lef We can't spare any more." With a nod Arlen urged, "Us the courts. See what they mean by 'justice for all.'"

"We will if we have to, Arlen. We know who we are, don we?" He sought confirmation in each face. "We've bee around for a hell of a long time. Against some pretty bi odds, we're still hangin' in there. Main thing is, we remem ber who we are."

"And we teach the children, so they know who they are, Arlen said.

"Cool heads. Sharp minds. That's what we need." Gid eon shifted uncomfortably. He hated calling for painki ers, but it felt like something was starting to eat at his ra insides again. "If this settlement fails, we go to court. The law's on our side. You hear anybody talkin' up the cracking-heads warpath, you bring 'em to me."

"What about the guy who did this?" Carl asked.

Gideon made a cutoff gesture. "They arrested him."

"You know they won't do nothin' but—"

"That's for the court to decide, too." He managed a fleeting smile. "We gotta work the program, Carl. Right? Do the best we can."

Peter's turn came that afternoon, after Raina had been ordered to "go across the street to the hotel and sleep off those raccoon eyes." He'd brought his mother some clothes, but he wasn't staying at the hotel with her. Now that Gideon was out of ICU *and* out of the woods, Peter didn't mind saying that he wasn't crazy about hospitals.

"I'm with you," Gideon assured him. "I can't wait to blow this pop stand." Then he added, "Sure has been one hell of a summer vacation for your mom, hasn't it?"

Peter avoided Gideon's eyes. "I know you saved my life. You took that bullet for me."

"I was going after the gun, not the bullet." Gideon chuckled. "I was bigger than he was. I thought I could take the gun." When Peter looked at him as though he were some kind of miracle worker, he protested with, "You think I'm crazy, or what?"

The boy shook his head. "I think you're pretty brave."

"I wasn't thinking about being brave. I wasn't thinking at all. I wasn't going to let anyone hurt you was all."

"You weren't even scared," Peter insisted. "You didn't look scared."

"It all happened very fast." Gideon thought back, then shook his head. "No, when I saw that gun I was scared. I hope you were, too."

"Why?"

"Because guns kill people. You take the gun away from that scene the other night, probably nobody would've gotten hurt. At least, nobody would have gotten shot." He reached for the water bottle on the bed table, and Peter fairly leapt to put it in his hand. Gideon nodded, gave a quick wink and offered a teasing aside. "I'm supposed to move around a little."

He was also supposed to drink plenty of water, and he was damn well determined to do whatever the doctor ordered so he could be on his way. He downed half the bottle before he continued. "People get mad, they get a little crazy, too. You put a gun in some hothead's hand—" He snapped his fingers. "That quick, somebody can be dead. It's too easy. Too damned easy."

"It wasn't supposed to be like that. It was supposed to be like we were standing up for our rights."

"We have to do that, too. And that can be risky." Gideon shoved the plastic bottle aside. "You have to be careful who you follow, Peter. You have to listen to what they say and really think it over. Maybe talk to some other people."

"Like you?"

"Your grandfather, your mom. People who show you how much they care about you by treating you right."

"What about you?"

"Just say the word," Gideon offered lightly, but his eyes said, *I'd lay down my life for you, son.*

"I..." Peter polished his knees with his palms. "I don't know what to call you."

"How about just plain Gideon?" The boy looked up, dubious. "We'll take it one day at a time, okay? You take your time figuring out who I am."

"I miss my...my dad a lot."

"So do I."

"So that's okay, huh?"

"It better be."

Paddling with his heels, Peter scooted his chair across the floor until his knees touched the side of the bed. Then, awkwardly, he flopped one arm around Gideon's middle, pressing his cheek to Gideon's shoulder. "I'm glad you're gonna be okay."

"*Mii gwech.*" Gideon was unaccustomed to the way his throat prickled as he ruffled Peter's hair. He had to swallow more than once before he could come up with a breezy "Careful, *ningozis,* I'm a wounded man."

"What does that mean? *Ningozis?*"

It meant that his shoulders, his hands, his tender side, would always be at Peter's disposal. "It means I've already figured out who you are."

When Raina came to the room that evening, she found him dressed in jeans and a T-shirt and sitting in a chair with a bed pillow at his back.

"You're up!"

"Dream on, honey. They just took out the last of the tubes, and I am one wilted puppy. Oh, you mean up out of *bed.*" He gave her a cocky smile, just to show her how really good he was feeling about his accomplishment. "Since you're looking so damn sexy today, I thought maybe you were out to seduce me, and I was gonna say..." He eyed her up and down. She'd bought herself a new flowered dress, similar to the other one, but maybe just a little clingier. "Mmm, I think I'm getting my, uh . . . strength back."

"That's good news." She glanced up at the TV as she pulled a chair close to his.

"Yeah, well, *that* isn't." He aimed the remote at the local news, clicking it off with a vengeance. "Some damn retired football coach just held court at a screw-the-Indians rally today. What gives him any authority to speak on Indian issues? Who appointed him lord of the walleye? What in hell is he talking about, special privileges? The man owns a million-dollar house, for . . ."

"Arlen was there, quoting chapter and verse from the treaties. Damn, that old man's got spunk." Gideon jabbed a finger at the dark TV screen. "And that jerk's answer is that Arlen's 'under the influence.' Under the influence of what? Time-honored traditional ways, that's what." He tossed the remote aside. "Damn pigskin-for-brains wouldn't know American culture if it kicked him in the butt. And Arlen doesn't drink."

"I'll say you're getting your strength back." She sat next to him, the way they used to on his porch.

"*Native* American culture," he reiterated, carefully enunciating each syllable.

"But you *do* know," she said. "And you're absolutely right. The man is making a fool of himself, casting bigoted aspersions like that, so I'm sure no one will listen to him."

"You kidding? Every damn sports nut in this state will listen to him." He scowled. "What am I talking about. *I'm* a sports nut. I'm a Timberwolves fan even when they're in the sub-basement, and I can fish the pants off that pinhead." He turned a sly smile Raina's way. "Without him even noticing his fly's slipped."

She laughed, and because humor always helped his people through the bad times, so did he.

"I have a buyer for the house," she told him. He raised his brow appreciatively. The warmth in his dark eyes was all for her, but it made her dance away from the subject she had intended to lead up to. Evasively, she wondered, "Do the nurses know that you're going around here barefooted?"

He glanced down at his toes and shrugged. "You wanna make a note on my chart?"

"Didn't they help you get dressed?" She could think of one in particular who probably would have jumped at the chance. The little brunette who jumped to do his every other bidding.

"Did it all by my lonesome," he said, his tone irresistibly cute. "You should'a been here."

Now that he was in a good mood again, she had to avoid his eyes and charge ahead if she was going to get this out. "Arlen says that since we're moving to Pine Lake, he's not going to ask for custody of Peter. You're the only other person who can . . . press the issue."

"Peter's almost thirteen years old. It's up to him to decide whether he'll let me be his father after all this time. Not the judge." Suddenly all anger and all frivolity had disappeared from his quiet, steady voice. "I told you I wasn't going to take him from you. I meant that."

"So he can live with me?"

"You're his mother. There's never been any question about that as far as I was concerned." His eyes held hers. "But there is one question you haven't answered, Raina. My offer still stands. You can both live with me."

"You offered that as the solution to a problem," she reminded him. "But the problem no longer exists."

"So that's it, then?" he asked tightly. A frosty glaze slid across his eyes. "You can sleep with me, but you can't be my wife? You won't marry me?"

"Why are you asking, Gideon? You wanted sex—" she glanced away "—and we've had sex. You don't have to..." No, that was silly. She knew very well that that wasn't the reason he was asking. "Why did you pull away from me sixteen years ago? Was it because I wasn't ready to—"

"*I* wasn't ready," he told her calmly. "I didn't have much to offer you, Raina. Except a good time. I wanted you. And God, how I wanted you to want me. But for what? What would you want from me?"

She looked up, puzzling.

He chuckled, remembering. "I couldn't let you know how bad I had it for you. A case of the hots, I figured, so I tried to be cool. Suave, you know. Figured if you'd go to bed with me, just once, you'd be mine."

He touched the back of her hand, hoping to loosen her tense grip on the arm of the chair. "But I scared you off, didn't I? I rushed you. And the hell of it is, I *know* better than to move too quick. I can wait out in the brush for hours, never move a muscle. Hell, I can stalk a deer all day long." He looked into her eyes. "You needed more time. Among other things."

"What other things?"

"The kinds of things I didn't have going for me back then."

"But Jared did," she surmised.

"Yeah. Jared did." He smiled wistfully. He'd loved his brother almost as much as... "I knew you'd like him. I knew he'd be just your type." He laughed and shook his head. "But, damn my eyes, I introduced you to him, any way. Beauty, meet Prince Charming."

"And then you rode off into the sunset, as I remember."

"No way," he averred dramatically. "Can't do that scene without a horse. I just sort of politely bowed out. Exit Beast."

"I never thought...." She turned her palm to his. "I never knew what to think, Gideon."

"About me? Come on, Raina."

"Listen, Gideon, you pulled away from me, and you pulled away from Peter. You say you weren't ready." Her eyes narrowed, challenging him. "But now you've been to hell and back, and I have to know why you want to marry me. It's not for sex, and it's not for Peter." He tried to pull away again, but she held his hand fast. "What are you afraid of, Gideon?"

It took him a while to answer, but at last, at *long* last, he put it into words that almost surprised him. "Not being good enough, I guess."

With some difficulty he turned his wounded body in her direction and affected a lighter tone. "What you see is what you get. This is it. A little banged up at the moment, but I'll heal. I always do."

She extended her free hand toward his cheek, but he caught it midpath, kissed her fingertips and gave a jaunty smile.

No pity, Raina. Whether it's good enough for you now, I don't know, but what you see ain't half-bad.

"I've got plenty of muscle," he told her. "You wanna go somewhere? I can paddle you all the way to Tahiti. You want an addition on the house? I can cut the timber and raise the roof beams myself. I'd never let you go hungry. I'd protect you, defend you. Hell, I'd stop a bullet with my—"

She closed her eyes. "Oh, Gideon."

"You want a child? I gave you one. You want anothe
one? I'll make as many babies with you as you want." H
drew her closer, and his voice dropped to an intimate hush
"And I'll give you so much pleasure in the making tha
when the pain comes..." His head tipped toward her, fore
head resting against forehead, and he closed his eyes agains
the wooziness he was beginning to feel. "But when it comes
I'll be there, just the way you stayed with me. Always. N
matter what kind of pain it is. I want to be your husband s
that I can be there for the good times and the bad."

The last confession pinched his heart—badly, this time
because everything else was out on the table, and his hear
was completely, absolutely vulnerable. "What I'm afraid c
is that all I can offer won't be good enough."

"Why wouldn't it be?" she asked, breathless from th
beauty of his vows, praying for just one more. "If you lov
me."

He raised his head and searched her eyes, wonderin
whether his whole heartfelt speech had fallen on deaf ears
"That's what I just said, isn't it? That I love you?"

"*You* tell *me.* Why do you want to marry me?"

"Because I love you. Because I loved you when I had n
business loving you, and now, here you are with..." H
caught her face in his hands. "And now there's no reaso
in the world why I can't love you. And I'll be damn good :
it, Raina."

She gave him a misty-eyed smile. "I think you alread
are."

"Then why are you making me jump through all thes
hoops?"

"Because I've already jumped through them for you.
She took his hand from her face and placed it on her breas
She moved it over her racing heartbeat, slipped it over an

under the neckline of her sundress and invited him to feel the hardness of her nipples. "To me, this means that I love you. You know that, don't you? There's no other way for me. And while my being in love with you was reason enough for making love..." Her hand sneaked into his lap, found his "wilted puppy" and gently caressed him. She smiled, for it was a puppy no more. "The recipe for marriage calls for *two* people in love."

"Two people making love?"

"Two people—one man, one woman—in love with each other. That's how you make a marriage."

"Looks like we've got the right ingredients, then." He figured he'd better get this hand thing under control before she had him howling. He enfolded both of hers within both of his. "Wanna make one with me?"

She laughed and cried, both at once. "I surely do."

Epilogue

The date was set for early October. Raina had gotten
started in her new school, Peter in his. Some of the changes
weren't easy to make, but, as Arlen had said, the sooner a
person learned the lesson of the willow, the smoother life's
road became. Flexibility. Learning when to stand firm and
when to bend could keep a person from breaking.

Gideon's ears tuned in to such wisdom wherever he found
it these days. The fate of the settlement rested with the state
legislature now, for the Pine Lake Chippewa had made their
offer. And the outcome of the vote, which would be taken
a few months down the road, looked like a toss-up. The
DNR and the attorney general's office were strongly in favor of the compromise, but those in opposition had finan-
cial clout. The sportsmen's groups, in particular, had
powerful allies and vocal lobbyists working for them. In the
end, the issue might very well be decided in federal court.
Either way, Gideon realized that the fate of the Pine Lake

Chippewa lay exactly where it always had—in the hands of the Chippewa people themselves and with *Chimaunido*.

For now, on this sunny October day, beside the sparkling blue waters of Pine Lake and with a blazing pink-and-yellow backdrop of sugar maples, there was a marriage to be made. During the feast, the people would launch the bride and groom in a red canoe, and he would paddle her across the water to their honeymoon bower—or as far as Tahiti, if that was her wish. His doctor had pronounced him fit to do anything he felt up to doing, and on this day he felt up to taking his bride to the paradise of her choice.

He was dressed for just such a journey. He wore jeans, along with moccasins and a buckskin jacket, both beaded in the traditional floral designs of the Chippewa. His hair was pulled back and tied at the nape. He had the ring. He was all set. Except that there was a knot in the dentalium shell necklace, and his hands were a little shaky. Must've had too much coffee this morning, he told himself.

There was a knock at the door of the room the lodge had provided him for dressing. Peter stuck his head inside. "Mom wants to know if there's a word in Ojibwa for two o'clock."

"Tell her the only word we've got for that is *Indian time*. When the time is right and the people are ready." Gideon motioned for the boy to come in and close the door. "And I'm ready, except for this damned knot."

Peter looked more than thirteen years' worth of sharp in his blue blazer and tan slacks. He smiled indulgently as he took over on the untying job. "You nervous?"

"Do I look nervous?"

"You look a little pale." He gave a quick shrug. It was the padded shoulders, Gideon thought, that made the boy look so much older today. "It kinda fits, though, because ever in the sun, Mom's really... We used to call her 'pale face.'"

"We did?" Gideon chuckled. "Maybe we could come up with something more original."

"*You* can. 'Mom' works for me."

"Did anyone ever tell you that I knew her first?"

Peter glanced up from the slow-yielding knot. "*Knew* her?"

"Met her first. Went out with her first. And, no, don' ask any more than that, because a guy never discusses hi private moments with his lady with anyone else." Gideor nodded instructively. It was becoming a habit. "You re member that."

"As far as I'm concerned, my mom's a virgin and always will be." Displaying his conquest over the knot, Peter's eye twinkled as he imitated Gideon's instructive tone. "A guy' mom doesn't do that stuff. You remember that."

"I'll be good to her, Peter. I do love her, with all my heart."

"Siiick! Who turned on the oldies station?" Peter clapped a hand over the pocket of his blazer and crooned, "Witl aaaall my hearrrrt." Then he cut Gideon a meaningful look "You'd better be good to her, with all your heart and what ever else you got."

"Gotcha. You wanna put that on for me?" Gideon asked seating himself on the bed to make the job easier. "I seem to be all thumbs."

Peter draped the necklace in place. "I feel like the mothe of the bride," he muttered, and they both laughed. Then a unsettled quiet fell over them. "You got a best man?"

Gideon shook his head, but damn, he was hoping.

Peter tucked the tied ends of the necklace under the back of Gideon's collar. "You want one?"

Gideon cleared his throat. "You available?"

"Somebody better make sure the ring gets there, nervous as you are."

Rising slowly from the bed, Gideon drew the gold band from his pocket and pressed it into the hollow of Peter's palm. He wasn't sure he could have said anything if he tried. His chest was full to bursting with love and pride. Maybe that sounded like the oldies station, too, but there was no other way to put it.

Peter looked up, his eyes filled with tears. "It's like I'm filling in for Dad. If he was here, this would be his job, because he was your brother."

Gideon nodded once. "If your father were here, this wedding wouldn't be taking place."

"You know what? I think my dad's here in spirit." He glanced away. "But I feel like my father's here in the flesh, too."

Gideon's arm went around the boy's shoulders. He closed his eyes and gripped a fistful of shoulder pad.

Peter pressed his cheek against the soft leather jacket. "It sounds confusing," he said, "but in my head, it works okay."

"Works great for me, too."

Then he saw Raina through the window, standing on the grass below. She was wearing a long-sleeved, soft white cotton dress, scattered with pastel field flowers. The gentle breeze lifted the long skirt and made it flutter as she walked. A broad-brimmed hat shaded her face. One of the girls from her class at school came running after her with a bouquet of wildflowers. She turned, took the flowers, then took the girl's hand.

"We're late," Peter warned.

"But not too late. God, she's beautiful."

And then they were on their way out the door. "One thing you gotta learn about Mom. She's always there when she says she will be."

Gideon smiled. "Then from now on, my time is her time."

*   *   *   *   *

Author's Note

ne Lake Reservation and the Pine Lake Band of Chippewa are purely fictitious. The Anishinabe, or Chippewa ands (many of whom prefer the name Ojibwa or Ojibwe), e an indigenous people of the Upper Great Lakes Region. Even though I chose to create a fictitious band, many aders will recognize that the issues with regard to Native merican treaty rights, especially as they apply to fishing ghts, are genuine concerns. The conflict between some ative American tribes (those who are traditionally fishermen) and non-Indian groups (among them some organizations formed to promulgate sport-fishing interests) came to head in the 1970s in the Northwest, in Michigan and in isconsin, as a result of a series of federal court decisions affirming the fishing rights of Indian tribes guaranteed by aty.

For the sake of authenticity, I have used the more recent ntroversy in Minnesota as the model for my story. In the

hope of avoiding the kind of violence that occurred in oth
parts of the country, the Mille Lacs Band of Chippewa n
gotiated a proposed out-of-court settlement, backed by t
Minnesota Department of Natural Resources and the sta
attorney general's office. Under pressure from various sp
cial interest groups, particularly sportsmen's groups, t
state legislature rejected the compromise. The issue w
likely be tested in federal court in the near future.

It should be noted that the vast majority of people wl
enjoy fishing as a sport have no interest in interfering wi
the relatively few Native Americans who seek to exerci
their treaty rights. Typically, non-Indians who question t
validity of treaty rights do so because they have limit
knowledge of their historical background, along with li
ited understanding of and respect for Native American cu
ture and its values. Historically, movements to abroga
Indian treaties have been fueled for the most part by
common motive, and that has been greed.

JINGLE BELLS, WEDDING BELLS:
Silhouette's Christmas Collection for 1994

Christmas Wish List

*To beat the crowds at the malls and get the perfect present for *everyone,* even that snoopy Mrs. Smith next door!

*To get through the holiday parties without running my panty hose.

*To bake cookies, decorate the house and serve the perfect Christmas dinner—just like the women in all those magazines.

*To sit down, curl up and read my Silhouette Christmas stories!

Join *New York Times* bestselling author Nora Roberts, along with popular writers Barbara Boswell, Myrna Temte and Elizabeth August, as we celebrate the joys of Christmas—and the magic of marriage—with

JINGLE BELLS, WEDDING BELLS

Silhouette's Christmas Collection for 1994.

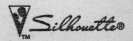

JBWB

MILLION DOLLAR SWEEPSTAKES (III)

No purchase necessary. To enter, follow the directions published. Method of entry may vary. For eligibility, entries must be received no later than March 31, 1996. No liability is assumed for printing errors, lost, late or misdirected entries. Odds of winning are determined by the number of eligible entries distributed and received. Prizewinners will be determined no later than June 30, 1996.

Sweepstakes open to residents of the U.S. (except Puerto Rico), Canada, Europe and Taiwan who are 18 years of age or older. All applicable laws and regulations apply. Sweepstakes offer void wherever prohibited by law. Values of all prizes are in U.S. currency. This sweepstakes is presented by Torstar Corp., its subsidiaries and affiliates, in conjunction with book, merchandise and/or product offerings. For a copy of the Official Rules send a self-addressed, stamped envelope (WA residents need not affix return postage) to: MILLION DOLLAR SWEEPSTAKES (III) Rules, P.O. Box 4573, Blair, NE 68009, USA.

EXTRA BONUS PRIZE DRAWING

No purchase necessary. The Extra Bonus Prize will be awarded in a random drawing to be conducted no later than 5/30/96 from among all entries received. To qualify, entries must be received by 3/31/96 and comply with published directions. Drawing open to residents of the U.S. (except Puerto Rico), Canada, Europe and Taiwan who are 18 years of age or older. All applicable laws and regulations apply; offer void wherever prohibited by law. Odds of winning are dependent upon number of eligibile entries received. Prize is valued in U.S. currency. The offer is presented by Torstar Corp., its subsidiaries and affiliates in conjunction with book, merchandise and/or product offering. For a copy of the Official Rules governing this sweepstakes, send a self-addressed, stamped envelope (WA residents need not affix return postage) to: Extra Bonus Prize Drawing Rules, P.O. Box 4590, Blair, NE 68009, USA.

SWP-S994

Dark secrets, dangerous desire...

Lovers
DARK AND
DANGEROUS

Three spine-tingling tales from the dark side of love.

This October, enter the world of shadowy romance as Silhouette presents the third in their annual tradition of thrilling love stories and chilling story lines. Written by three of Silhouette's top names:

LINDSAY McKENNA
LEE KARR
RACHEL LEE

Haunting a store near you this October.

Mavericks

Stories that capture living and loving beneath the Big Sky, where legends live on...and the mystery is just beginning.

This October, discover more MONTANA MAVERICKS with

SLEEPING WITH THE ENEMY
by Myrna Temte

Seduced by his kiss, she almost forgot he was her enemy. *Almost.*

And don't miss a minute of the loving as the mystery continues with:

THE ONCE AND FUTURE WIFE
by Laurie Paige (November)
THE RANCHER TAKES A WIFE
by Jackie Merritt (December)
OUTLAW LOVERS
by Pat Warren (January)
and many more!

Wait, there's more! Win a trip to a Montana mountain resort. For details, look for this month's MONTANA MAVERICKS title at your favorite retail outlet.

Only from ▼ *Silhouette*® where passion lives.

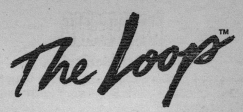

Silhouette Books
is proud to present
our best authors, their best books...
and the best in your reading pleasure!

Throughout 1994, look for exciting books
by these top names in contemporary
romance:

DIANA PALMER
Enamored in August

HEATHER GRAHAM POZZESSERE
The Game of Love in August

FERN MICHAELS
Beyond Tomorrow in August

NORA ROBERTS
The Last Honest Woman in September

LINDA LAEL MILLER
Snowflakes on the Sea in September

*When it comes to passion,
we wrote the book.*

BOBQ3

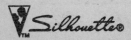

HE'S AN

AMERICAN HERO

They're back! Those amazing men whose heroic spirits inspire passion and pride in the hearts of women everywhere. And they're yours for the reading.

In October: NIGHT SMOKE by Nora Roberts—Rugged arson inspector Ryan Piasecki wasn't prepared for the blaze of desire that coolly beautiful Natalie Fletcher ignited in him. But he was more than ready to deal with the vengeful arsonist hot on Natalie's heels.

In November: CALLAGHAN'S WAY by Marie Ferrarella—Kirk Callaghan had returned home in search of peace, but he soon found himself playing surrogate dad to Rachel Reed's son—and playing for keeps with her heart.

In December: LOVING EVANGELINE by Linda Howard—Robert Cannon had vowed to destroy the thief who'd stolen classified information from his company. But when the trail led to beautiful Evie Shaw, Robert found both his resolve—and his heart—melting fast.

AMERICAN HEROES: Men who give all they've got for their country, their work—the women they love.

Only from

INTIMATE MOMENTS®
Silhouette®

IMHER010

Return to the classic plot lines you love, with

In October, Justine Davis delivers LEFT AT THE ALTAR, IM #596, her telling twist on the ever-popular "jilted" story line.

Sean Holt had never forgotten the pain and humiliation of being jilted five years ago. Yet runaway bride Aurora Sheridan had had her reasons—dangerous reasons that had just turned deadly.

And there will be more ROMANTIC TRADITIONS titles coming your way in the new year, starting in January 1995 with Beverly Barton's THE OUTCAST, a bad-boy book you won't want to miss. So come back to the classics—only in